M000298496

DESTRUCTIVE
King
A MAFIA ROYALS ROMANCE

by
RACHEL VAN DYKEN

Destructive King
A Mafia Royals Romance, Book 3
by Rachel Van Dyken

Copyright © 2021 RACHEL VAN DYKEN

This is a work of fiction. Names, places, characters, and events are fictitious in every regard. Any similarities to actual events and persons, living or dead, are purely coincidental. Any trademarks, service marks, product names, or named features are assumed to be the property of their respective owners, and are used only for reference. There is no implied endorsement if any of these terms are used. Except for review purposes, the reproduction of this book in whole or part, electronically or mechanically, constitutes a copyright violation.

DESTRUCTIVE KING
Copyright © 2021 RACHEL VAN DYKEN
ISBN: 978-1-946061-74-4

Cover Design by Jena Brignola
Editing by Kay Springsteen
Formatting & Editing by Jill Sava, Love Affair With Fiction

DEDICATION

To all of the readers, new and old, experiencing this mafia world— thank you for your constant support. I would be nothing without you guys! And appreciate you more than words will ever describe! Oh, also... grab some whiskey; it's gonna get worse before it gets better...

LOL,

blood in, no out!

AUTHOR
Note

This is the third standalone within a brand new series; I know you probably already know that since you picked up this book, but hey, let's just repeat it again! ;) If you recognize some of the names in this book, it's because back in 2010, I wrote a series called Eagle Elite, and the parents in this series are the OG's of Eagle Elite. That series got extremely long (as you can imagine), so I decided we needed fresh blood back at Eagle Elite University, and that started with Ruthless Princess and continues the saga with Scandalous Prince and now **drumroll** Destructive King.

If you are an EE fan, then this is the part where you may nerd out and want a family tree; I have that on the very next page, NEVER FEAR! If you're new, just scroll on by, it won't matter to you, haha, and you'll be like yeah, I don't care. And you don't NEED to know any backstory, because again, this is a new series (do you like how I keep repeating that), oh by the way, it's a new series.

So if you've made it this far, this is the part where I tell you that this book is a bit different from the first two. I'm lucky to have amazing readers who, when I was plotting this book out and going back and forth, really helped me see how important it was that the characters not only allow themselves to feel even if it hurts but that we need to visually see that process on the page, even if it makes us reach for the whiskey (thank you btw, Krystal R for your honest feedback!).

This book will make you laugh on one page, and on the next, you may want to strangle Ash alive; just keep with it. You'll notice that I was probably a bit emotional writing it because, during this book, we were in the process of adopting, so I was feeling all the things as I was sitting in that hospital going, are we going to get baby, are we not, what's going to happen, etc. One thing I've learned is no matter what, you must allow yourself to feel things. 2020 has been extremely hard on EVERYONE, so I just wanted to add that in—that we're all human, we all go through pain even if social media doesn't make it seem that way. In reading this book, I hope you'll allow yourself to feel, to maybe deal with a loss that you've never dealt with before. I hope you heal. You laugh. You have fun. I hope, hope, hope you NEVER look at mafia books the same again, and that you go back and read the rest of the series or even the original (aka OG) Eagle Elite books!

Phew, enjoy my bloodthirsty readers, enjoy!

Blood in. No out. Let's go meet our Angry Ash, royalty, Destructive King. May God have mercy on your soul… because he—will not.

WHO'S WHO IN THE
Cosa Nostra

Nixon and Trace Abandonato. Nixon is the boss of the Abandonato Family; he's a bit psycho, has a lip ring, and in his mid-forties, looks like a freaking badass. Think if Jason Momoa and Channing Tatum had a baby. SURPRISE, Nixon! Trace is the love of his life. Nixon's daughter, Serena, is his pride and joy; she's the heir to his throne and in love with Junior Nicolasi. His adopted son Dom is ten years older than Serena. At thirty and married to Tanit, he's ready to step in if he needs to, but he really doesn't want to, not that he's thinking about a family of his own. Nixon's youngest, Bella, was a most welcome surprise.

Phoenix and Bee Nicolasi (formerly De Lange) have one son, Junior, and he's everything. The same age as Serena, he has only ever had one thing on his mind. Her. And now he has her. Pursuing her was like signing his own death sentence. The one rule that the bosses gave all the cousins, all the kids, no dating each other, it complicates things. They all took a blood oath. But he risked it all, for just one taste—and is still here to tell about it (Ruthless Princess).

Which brings us to Chase and Luciana Abandonato, their love story is one for the ages. He had Violet first, gorgeous, Violet Emiliana Abandonato, now married to her own boss Valerian Petrov (Scandalous Prince). And then he had twins, God help him. Asher (Marco) and Izzy. All are attending Eagle Elite University. Violet is more into books than people. And the twins, well they are polar opposites. While Izzy is quiet and reserved, taking after her uncle Sergio in the tech support part of the mafia, Asher was an assassin at age twelve. He takes care of everyone even though he's younger than Serena and Junior. He feels it's his job to make sure everyone is safe, so when he was unable to do that for his girlfriend, Claire—he was inconsolable. She was his soul mate, and he'd do anything for her. And don't forget the baby of the family, Ariel, who everyone dotes on.

Tex and Mo Campisi. He's the godfather of this joint, gorgeous, he's a gentle giant unless he's pissed, and his wife, Mo, is just as violent as he is. They have two sons, Breaker and King. Breaker their adoptive son is really Valerian Petrov, he just took over as the boss of the Petrov (Russian) Family releasing Andrei Petrov Sinacore from that role. He's now married to Violet Abandonato, the love of his life (Scandalous Prince). King, on the other hand, is vying for top whore at Eagle Elite University, going as far as to seduce his own older… tutor (that he doesn't need).

Sergio and Valentina are also Abandonatos. While Val is quiet and reserved, Sergio is the resident doctor of the Families. He's also really into tech and loves spying on people. They have two gorgeous daughters. Kartini has her daddy wrapped around her little finger. He just hopes he survives her first year of college without shooting one of her boyfriends. With Lydia, he knows she can take care of herself. She already beat up the class bully, making Sergio quite proud.

Dante and El don't have things easier; they're one of the younger mafia families, he's the head of the Alfero Family. And he has two twin girls at age eleven who are making him pull his hair out. Raven and Tempest are adorable, but they're feisty like their mom. He lets them have more screen time than he should, but they say he's their favorite in the world, sooooo… he lets it pass.

Andrei and Alice have been through a lot. Their name single-handedly brought the Russian Mafia into the Italian fold then successfully handed over the Russian throne to the true rightful heir, Valerian. Andrei is both Petrov and Sinacore, meaning that the oldest Italian mafia family is now part of the Cosa Nostra. Forever and will stay that way if he has anything to say about it. Their son's name is Maksim, and weirdly enough, he's a total flirt; he takes nothing seriously but can flip a switch in a minute if someone he loves is threatened. Anya is his little sister, and he would do anything for her; she seems fragile but studies Krav Maga, so nobody messes with her.

These are the Families of the Cosa Nostra.

Welcome to the Family.

Blood in. No out.

MAFIA Royals

Mafia Royals Romances

Royal Bully — *Royal Bully is a prequel novella*
Ruthless Princess
Scandalous Prince
Destructive King
Mafia King
Fallen Royal
Broken Crown

DESTRUCTIVE
King

"*Do not stand at my grave and weep, I am not there; I do not sleep. I am a thousand winds that blow. I am the diamond glints on snow. I am the sun on ripened grain, I am the gentle autumn rain. When you awaken in the morning's hush I am the swipe uplifting rush, of quiet birds in circled flight. I am the soft stars that shine at night. Do not stand at my grave and cry. I am not there; I did not die. — Mary Elizabeth Fyre*

PROLOGUE

"Death is not the opposite of life, but a part of it." —
Haruki Murakami

Annie

I'd been living at the Abandonato compound, aka house, for two days, and already I felt like I was going to go crazy.

It was huge.

Like a mausoleum.

The only thing that helped was Ash's mom Luc's amazing cooking and the fact that Chase, underboss to the Abandonato Family and current US Senator from Illinois, reserved his terrifying mafia face for his children.

But me?

It was like he saw past the sweaters I couldn't help but button all the way up to my chin.

He saw past the shyness.

He saw it all.

So when he looked at me, it was with respect.

If only that trickled down into his one and only son, Ash.

The same son who'd been spiraling since the death of his fiancée.

A chill wracked my body as I shot up from the bed in search of a sweatshirt I could put on. Why did they always keep the house so frigid? It was like they didn't believe in heat or something, not that I wasn't thankful for having a roof over my head after my adoptive parents' death.

I blocked out the memories.

Just like I blocked out the blood that seemed to still be staining my hands even though I hadn't done anything.

No, that had all been Ash.

I'd never seen another person so full of rage, so full of uncontrollable sadness that you couldn't help but feel it every time you were in their presence.

Thunder boomed outside my window as the late fall rain pounded against the rooftop. I'd always loved storms, even more so now that I had a ginormous room with a balcony that overlooked the pool—including the pool house where Ash was currently brooding.

Memories of kissing him in that pool assaulted me until my feet took me over to the door, until I was opening it and peeking my head out to get a glance at the shallow end where he'd pushed me up against the wall and kissed the hell out of me.

To the footsteps I'd taken from the pool in a stupid immature move that probably could have ended with my blood on his fingertips—he'd been that angry.

I stared at his door and willed it to open.

And when it did, I nearly dropped to the ground so he couldn't see me.

Instead, he just looked up at the sky, swaying on his feet as a bottle of pills fell from his hands onto the cement; he barked out a laugh and tilted back whatever was left of the fifth he'd chosen that night.

His full lips were pulled back into an amused smile as the rain attacked whatever shreds of good sense he still possessed.

"Are you happy now?" He roared up at the sky, then threw the bottle against the side of the pool house as the pills on the ground washed away. "Answer me!" He grabbed a chair and threw it into the pool. "Are you fucking happy?"

His screams were going to wake up the only neighbors we had—two miles away.

As it was, he was one more mistake from getting chained in the dungeon. I knew this because Chase had said so during dinner the night before, and when I laughed, and nobody else did, I realized they did, in fact, actually have a soundproof room in the basement.

Something told me people didn't exactly come back from that.

It was his own child, but it was also the mafia, and even though nobody ever explained the rules—I knew one thing. They were killers. All of them. So chaining your son to a chair in the basement?

Probable.

I hesitated for a minute, but when he grabbed another chair and threw it, I snatched my sweatshirt, told myself that I'd faced angry before and knew how to calm it, and ran down the stairs and out the kitchen door.

Rain pelted my gray hoody as I jogged over to Ash and yelled, "Stop!"

He was holding the chair midair as he turned to me, his icy blue eyes void of all emotion.

Lost. He was so lost my heart cracked bit by bit as his chest heaved with more rage than a human was capable of holding—capable of coming back from.

A tear slid down my cheek, mixing with the raindrops.

He had everything.

And yet, he focused on the one thing he had lost.

I didn't want to judge his mourning, but that's not what this was—this was devastation pure and simple. This was carnage in its rarest form—this was death while still living.

A damned purgatory I wasn't sure anyone would come back from, especially since he chose to punish himself because he was left behind.

And Claire?

In Heaven with their unborn child.

"Go. Away," he said through clenched teeth, but at least he lowered the chair to the ground.

I took a deep breath and then a step forward. "You're drunk and, from the looks of the pills you spilled, high. Just sleep it off, Ash—"

"Why the fuck does everyone suggest I sleep it off? Like I could just go to bed, close my eyes, and when I wake up in a blanket of fucking sunshine, I'll have her back? I'll have our baby back? That's not how life works, Claire…" He stumbled toward me, then swayed on his feet as he rubbed his eyes with his right hand.

He'd called me Claire.

The knife twisted deeper into my chest as I took the second step, raising my hand to put it on his shoulder. "It won't be better. I never said it would be better; I just think it's best that you go inside so you don't die from pneumonia or force your dad's hand any more than you already have."

He flinched a bit.

He worshipped his dad.

He was, after all, a carbon copy of Chase right down to the tattoos, good looks, and insanely out-of-control temper when he had no outlet for his feelings.

Luc calmed Chase the way Claire had calmed Ash.

And now…

Destruction.

"Ash." I squeezed his shoulder, his full weight collapsed against me, thank God I was stronger than I looked as I helped him walk back into the pool house, completely soaked.

We made it as far as the couch before he fell against it. I decided to use gravity to shove him down.

He groaned and flipped onto his side, eyes empty as he stared straight ahead, droplets of water slid down his sculpted jaw onto the black leather.

I cleared my throat. "Let me just get you some dry clothes and some water…"

He squeezed his eyes shut.

At least he wasn't yelling anymore.

It took me at least ten minutes to grab some clean clothes from the chaos that was his room. I finally located a dry shirt that didn't smell like whiskey and a pair of Nike sweats that looked clean-enough.

By the time I made it downstairs with one of the bottles of water he always kept by his bed, along with his clothes, he was nowhere to be found.

Seriously?

Ugh, I so did not sign up to play babysitter tonight. I had class in the morning—early. And my only shot at survival was keeping my scholarships and actually graduating so I could get a job and get away from killers.

Not that I wasn't thankful.

At this point, I would have agreed to be their live-in cook full time if it got me a place to stay—plus, they protected me from the outside.

And I knew it was only a matter of time before someone came after me, mistook me for someone else, tried to hurt me, or just found out what pain I was hiding.

Better to keep your enemies close even if they are terrifying.

"Ash," I called.

A light flickered from the bathroom.

I sighed in relief, then went over and knocked, the door creaked open, and there he was, sitting in the bathtub completely naked.

It was impossible not to notice his perfect physique; even drunk out of his mind, he was beautiful—like a fallen angel that forgot his place was in Heaven—not his own personal hell.

"You know…" He held out a giant knife and thumbed the blade, studying the point as a trickle of blood trailed down his thumb. "Most people do it wrong…"

I froze. "You're drunk, Ash. Let's just get you some clothes—"

"Fucking idiots." His pupils were pinpoints as he looked at me over the blade of the knife. "They cut against the vein forgetting that you're supposed to cut with it. But there's other ways, Claire—other ways to join you…"

He was out of his mind. My chest heaved with panic as I weighed my options. He was an expert at killing things, even drunk. I was a college nerd on scholarship who had zero hand-to-hand combat skills.

Let alone against a proven killer.

"Three seconds," he rasped as he lowered the knife to the inside of his right thigh cutting the side like he was testing the sharpness of the knife. "Three seconds, and I'll see you, sweetheart. Three seconds and you'll be real again, three seconds, and we'll be a family." Tears streamed down his face. "That's all, Claire. That's all it would take."

The knife was so dangerously close to his femoral artery that I had no time to call Chase or the ambulance.

No time but to figure out a way to save his life.

No other way.

"Don't," I whispered. "Ash, please… don't."

"I have to." He sobbed. "I have to!"

"Please!" I choked on my tears. "Please don't, Ash, please! Just stay, stay with me, right here, right now—hand me the knife."

"Three seconds, Claire."

"Ash, Claire would want you to live."

"I killed you…" He grabbed the blade with his other hand and squeezed as blood spurted all over the bathtub. "This may as well be your blood. You were my soul, and I spilled it, I spilled it all. I didn't see, I didn't—" The knife slipped out of his bloody hand.

I lunged for it and barely grabbed it in time before he did; he was thankfully too slow.

I threw the knife away from us; it clattered against the bathroom floor as I tripped against his legs as they dangled out of the tub.

With a grunt, I fell on top of him.

He held me there.

Bleeding on me.

Sobbing.

His arms came around me. "You're gone, you're gone!"

I squeezed my eyes shut as he held me close, and then he was kissing the back of my neck.

"It's Annie…" I moved away from him. "I'm not Claire—"

"Claire…" He moaned. "Please…"

"Ash," I said it more firmly that time. "It's Annie."

I finally broke free from him, but he was fast; he grabbed me again, this time shoving up from the bathtub and reaching for me, jerking me against his chest as he pressed a hungry kiss to my mouth.

Every time I tried to pull away, he pulled me back.

And then he was turning the shower on.

My sweatshirt was coming off.

Escape was futile.

"Claire—"

"Ash." My heart cracked in half.

He stole it then.

He stomped on it.

He wrecked it like he wrecked everything.

And I let him because I was too afraid he'd kill himself.

Too afraid that he'd snap.

I'd always been too afraid.

And half in love with a man who loved a ghost and would do anything to follow her into Heaven.

"Until the sky falls…" he whispered as he kissed me again and again, so I said the only thing I could say back.

The only thing I'd ever heard Claire repeat over and over again.

"Until," I whispered, "if the sky falls, Ash."

"You're here…" He smiled for the first time. "Finally… finally…"

A tear slid down my cheek and joined the blood, and whatever was left of my broken heart as I swore to take this to my grave.

Right along with any feelings I'd ever had for Ash Abandonato.

He may as well be dead.

I may as well have let him do the digging.

"Goodbye, Ash," I whispered under my breath.

This time I kissed him.

This time I pulled him.

This time I gave him what he'd been wanting since yelling into the dark night sky—Claire.

I gave him Claire.

CHAPTER
One

But our love was stronger by far than the love of those who were older than we—of the many far wiser than we—And neither the angels in Heaven above Nor the demons down under the sea Can ever dissever my soul from the soul of the beautiful Annabelle Lee. —Edgar Allan Poe

Ash

Ten months later...

Shit always hits the fan when the storm is calm.

And I'd like to think that I was finally able to calm the hurricane inside—mostly. At least now I wasn't suicidal.

At least now, I wasn't drinking my way through the day and hallucinating that Claire was an angel sent by Heaven to give me one last moment—one last time with her—closure.

Glimpses of that night—those memories—haunted me on a daily basis. Had she really been there? Had I been that far gone that I'd seen her face? Felt her kiss?

I'd woken up with the hangover from hell and puked my guts out most of the day. I literally had to go to Sergio, our resident doctor, and ask for an IV bag.

Junior, my best friend, still refused to let me live that down the fact that I had walked around the pool house rolling an IV pole.

Miserable.

I'd been fucking miserable.

And now?

Now at least I didn't want to slit my wrists every second of every day—nah, it was more like every other second.

See? Progress!

"This came for you." Dad tossed a package onto my bed and leaned against the doorframe. "You know her plane lands in an hour."

"Yup." I didn't look up at him. I knew what I'd see.

Disappointment.

We weren't at odds with each other anymore, but that didn't mean my dad wasn't still looking at me like I shit on the unicorn that was Annie Smith and sent her running away screaming.

Mom was still pissed.

Violet.

Safe to say, my entire family wanted to burn me alive for fighting with her that next day.

Again, I'd had a hangover.

I wasn't in the mood to talk about my feelings.

She'd come over to check on me.

Her eyes haunted.

And the skin around her wrists slightly bruised.

I still wore the scar from the cut I'd made against my skin—

and still remembered waking up in a bloodbath of my own making wondering how the hell I was still alive with all that blood—again, confirming I'd dreamt up the whole thing.

When I'd asked Annie about the bruises on her wrist, about the blood in my bed, she'd just stared at me like I'd run over her favorite puppy and laughed.

"Who hurt you?" I asked without looking up, ready to puke all over her white Keds.

I mean, really? White Keds? Was she six?

"You don't—" Her voice cracked. "You don't remember last night? Throwing a tantrum and chairs? Coming back here—"

"Look." I winced as the need to puke surged closer to the surface. "I'm sorry if I said some shit that was hurtful; I was drunk, high off pills I should have never had in the first place. And sad, so fucking sad." I finally looked up at her as a wave of tension pulled tight between us. "All I remember is waking up in my bed, so if you're the one that helped me..." God, this was painful. "Thank you."

"Ash..." She chewed her lower lip as tears filled her eyes. "You really don't... you really don't remember anything else?"

I squeezed my eyes shut and smiled. "I remember her."

"Her?" She gulped.

"Claire," I whispered. "Look, I know I sound crazy, but she was there, maybe, maybe it was the drugs, I don't know, but if I have to keep talking, I can at least promise you that I'm going to start puking."

"Sorry." A tear slid down her cheek.

"Why the hell do you cry so much?" I snapped, my head pounding at the temples so hard that I thought I was going to die from the pain. Besides, her tears reminded me of so much hurt that I'd yet to process it reminded me I needed to grieve,

which reminded me she was dead. Which meant every time Annie cried…

I thought of Claire.

She jumped a foot. "Wh-what?"

"See, that's what I mean!" I needed someone to be angry with, and I sure as hell didn't want to be angry with myself, and she was standing there so fucking perfect in her fucking sweater looking like sunshine.

And I hated her for it.

When you're suffering, you want everyone around you to suffer. Everyone.

Most of all, the ones who seem to have more happiness than you. Because if you can just steal away some of that happiness, maybe your sadness won't be so heavy.

If you can punch the hell out of their smile.

It won't hurt so much when you frown.

"I don't understand." Her eyes narrowed, filling with more tears. "I was just checking up on—"

"I don't like you." I snapped. "At all. I don't want to fuck you. I sure as hell don't want to be your friend, Annie, so you don't need to check up on me because I'm not that guy. I'm not gentle. If you were sick, I'd probably tell you to toughen up and then drop off soup at your door in case you're contagious. I'm not that guy, so I don't know why you keep trying. It's like you think you see something in me that you can save when I don't want saving. I don't need rescuing. And I would never pick you of all people to be my hero, even if I did."

Her eyes widened, and she stumbled backward, her head shaking like she couldn't believe what I was saying when I'd never promised her otherwise. It was confusing as hell.

I sighed. "Look, just because we almost screwed after the pool house means nothing." I knew it was a mistake, letting her play that part months ago while Valerian snuck into my house.

She was supposed to be the slutty distraction.

And I wasn't supposed to get so hard that I wanted nothing more than to take her into my bedroom and strip.

I'd been depressed.

Angry.

And she'd been easy.

That was it.

I didn't even realize I'd just said all of that out loud until she gasped and put her hand over her mouth.

"Shit, Annie—"

"No." She held up her shaking hands. "It's fine. I'm fine." Her smile was so damn forced.

She'd always been gorgeous.

But so damn pure that it was impossible not to hate her.

We always hated what we couldn't have.

And she had peace.

I was a son of war.

The two would never... could never meet.

She turned on her heel and muttered something about letting me drown in my own vomit before slamming the door behind her.

Huh, maybe she did have some spunk.

"Ash." Dad's voice brought me back to the present. When I looked up, all I saw was rage.

Fantastic.

Scary Dad was gonna go in for the kill.

In three.

Two.

One.

"You owe me." He clenched his jaw. "The only reason

your mom doesn't know about the pills is because I kept it from her—from your friends, your family. So here's how this is gonna work."

I clenched my teeth and waited for it.

"You're going to put on a shirt that doesn't have bloodstains on it from sparring with Tank, you're going to get your ass in whatever car that's going to get you there faster. You're going to put a fucking smile on your face, and you're going to pick up Annie from the airport. If she wants French fries because she's hungry, I expect you to stop at no less than five places so she can pick her favorite. If she wants you to take her shopping, you hand over the Amex. If she wants you to start rapping? You fucking ask her which song she wants to hear. You. Are. Her. Slave. Do you understand me?"

"But, Dad—"

"No 'but Dads.'" He jabbed his finger at me. "Consider your atonement finished only as long as she gets back to this house without looking like she's been crying. You don't deserve to breathe next to her, let alone be the reason for her tears."

"You do realize I'm your son, right?" I sneered.

He grabbed me by the shirt and shoved me against the nearest wall. His smile was cruel. "My son died that day; I've yet to see him return."

Slitting my throat would have hurt less.

We stared each other down.

The room was heavy with tension.

Sick with sadness.

God, when would it finally end?

"That was a low blow, even for you, Sen…a…tor." I drew out the title, knowing he hated it—especially coming from his only son.

His eyes flashed. "Baiting me won't make you feel better, believe me." He shoved me back against the wall, then adjusted his tie and cracked his neck. The tats on his hands seemed to come alive with warning as he moved like he wanted me to know he would punch his own son in hopes of knocking some sense into him.

"Fine." I looked away so I wouldn't see the disappointment in his eyes. "I'll take the Tesla, as much as it pains me to admit, it's faster than the Lambo."

He let out a snort. "Never let Tex hear you say that."

"I think he wept the day an electric sedan beat his sports car." I sighed and then went over to my dresser to grab a T-shirt.

"It will get easier," Dad whispered. "One day. Not today, not tomorrow, I don't know when, but one day, you won't feel like you're in purgatory."

"I don't feel like I'm in purgatory, Dad..." I looked over my shoulder. "I feel like I'm reliving Hell."

His eyes softened for a minute before he gave me a nod and then turned around and left.

I kicked my dresser a few times before finally pulling a long-sleeve black tee over my head then grabbing my wallet and cell phone.

One thing I was one hundred percent certain about?

Annie was going to shit a brick that enemy number one was picking her up—which to a masochist like me? Had me smiling the entire drive to the airport.

CHAPTER
Two

Time is too slow for those who wait, Too swift for
those who fear, Too long for those who grieve, Too
short for those who rejoice, But for those who love,
time is eternity. — Henry Van Dyke

Annie

e was late.

I tried to shove every last nerve down into the pit of
my stomach and keep it on lockdown.

Almost a full year had passed.

The memories of his words were as new and hurtful today
as they had been the day he said them.

But Ash Abandonato could just... rot in hell for all I cared.

That was why I'd left.

Well, it wasn't exactly part of the plan, but when Chase
had found me that day sobbing uncontrollably in the kitchen,
nearly ready to collapse against the ground, it had taken
everything in me not to rat Ash out.

But Chase knew.

His eyes had left mine and slowly gazed around until they landed on the sliding glass door and the pool house across the way.

"Tell me everything," he'd rasped.

Then and only then did I find out that I was vetted through the Family because they truly knew everything.

And their only way of protecting me?

Protecting what was going on?

Keep me safe.

I should have known better.

Then again, they'd very carefully kept me alive, and when Chase offered me an out for the next ten months, I'd jumped at the chance. I'd always loved art anyway, and to be able to travel to a foreign country by myself? To be given the type of freedom I'd only ever dreamed of with my own shiny black credit card and the blessing from one of the most powerful men in the states?

I would have kissed his feet then begged to shine his shoes for the rest of my life.

He'd kissed my forehead then.

He'd apologized on his son's behalf.

And I think a part of Chase died that day, the day he had to carry the sins of his son when he was already too busy carrying the sins of the world—the sins of the Family.

My time in Italy had been incredible.

Studying abroad had been a pipe dream, but now that I was back and ready to finish the last few classes I needed to graduate, I felt deflated.

In Italy, I'd seen myself as brave.

I'd learned to love myself.

I'd learned to put on lipstick, much to the amusement of all the cousins I already missed so much that there was a huge chunk of my heart missing where they were supposed to be.

Whatever preconceived notions I had about living with another mafia family went completely out the window when they hosted a party in my honor upon arrival.

So. Much. Wine.

So much food.

So much laughter.

I swiped at the stray tear on my cheek and quickly put on my black Prada sunglasses—a parting gift from Aunt Sophie.

"Boys who make girls cry, they are not worth your time, Bellissima." She lifted my chin with her fingertip, slid the black glasses onto my nose, and whispered, *"We Italians, we do not let them decide our emotions. We decide for ourselves. And then we raise hell, capire?"*

"Capire." I'd smiled through my tears only to be hugged within an inch of my life and told I was again too skinny and needed to eat.

With a sigh I checked my phone again, where was he?

"Annie!" A familiar voice sounded my name, and just like that, the anxiety lifted as I turned around and laughed at my friend Tank as he jogged toward me.

He was wearing a black beanie; his brown hair had grown out since I'd last seen him, curling near the nape of his neck as his green eyes drank me in, crinkling at the sides. One small dimple made itself known as his megawatt smile fell onto me like a day in the hot sun.

He'd always been like that.

Intense yet warm, in a way that I'd never been able to explain. As he got closer, I noticed the coldness that had started to seep into his eyes—that was what this life did, after all—the mafia life. He'd been recruited by Ash, and now—well now that was who he answered to no matter what.

Now he was in this, whether he liked it or not.

The warmth dissipated as fear replaced it. Fear for my friend and for the uncertain future under such a cruel royal rule.

"Tank." I grinned and then held out my arms as he pulled me in for a tight hug. He always smelled so good, like a hot guy should smell, though it was almost as if I could still sense the faint hint of blood in the air.

So much had changed since he'd been my savior last year at Eagle Elite University.

Next to the OG bosses, he was the only one who knew everything about me, who basically grew up next door and promised to one day come back and let me ride with him on his white horse.

Too bad it ended up being more black Chevy Impala, but still. In his own way, he'd tried to save me.

But sometimes, the girl had to save herself, and with my newfound freedom, I discovered I preferred that.

Being my own hero.

Straightening my own damn crown.

I was better at it.

Because people let you down.

But me? I was still standing, wasn't I?

Then again, I'd yet to be put in a position where I'd tested my own theory, but in my daydreams? I was a badass. So what if I couldn't throw a punch without wanting to cry and nearly hurled when I saw blood?

"Wow, girl." Tank's grin was wide. "FaceTime chats did not do you justice." He reached for my thick chin-length hair and gave it a little tug. Butterflies erupted in my stomach. He'd always been so beautiful. Safe. "It suits you."

"I was too hot over there." I lied.

Ash had said my hair was pretty.

The first thing I did overseas was cut it.

His eyes flickered to my mouth briefly, and then he was reaching for my black suitcase, tugging the handle up with one loud click. "Just this one?"

Warmth rushed to my cheeks. "Yeah, thanks, by the way, for picking me up."

I'd almost lost my nerve when I'd texted him, no idea why, but now I felt nervous around one of my best friends.

Great.

Tank just shrugged. "I figured you'd need reinforcements going back to that hellhole."

He clenched his teeth and looked away; it looked like he was thinking about killing someone.

I never told him exactly what happened.

But it was *Tank*.

And he was around all of the Five Families twenty-four seven as both an FBI informant and as a made man.

He could probably make an educated guess that things went horribly wrong the minute I stepped inside Ash's domain.

Then again, he had problems of his own.

One day he would have to choose.

Right now, he just straddled the line.

He was living with Sergio's family for the time being since Sergio was one of the ones who had the most experience with the FBI next to Phoenix.

And me?

I was the orphan that got to rely on the charity of the great

Abandonato Family. I had to admit, I did miss Luc, Violet, Izzy, and Chase—a lot.

But Ash?

My heart sank.

Was he still depressed?

Still angry?

Hateful?

Horrible?

Why did I even care?

Finish classes and get the heck out—my only job at this point. Besides, once I lost my usefulness with The Family, I'd probably be kindly asked to leave anyway. Sent packing with enough money and a new identity, isn't that what they did in the movies? Well, I mean either that or off people. Did they say it like that still?

I worried my lower lip and nearly ran into Tank's muscled back as he muttered, "You've got to be shitting me."

A black Tesla screeched to a halt directly in front of the curb.

I peered around Tank, digging my fingers into his biceps to keep myself from falling over because…

Ash Abandonato.

Of course, the angry one looked sexy.

Of course, he seemed to be walking toward us in slow motion.

His aviators only accented his chiseled jaw, pretty much perfect six foot three body, tight long-sleeve black shirt and ripped jeans. Was it so much to ask for him to look as bad as he'd made me feel that night?

Who was I kidding?

Multiple nights.

I willed the tears to stay in.

I was over it.

Over his stupid kiss.

Over those gentle words that night.

"Until the stars fall, Claire." *He'd messed up their phrase, making it feel new like it was ours when it had only ever been their sky, not our stars. His mouth was so tender as he pressed me back against the mattress. His expert tongue sliding past every defense I thought I'd erected.*

Our bodies molded together.

Was this what people talked about when they said they just knew?

This feeling right here?

He pulled away, his eyes glassy, filled with tears. "Miss you so fucking much."

"Do better," I whispered. "Be better than this, Ash."

"How?" His voice cracked.

"You live the life they would have wanted you to live. You need—" A tear ran down my cheek. "—you need to let go."

"Anything but that." He shook his head and then buried his face beneath a blanket of my hair. "I'm not good without you."

"Yes." I took a deep breath. "You are."

Tank's possessive stance then sudden shove backward pulled me from my memories as I waited for the gates of Hell to open and swallow its number one sinner whole. When I glanced down, I wanted to commit murder. How was he able to even make Adidas slides look expensive and sleek?

I didn't think it was possible to hate him more, but I did. I so did. Because how dare he smile at both of us like he had a right to even look at me?

In front of me, Tank tensed, every muscle on high alert.

In a huff, I moved around him and put my hands on my hips; clearly, Italy had been good for me because I was ready for a fight. Ready to hand my sunglasses to Tank and throw a punch even though I'd probably break my hand.

Or so I thought.

And then he made eye contact.

And I lost all nerve, ready to dive into the nearest trashcan and rock back and forth.

"Hey." Ash frowned down at me, and then slowly, a sultry smirk appeared on his face as he glanced back at Tank. "Who's your friend?"

I opened my mouth, but Tank shoved me behind him again and laughed awkwardly. "Nobody, man, just a friend."

"Your friend have a name?" I could almost imagine Ash's sexy grin; the way it could literally melt clothes off a girl's body was so infuriating, I had to imagine setting him on fire in order to feel better about my life.

"Nah, I think I'm keeping this one for myself." Tank shrugged. "You know how we all like our secrets, yeah?"

"Yeah…" Ash drew out his response.

"So you need anything else, or…?" Tank was already violently tugging me in the opposite direction. I stumbled after him, nearly faceplanting against the concrete.

Ash sighed in annoyance, following after us. "Look whatever. My dad's gonna kill me. Traffic was complete shit—"

Tank halted and shot him a glare over his shoulder. I tried but couldn't keep my eyes off this man who had yet to really acknowledge me. What an ass!

Holding up a hand in surrender, Ash released a soft laugh. "Not the point, have you seen Annie? You know, about yay high."

I was NOT that short!

His hand was literally halfway to his chest, the bastard!

And the gorgeous idiot just kept going. "Constantly has her nose in the air, most likely a pair of pearls wrapped around her neck." He sighed and shook his head in what appeared to be disappointment. "I just hope she burned the Keds and cardigans... Then again, sometimes the cardigans did do something for me—"

"Stop talking," Tank said through clenched teeth.

But it was Ash, so of course, he just put his hands on his hips and kept right on going. "Bro, what's your deal? You still upset that I kicked your ass yesterday? It's how we're training the new recruits, you know? It sucks—hey, did you ever find your missing molar?"

Tank shifted between his feet. "No, but it's fine; teeth can be replaced."

"And dicks cannot." Ash nodded solemnly like he was spouting wisdom. "Anyway, back to Annie, seriously, have you seen her?" He scratched his head like he was dumbfounded about why I wouldn't be waiting for him at the airport. Was he insane? "Her plane was supposed to have just landed, bro. Come on, you know Annie! Looks like she's always late for Sunday school." He gave a sarcastic grin. "Either that or late to teach it." He laughed at his own joke.

That bastard!

All right.

I was done.

I shoved Tank to the side, which meant he moved maybe two inches, and I made my appearance, jamming my hands on my hips. "Had I known the devil was coming to pick me up, I would have put on some garlic instead of my pearls."

In one fluid movement, Ash jerked off his sunglasses and stared down at me in confusion, and then squinted harder, taking in my black leggings, black combat boots, and cream sweater. "I'm sorry, who are you again?"

I shoved both hands against his chest, sending him stumbling backward, then yanked off my sunglasses. "Apparently, your new Sunday school teacher. Spoiler alert, you're going to hell!"

His eyes widened as he eyed me up and down and then seemed to realize it looked like he was checking me out and quickly looked away, jaw clenched, anger back.

Was it always going to be like this?

My heart was already so wounded at this point, right along with my pride, they were getting wheeled toward the emergency room as if the year of healing hadn't even happened.

"Take me home, Tank." I was suddenly exhausted as I tried sidestepping Ash, only to have his arm jerk out and grab my wrist. "Let me go!"

"No," he snapped, his fingers digging into me, reminding me of that night, of my mistake and gross mistrust. "I promised my dad I'd pick you up, ergo, you get your ass in my car, not his truck."

Tank lunged for him only to have Ash hold up his hand like he was God. I hated that it stopped Tank in his tracks. Hated it.

"Remember who you serve, Tank," Ash said in a cocky tone that basically meant Tank's hands were tied even though I was convinced he wanted to cheerfully strangle Ash.

According to their stupid mafia rules, Ash was basically Tank's boss. Nobody crossed him, least of all someone who hadn't even been given the title of captain yet. Though he deserved it, I knew why they waited; they wanted to make sure they could trust him.

Which meant right now?

I would have to get in that stupid Tesla and try not to cry.

Because if I cried, he'd make fun of me.

He'd ask me why I was crying again.

And I wasn't sure I could handle Ash making fun of me ever again.

It was already hard enough breathing around him, let alone having to listen to the poison that fell from his mouth.

I straightened my shoulders. "It's fine, Tank; I'm a big girl." I jerked my head toward Ash. "Get my bag."

"No please?"

"Nope." I popped the P then smiled sweetly. "You don't deserve manners; why would I even waste words on you at this point?"

He scoffed. "That's rude."

I snorted. "Coming from you, I think that's almost a compliment."

Tank opened the passenger side door, worry etched all over his preppy looking face. He was almost too All-American, too pure to look the part, but I knew his secrets.

What he'd done.

Who he'd silenced.

Such a nice ruse.

We all had them.

I guess everyone but me.

Maybe that was why Ash hated me so much.

I didn't know how to pretend.

How to verbally spar.

How to physically fight, at least well.

I was just… me.

And it bored him to tears, made him lash out, made him angry that I didn't try to pretend to be anyone but who I was born to be.

A girl who loved art.

Who wore cardigans so people didn't see too much.

A girl who wore pearls because it was the only thing that was left of her dead parents.

No, Ash wouldn't want to know those boring details.

He may discover he actually had a heart if he did.

And the last thing I needed was Ash discovering he wasn't as scary as he thought he was.

No, he was more terrified than scared.

Terrified, of losing everything.

Tank reached for me. "Annie, text me if—"

"She's safer with me than anyone else in this city, or do you doubt my ability to protect her?" Ash crossed his arms in a challenge as I sunk down into my seat and prayed for the apocalypse.

"Sorry, Ash." Tank straightened. "You're right; I'll just check in later."

"Do that," Ash snapped.

He opened the driver's side door, slammed it, then seemed pissed that the car wasn't making enough noise as he sped out of the airport.

I gripped the door handle to keep from getting flung through the actual door as he sped in and out of traffic, his long, lean fingers bracing the steering wheel as he stared straight ahead.

"Hungry?" he asked with a gruff bark that had me jumping in my seat.

Was he still doing pills? Drinking? Should he even be driving?

"I'm fine," I said softly.

Do. Not. Cry.

I lifted my chin a bit, remembering Aunt Sophia's words.

He gave me major side-eye and then jerked his head back toward the road. "You're skin and bones."

I squeezed my eyes shut.

When Aunt Sophia said it, she said it out of love because I couldn't eat anything for the first few months.

I had trouble existing, let alone eating.

My lower lip trembled as I looked out my own window. "I got sick in Italy. I'm fine now, thanks for asking. It's not because I'm choosing not to eat." Jackass.

"How sick?" He asked, again his voice so gruff that I wanted to shake him. Would it kill him to soften up a bit?

With a sigh, I answered, "Sick enough that I had a rough first few months."

"Did you see a doctor?"

"Do you even care?" I snapped.

His grip tightened on the steering wheel. "I'd be an animal not to care."

I just stared at him, letting the silence do the talking.

He glanced over at me, then back at the road, then at me again. "You're shitting me. You hate me that much?"

"Pretty sure the hate's mutual, Ash, which suites me just fine."

"What the hell did I ever do to you?" he roared.

I was already exhausted. "The fact that you even have to ask yourself that question tells me all I need to know." I grabbed my cell. "Can you take me over to Sergio's first?"

"You don't live at Sergio's," he pointed out. "You live with me—us."

"I know where I'm currently staying, thanks." My voice cracked. God, it was like he would never let me forget it. "I just want to hang out with Tank for a little bit before dinner—"

"No," he barked.

"No?" I argued. "Who died and made you my dad?"

"You said you were sick. If you were sick, that means you need to rest, and you need food, no hanging out, no shopping, no guys. Just... no guys."

I gaped at him like he'd just grown a second and third head. "Are you even hearing yourself right now?"

"Honestly, wish I wasn't hearing myself." He slammed his hand against the steering wheel. "Fucking hell!"

I jumped a foot.

"Sorry." The fact that he actually apologized was more confusing than the outburst. "I'm... never mind. Long day."

"Tell me about it," I muttered.

The rest of the ride was quiet as we pulled up to the house. I missed it. It was like something out of a magazine, the perfect house to do a photoshoot in front of with its huge fountain in the middle, perfect brick, expensive cars parked out front.

My life now.

Weird.

Ash grabbed my bag without me asking and then opened the front door for me just as Izzy popped into my line of vision. "You made it!"

I was engulfed in a hug before I could say hi.

She held me tight, then whispered. "You have no idea how

much we need to talk about."

My smile felt strained. I really was tired.

"Shit, Iz, let her at least change before you start terrorizing her." Ash came to my defense.

I narrowed my eyes at him.

He narrowed his right back.

What was this?

I leaned in.

"What are you doing?" He smirked.

I waved in front of his face. "Are you still taking—"

Ash's eyes went wide as saucers as he slammed a hand over my mouth and started dragging me down the hall. "Adult conversation, be right back. Iz, take her stuff up to her room? Thanks, you're the best; I'll do the dishes, okay bye!"

He dragged me all the way back outside, around the pool, into the pool house, and all the way up the stairs into his room.

It was impossible to fight him, and I really just wanted to be anywhere but there.

"Get off!" I shoved him when he finally shut the door to his bedroom. "What the hell is your problem?"

His eyebrows shot up. "You dare talk to me like that?"

"You dare kidnap me in your parents' house?"

"Hardly kidnapping." He scowled. "I didn't even use duct tape."

"What's sad is you're probably not joking."

"I never joke about a good kidnapping."

I sighed; I was on borrowed time with the tears as it was. "What did you need this much privacy for, Ash?"

His eyes roamed over me before his jaw ticked, and he looked away. "They don't know."

"They don't know what?"

He cleared his throat and looked down at his feet. "About the pills."

"You idiot!" I stomped over to him and smacked him in the chest. "You're still taking pills? Are you insane! You're going to kill yourself! I guess you really do want to die, don't you? Do you even know how bad that is for your liver? Or all the things that could happen to the people you love? It's like a gateway to heroin, and I'm not going to sit back and watch someone I—" I stopped myself "—I won't do it, Ash! I'd tell the whole damn world before keeping your secret!"

By the time I was done, my chest was heaving.

And Ash was smiling down at me.

"Stop smiling!" I gave him a shove. "I hate you! I hate you!"

I didn't realize I was screaming until he cupped his hand over my mouth again, then very slowly removed his fingertips one by one.

"Feeling's mutual," he rasped. His eyes were filled with hatred and something else I couldn't put my finger on. "And I'm not doing drugs, okay? My mom and sisters just don't know." He pulled away from me then. "So I would appreciate it if you'd stop the whole Sunday school teacher act and actually not tell everyone all my sins."

"I can't count that high anyway," I said sweetly and followed up with a pasted-on smile.

He barked out a laugh. "Wow, Italy changed you. Last year you would have cried, and now I'm half afraid you're going to scratch my eyes out."

"The night's young." I snapped, then walked over to his bed and picked up a package.

It looked funny.

I wasn't sure why I thought that.

It was from China, but *"Toy Distribution"* was stamped on it. "What's this?"

He held open his hands, so I tossed it to him, and he tore it open in annoyance. Hands trembling, he dropped whatever white thing it was to the ground and rushed me until I was slammed up against the wall, his body protecting mine.

"Ash?"

"Shhhhh. Just wait…" His eyes were furious, his body strained as he held me captive, and then he very slowly slid his hand into his pocket, pulled out his phone, and pressed a number. "Yeah, Dad, white horse… I'm not sure; send Junior just in case—Dad, Junior would want it that way… No, Phoenix would get it… Call Valerian too while you're at it—I don't know. I don't fucking *know!*" His hands were shaking by the time he ended the call.

"Ash?" My voice shook, even then, I didn't move a muscle, too petrified something bad would happen if I was reading his body language correctly, and by the heat coming off his chest, the rage burning from the inside of his soul. "What's going on?"

He locked eyes with me, his whisper gruff. "Nothing huge… Someone just wants me dead."

I jolted like I'd been slapped as tears filled my eyes. "And the package?" Panic pitched my question two octaves too high.

Sympathy mirrored in the depths of his gaze. "I need them to make sure there's no bomb."

"Then why are you still here?" My voice trembled. Why not let me die?

"Because here is where you are." He leaned in, licking his lips just as the door to his room flew open admitting Hell's scariest demons.

The men of the mafia.
Lovers.
Killers.
Family.

CHAPTER
Three

"If I should go before the rest of you. Break not a flower nor inscribe a stone. Nor when I'm gone speak in a Sunday voice. But be the usual selves that I have known. Weep if you must. Parting is hell. But life goes on. So sing as well." —Joyce Grenfell

Ash

My heart was pounding so hard I was convinced she could hear it. Every muscle was on high alert as I tried to shield her with my body.

It had been pure instinct.

Pure adrenaline.

She didn't know that the last horse sent to Nixon's had taken out part of the kitchen.

Thankfully, no one in the family had been home.

But it had put two associates in the hospital with burns and burst eardrums. All I could think of was keeping her safe.

Amidst the hatred.

The shame.

The tension between us.

My brain had shut down.

And my heart had demanded, *"protect."*

"Stay there!" Junior shouted at us as I pressed Annie harder against the wall. I didn't need to be so aggressive, but she didn't know that, so I enjoyed the moment while I could, aware that once my brain kicked back into gear, I'd scowl and push her away like I always did.

Because even if there was a slight attraction there...

The hatred burned brighter just like the blame; it always did, it always would.

"Got it," I called back and then lowered my head until my lips grazed her right ear. "Try to stay calm; Junior's one of the best."

She slowly nodded her head, but her breathing picked up.

Was it me or the potential bomb?

Both?

I moved my hands to her hips, holding her there, pressing my body up against hers in a way that to anyone else would look protective.

Instead, I just couldn't help myself.

She let out a shudder, one of her hands slowly moved to my hip. She rested it there, her palm burning a hole through my jeans and part of my skin since my shirt had ridden up in all my haste to protect her.

"Junior!" Phoenix bit out a curse. "The hell is taking so long?"

I could hear my dad roaring insults into what I assumed was a cell phone, most likely a safe distance from my bedroom door.

Of course, Phoenix wouldn't be kept downstairs; his son was acting as bomb expert—his only son.

"Ash!" Serena called my name. "Why are you so extra?"

I rolled my eyes. "Could you not right now, Serena?"

"Stupid cousin," she fired back.

"Love you too," I called.

"Is Annie okay?" Izzy was next.

"Phoenix, why the hell are you allowing the girls up here?"

I could practically feel Phoenix's sigh. Nobody said no to my cousin and sister. Nobody.

Not even the great Phoenix Nicolasi.

The thought had me smiling until I locked eyes with Annie again; she had tears streaming down her face.

"Hey, hey, hey." I cupped her face wiping her tears with my thumbs. "You're going to be fine; besides, the blast would take me out and keep you alive."

Her pouty lips parted. "I don't think I could survive that sort of guilt twice, Ash. Next time—" Her lip trembled. "Next time, please just let me die."

I dropped my hands. "Are you fucking kidding me?"

She looked away. "Are we safe yet?"

"Almost there…" Junior said, all casual, and then started fucking whistling Shawn Mendez. Sometimes I hated him. "And wires cut…" He sighed. "You're lucky it was a dud, or you would have been *ash*." He laughed. "Oh shit, sorry, I couldn't help myself."

"Jackass!" Serena yelled, barging into the room as Annie slipped out from underneath me and made her way toward the door.

Izzy was there in an instant pulling her into her arms. "Are you okay?"

"Yeah." Annie sniffled.

"Annie!" Tank's voice was more unwelcome than the bomb.

"You sure it's a dud?" I jerked my head toward the small stuffed white horse. Because if it wasn't, I had someone I was going to throw it at. Hah, watch him explode into tiny little Tanks all over the house.

The hell was wrong with me?

Tank shoved his way into the room, basically jerked Annie out of Izzy's arms, and hugged her so tight that I was afraid her head would pop off.

"She's fine," I barked.

"Why was she even up here in the first place?" Tank scowled over Annie's head, his green eyes flashing.

I just grinned like it was for nefarious purposes and then lifted a shoulder in a bored shrug. "Does it matter?"

"You." Tank jabbed a finger at me.

I tilted my head. "Yes?"

"Tank." Serena patted his back. "Leave it alone, big guy. As much as I like watching people fight, you would lose, and Ash's running on enough adrenaline that I'm afraid he'd wrap your tongue around your own head then set you on fire."

"Always so fucking graphic, my girl." Junior winked.

Looking remarkably at ease in her black pants and matching crop top, she carried out a mock curtsy, then crossed her arms and stared at both Junior and me. "So what are we dealing with?"

"Evil horses." Phoenix marched into the room and grabbed the package. "Good job, son. You did this one in under a minute."

Serena pushed Junior in the stomach, her way of giving him a high five. Psychopath.

Junior ran a hand through his newly buzzed hair. "Thanks, Dad."

Phoenix just nodded his head and then waved the package at us. "I'll be with the other bosses trying to figure this shit out. You guys get any more packages, don't bring them into the house, all right?"

"Yup." I saluted him. "Though that one's on my dad…"

Phoenix froze, his blue eyes narrowing. "He brought it in?"

"Tossed it on my bed."

"Huh." He licked his lips. "Wonder why our underboss is suddenly so careless…"

All eyes fell on me like it was my fault.

Well… it probably was.

He'd been pissed at me again.

I'd been like an angry zombie going through the motions.

"Shit." I lowered my head. "I'll talk to him."

"Better yet," Phoenix said, his voice icy. "Fix it."

"Fix what?" Serena asked, even though I knew she wasn't clueless.

"All of it." Phoenix smirked. "Annie, always a pleasure to see you; I like the hair. It suits you."

Her cheeks pinked. "Thanks, Phoenix."

The hell? He gives her a compliment, and she looks ready to write him a note during math class! I compliment her and… Well, I didn't actually compliment her, but in my head I know I said something like, *"damn nice hair."*

Fuck.

"Are you sure you're all right?" Tank tilted her chin toward him and studied her face.

"She's fine," I snapped. "She was with me, or did you forget so quickly?" I crossed my arms while both Izzy and Serena gave me funny side-eyed looks. Junior was suddenly staring down at his phone like he was seconds away from curing cancer.

And Tank?

Well, every muscle seemed flexed.

I hated that I was the reason he'd gotten more cut in the last year. I'd trained him, for shit's sake, and now he felt more foe than friend.

"I'm staying for dinner," Tank announced, wrapping an arm around Annie and leading her out of the room.

Izzy skipped after them, then looked over her shoulder and stuck out her tongue at me.

I flipped her off.

Her cackle could be heard all the way down the hall.

With a sigh, I collapsed onto my bed.

Junior was first. "Sooooo, Annie in your room?"

"Long story." I lay down on the unmade bed and wiped my hands down my face. "Don't worry about it."

Serena was next. "You know, it's okay to—"

"Finish that fucking sentence, and I'm pulling a gun."

She snorted. "Please, I'll just kick it out of your pathetic hand, you weak little lamb—besides, you've got a crush, which means you have a blind spot; I'd eat you alive cousin."

I peeked through my fingers and burst out laughing. "Shit, you're trying to get me to fight, aren't you?"

She shrugged. "Junior's not rough anymore."

"I could have gone my entire life without hearing that sentence, Serena," I grumbled while Junior winked at her like he had plans later.

"Hate you guys." I shot to my feet. "Where's Valerian when you need him?"

"Actually, Dad said he's flying down later this week. The

Russians are concerned that if something happens to us, they'll lose some of their most powerful allies."

I frowned. "How sweet and uncharacteristic of them."

"Exactly." Junior snorted. "Oh, also, we're staying for dinner too."

"Is everyone staying for dinner?" I was already exhausted.

"With Annie and Tank here? It's gonna be dinner and a show." Serena rubbed her hands together. "And just so we're all clear—you still hate her?"

"With every fiber of my dark soul," I muttered.

Annie suddenly appeared at the door, her face blank. "Sorry, I uh, dropped my cell." She scurried past Serena picked her phone off the floor, and then sprinted out of my room.

Most likely cursing me to hell the entire way.

"Did that on purpose, didn't you?" I said to no one in particular.

"Course she did." Junior winked. "She's evil."

"Aw." Serena put a hand to her chest. "Thank you!"

"My evil queen," he said gruffly.

"My wicked queen." She jumped into his arms, wrapping her legs around his waist.

"Leave before I bleach my eyes!" I roared as they started making out right in front of me. "What the hell have I ever done to deserve this?" She was fucking climbing him like a tree.

And I wasn't jealous.

At all.

Of the fact that they had each other and I had no one.

Or that even Tank—of all people—had the one person I hated more than anyone in this world.

So why had my heart felt like it missed a few beats when I'd thought there was a bomb?

And why did the thought of him touching her send me into an angry spiral that had me ready to break him in half?

Hate was a weird emotion.

But hate for the woman who you held responsible for your fiancée's death?

Impossible to explain.

It could only be felt.

And I hated that every time I felt it—it felt wrong.

CHAPTER
Four

Where do people go when they die? Somewhere down below or in the sky? 'I can't be sure,' said Grandad, 'but it seems they simply set up home inside our dreams.'— Jeanne Willis

Annie

Tank brought me back to my room and then said something about sparring down in the basement. He was so comfortable in this house, and yet I was the one who had lived here.

Who had a room here.

And I still always felt like I was an interloper.

Even though everyone treated me like family.

My room was the same, a dark navy blue with spouts of white on the walls, a gorgeous sitting area by a fireplace, and my own outdoor balcony.

I blamed that balcony for everything, so I gave it a wide berth as I slowly put my clothes away.

My eyes fall upon the cute pair of jeans I'd bought and the crop top that I'd been brave enough to purchase only because I'd had two full glasses of wine with my aunt before she took me to get new clothes.

Her idea.

She loved spending Chase's money; she said so every time she swiped.

And maybe, just, maybe she knew that I felt too guilty to do said swiping, so took it upon herself to make sure it was used.

Both items still had tags on them.

Sad that I would probably never wear them.

"You're wearing that." Izzy's voice fills the room.

"Agh!" I dropped the clothes. "Are you trying to give me a heart attack?"

She waved me off, tossing her long dark hair over her shoulder. "Stop being dramatic. If I was trying to give you a heart attack I'd just inject you with one of the handy needles we keep in our cases, stops your heart instantly doesn't even leave a mark, genius really—" She stopped talking, probably because I'd felt my body sway as all the blood drained from my face. She scrunched up her nose. "Sorry, I tend to get too detailed."

"It's okay." I put a shaky hand to my chest. "Just not used to all the casual killer talk."

"Meh, you'll get there one day." Her blue eyes lit up. "Okay so, I'm pretty sure Tank has the hots for you. He wouldn't stop talking about picking you up the other day, which is weird since Ash was the one who— You know what? Never mind, Ash is an idiot; we don't count him in this scenario."

"Definitely not." I swallowed the lump in my throat. "Plus,

46

he hates me with every part of his soul, and that's a direct quote, mind you."

She winced. "He said that? Out loud?"

"Yup." I refused to let it bother me even though it was kind of impossible not to. I mean, it was never fun hearing how much someone hated you despite trying to save his life.

Boys were weird.

That one in particular.

I took a deep breath. "Anyway, this is a fresh start, and I like Tank. He's… hot, and we've been friends since…" I frowned. Did I tell her? That it had been longer than just college? That that part had been a carefully constructed ruse by Tank himself to infiltrate?

"Since last year." I lied, hoping she wouldn't see through it since I was one of the worst liars ever. "Anyway, I just want to forget about—all of it."

"And by all of it, you mean Ash having a nervous breakdown and throwing chairs in our pool or all of it being him making out with you a week after Claire died only to push you away and blame you for her death?"

I was quiet for a minute as my emotions rolled around in my chest, colliding with each other, wreaking havoc. "All of that."

"Good!" She jumped to her feet. Her purple Jordan high tops were matched with ripped jeans and a loose T-shirt; out of all the girls, she'd always had the most relaxed style.

Last year she said it gave Maksim easy access.

This year?

I still hadn't seen him. And she hadn't talked about him.

So I assumed Maksim was either murdered by Chase or warned away.

And since she wasn't sobbing, he was probably just threatened with a beheading.

Typical Chase.

Izzy jerked the tags off the clothes and tossed them to me. "Trust me. He won't be able to take his eyes off you, plus this is your first family dinner since up and leaving without telling us. You need to look hot. Now, where's your makeup?"

"Why? Do you need some?"

She snorted. "Uh, look at me? Do I look like I need makeup? I'm a damn masterpiece. No, I mean for you."

"Oh, I have some on—"

"I'm gonna stop you right there. You have very little on, and while it looks natural and pretty, I want you to look like you just walked off the runway. Tank will love it."

And maybe even Ash.

No!

See! This was the reason I hated watching TV. The girl almost always fell for the asshole when he had zero redeeming qualities!

Plus, how did you even begin to navigate a relationship with a guy who only saw his dead fiancée when he looked at your face?

You didn't.

You couldn't.

It was irreparable.

And it was my fault.

"Hellloooo." Izzy snapped her fingers in front of my face. "Makeup bag. Now."

"Over there." I pointed to my carry-on. "Just don't make me look crazy."

"Please." She rolled her eyes and snatched the bag. "I'm a damn professional at this point."

"You're twenty," I reminded her.

"Exactly. Makeup tutorials are my life."

"Okay…"

"Yes!" She pointed to the bed. "Sit."

"Is, um, Maksim coming tonight?"

Her smile fell, and then her face was back to its neutral self. "Maybe, maybe not. But say his name again, and I'm going to make you look like a street whore on a bad acid trip, understood?"

"And to think I always imagined Serena as the scary one," I mumbled, giving my shirt a nervous tug while she stood proud in front of me.

Izzy grinned. Her smile dazzling like always. "Oh honey, when I grow up, I'm gonna make the world shudder in fear every time my Jordans' slam against the street."

"Ummmm."

"Now hold still."

I was too afraid to move anyway.

CHAPTER
Five

If only we could know the reason why they went. We'd smile and wipe away the tears that flow… And wait content." —Author Unknown

Ash

It was going to be the longest family dinner of my life.

What was supposed to be a small surprise party for Annie with just our family turned into my mom calling all the bosses and using the excuse of the whole bomb thing for them to meet at the house.

After all, what better way to celebrate taking apart a bomb then over pasta and bread? I was currently sitting between Junior and Serena because last time they sat together, Nixon nearly took off Junior's head; something about Junior's hand down Serena's pants made Nixon grab his gun even though they were basically married already in their own heads.

It took four men to take the boss down.

And Junior had paled to the point of being unrecognizable after getting caught.

Come to think of it, that was a good night.

And now?

Now everything was awkward.

My sister Violet was gone, married off to Russian royalty, and living in Seattle, though I was excited she was visiting soon.

Maksim and Izzy had been sleeping together only to have my dad and Andrei find out because they were lazy.

Not lazy as in they got caught because they got comfortable but fucking loud.

They'd both been naked.

And Maksim, the jackass, had backed off after my dad politely asked him to—at gunpoint.

Which just pissed Izzy off because she was young, and Maksim was, according to her, sexy as hell. They'd been inseparable for years, so the fact that he just shrugged and moved on made her want to commit murder, which was why he was at the opposite end of the table and currently looking anywhere but Izzy as she sharpened a fucking knife in front of her empty plate.

Any other day and I would have laughed.

But not today.

Today I felt nothing but the usual numbness.

Funny, how I used to pray to feel nothing.

And now that I did?

Now that I tamped it all down, I would do anything to feel again.

Anything to not hate myself as much as I did.

Anything to not hate everyone else as much as I did.

But after my break.

After Claire said goodbye in my dreams.

After I let her go.

All I could see was her face in that hospital bed.

"She's not coming back, son." Nikolai Blazik, doctor to the Russians and scary as shit associate, handed me the needle then. I knew it would stop her heart. I knew it would give her an honorable death.

But I couldn't do it.

I couldn't shove the needle in.

So I sat there.

Holding her limp bandaged hand as the machines breathed for her and I counted all the bandages.

Twenty-seven.

Then I counted all the bruises.

Sixteen.

Then I counted each of the breaths the machine took for her, one, two, three… The slow hum of the room reminded me that when I walked away, the humming would stop.

There would be nothingness.

I would be left.

With tears streaming down my cheeks, I placed a hand on her still flat stomach. There used to be a heartbeat there.

Today there was silence.

"I bought a onesie," I confessed. "I was going to surprise her and start on the baby room." My hands shook—one held the needle that would release her from this broken body, one was pressed against the life that had been taken from us.

The life that had terrified and excited me.

I choked out a sob as Nikolai put his hand over mine. "The baby didn't suffer, and neither did Claire; you have to believe me when I say—the way she was hit was a kindness compared to what could have happened."

I squeezed my eyes shut as tears slid down my cheeks in rapid succession. "But what about those few seconds before she died? What about those seconds of fear, Nik? Where I wasn't there? Where she knew in her soul that something was happening, but she couldn't do anything? How do I live with the fact that she always trusted and expected me to protect her in this life—and I failed? I fucking failed! And those three seconds, she had to feel scared, petrified, Nik. And I wasn't there to take away that fear, and I can't take it away now. All I can do is imagine the moment over and over again."

"Ash." Nik's eyes blurred with tears. "I wouldn't wish those three seconds on my worst enemy."

I sucked in a painful breath.

He sighed. "You expected me to lie, to make you feel better?"

"Maybe."

My lips tasted salty as I leaned down and kissed her stomach, laying my ear against it, willing there to be life inside her body when I knew there was nothing but death.

"One. Two. Three," Nikolai whispered. "And then nothing but your body's natural response to trauma. I imagine that when we're in coma's we dream about our favorite moments, so yes, those three seconds were horrible, I'm sure of it, just like I'm convinced that her dreams for the last hour have been full of love. Full of you."

I burst into uncontrollable sobs. "I can't survive this. I won't."

Nikolai gripped me by the shoulders, his fingers digging into my skin as his dark eyes held me captive. "For the sake of your family. You. Must. This is your cross to bear, and you will bear it."

A soft moan escaped Claire's lips.

Nikolai jerked back and gently pulled the equipment from her mouth as she choked.

"You're awake! Nik, she's awake!" I cupped her bruised cheeks. It was a miracle! "Claire, sweetheart, can you hear me? It's Ash. I'm here, I'm here, you're going to be fine."

She shook her head as a solitary tear ran down her cheek. "Take care."

"I'm fine, you're fine. Everything is going to be fine!" My heart was pounding so hard. She was going to be okay! She was awake.

"No." She squeezed her eyes shut as a trickle of blood ran from her lips. "Annie. Take care."

The fuck! "You're delirious, I love you, I love you."

"Love you." More blood trickled down from her mouth as she turned her head to the side and whispered. "Annie, take care…"

I opened my mouth to ask what she was talking about when she suddenly coded.

"Claire!" I roared. "Nikolai, do something!"

He rushed over to the paddles. "Move her gown, now!"

He rubbed the paddles together and pressed them to her chest.

I started counting again.

The seconds.

And how many went by as he tried and tried and tried again only to finally stop as sweat poured down his face and he shook his head.

Rage pounded into my body.

At Annie for stealing those last moments.

For it being her fault in the first place.

And at Claire—for leaving me. For using the last few seconds of her life to still protect the one reason, she was dead in the first place.

I would take it to my grave. How much I resented Claire. How much I refused to confess my anger at her for leaving me.

For caring more for Annie.
Than her fiancé.

"Helloooooooo, Ash?" Serena elbowed me in the gut. "You're awfully quiet for someone who said he was so hungry he could eat Tank five minutes ago."

I shook myself out of the memory and pasted a fake smile on my face. "I think I'd rather just kill him."

"Right here, sitting across from you." He glared, sweat still visible on his chiseled face. We'd sparred for the last hour. I got a few good shots in, but unfortunately, he was getting better, which meant he bruised my kidneys.

I was pretty sure I'd be peeing blood later.

"I know." I grinned. "Why are you here again? You're not family."

"Ash, why the sudden hostility?" Serena gave me a knowing grin.

I grabbed a dinner roll and shoved it in her mouth. "You looked hungry."

She spat out the roll, grabbed her knife, and held it to my throat. "Try that again, see what happens."

"Junior… call her off, man. I can't tell if her knife has sauce on it or blood."

"Both. She's crazy." He smiled through his bite and then winked over at her. "And I mean that in the sexiest way."

"I know." She pulled the knife away from me and grinned.

Most everyone had already dug in, even though not everyone was at the table yet.

Nixon finally came over and sat, and then my dad strolled into the room with Tex the Capo in tow. "Savages just started eating without praying first?"

"I prayed," I lied. "Right Tank?"

His eyes narrowed. "Sure, is that why I just heard thunder? Lightning gonna strike here any time soon?"

Dad sighed. "Everyone sit. Where's our guest of honor?"

The moms were pouring wine in the kitchen and making their way over to the giant buffet table, all of them talking so loudly that if Dad really did want to say a prayer, he'd have to scream it.

It was ridiculously crowded even in our giant dining room—then again, at this point, we had to have two tables.

One for the older kids and adults.

And another for the littles, so they didn't get blood splatters on them.

Not even kidding. If I even hint at the incident at Christmas in 2016, my dad looks ready to flog me.

"Here!" Annie rushed into the kitchen at around the same time I took a huge sip of wine.

"Damn…" Junior hissed under his breath.

I tried to hold the cough in. My eyes watered, and my throat burned with the need to choke.

I lasted maybe three seconds before I started hacking the wine that went down the wrong tube out of pure shock at what was in front of me.

Serena wasn't helpful with her sudden hitting of my back. "You okay, cousin? Something wrong?"

I grabbed my napkin and wiped my mouth. "Wrong tube."

"Suuure," Junior said under his breath while Maksim looked between the two of us like a show was about to start.

He mimed eating popcorn, then elbowed King as if to say, *pay attention to the show!*

I glared at the two of them.

It did nothing to deter the little shits.

I swear everything just encouraged Maksim's bad behavior these days.

"Sorry." Annie didn't meet my eyes, instead looking everywhere but my face. Hell, the plant in the corner got more action than I did. She pulled out her chair next to Tank and gave him a cheerful grin. "Izzy wanted me to change."

Tank smirked. "Remind me to give Izzy a hug later."

"You're welcome." Izzy beamed, lifting her glass of wine in the air only to have my dad pull it from her hand and shake his head no, mainly because she'd already had two glasses.

She pouted.

Typical.

And of course, he immediately cracked, handed the wine back, and said, "But only a few more sips."

I willed Annie to look at me.

And I had no idea why.

I hated her, right?

She was the reason for my suffering.

For my numbness.

And hers was the last name on my soul mate's lips.

She was wearing a white crop top that fell over her shoulders and low slung jeans that showed more skin than I think I'd ever seen her show in my entire life.

She didn't look like herself.

What the hell happened to her over in Italy? And why did it piss me off so much?

I could admit she looked hot as fuck—but she didn't look like the Annie that cried at the drop of a hat.

The Annie I knew.

The one I hated.

Did that mean I was allowed to stare this stranger down?

Drink her in and let her beauty consume me? Was she wearing pink lipstick?

Tank put his arm around her and squeezed. "Still shook up?"

She gave him a small nod then leaned into his chest. Fucking idiot looked ready to preen like a peacock all over the dinner table.

"Of course, she's shook up." I just had to start talking. "She could have died. I'm curious, do you report everything to the FBI, Tank, or only the things we let you report? Because bomb threats, that's pretty huge, right?"

He shifted uncomfortably. "If you're asking if I've been feeding them information, that's a no. I only tell them what you allow me to tell them, and even then, you know I'm going to have to pick a side soon; they only believe the whole deep cover story for so long."

"Complete shit that they even believe it now," I admitted. "What with you coming over to family dinner—why are you here again?"

He grinned knowingly. "You asked that already."

"Did I?" I reached for a roll. "Sorry was distracted by almost dying earlier and saving Annie's life. You know how it is—" I snapped my fingers. "Oh wait, you don't. Because you weren't here then, but you're here now." I frowned. "I'm confused. Is it a convenience thing or—"

"Ash!" Dad barked. "Leave Tank alone. If you need someone to pester, take Junior downstairs and get a few hits in."

"Great," Junior grumbled. "Can't I tap Maksim in? Ash nearly broke my jaw last week."

I made a face. "Bullshit. You should have ducked and weaved."

"I DID!" Junior roared. "You cheated!"

"Boys." Tex pounded his fist onto the table, causing all the silverware to jump then resettle haphazardly. He poured himself a glass of wine. "Junior, I'm disappointed you'd back down from a fight. You growing soft now that you're getting laid on the regular?"

"Oh God." Nixon reached for his wine while his wife Trace snorted into hers. "Tex, could you not give me that visual of my daughter having sex? It makes me want to grab a steak knife."

"Oh, we hid those." Tex's wife grinned. "You know, after Chase stabbed our son repeatedly in the back with one." She lifted her wine glass. "Cheers."

My dad, at least, had the decency to say sorry. Last year he'd been so pissed to learn that Breaker, aka Valerian, wasn't dead and was cheerfully married to Violet, well let's just say it was a shit show, and we all learned something very important that day.

When all else fails, a steak knife works just fine.

The rest of the dinner went by with awkward small talk about bombs. My entire appetite was gone; every single time I heard Annie laugh, I wanted to stab something.

I just couldn't figure out if it was hate or something else.

All I knew is that I was minutes away from using Tank as target practice and gathering all the forks.

Tank looked down at his phone as it went off. "Speaking of bombs and work, am I telling them or not? It's my superior?"

Tex leaned back in his chair. "Tell them. You can even bring the evidence in, and if they ask what the white horse represents, make sure you let them know it's what we send someone when they're a rat—which should also be a reminder to you about what happens to those who betray us." He smiled and raised his glass toward Tank. "Cheers."

"Right." Tank grabbed his phone and then leaned down and kissed Annie on the head. "I'll be back later to check on you, all right?" He shot me a dark look then left the table.

The sound of the front door slamming was like Christmas fucking morning.

I finally relaxed.

Assuming Annie would at least scowl at me, instead, she quietly ate the rest of her food and kept easy conversation with Izzy, never once looking in my direction.

Then again, she did hear me say something about hating her with my entire soul, but still, I always said shit like that, and she always came back for more.

What made this time so different?

And why the hell did I care?

I jerked to my feet and started gathering dishes. "Anyone else finished?"

The entire table fells silent.

I frowned. "What?"

My mom stood then leaned over and felt my forehead. "Are you getting sick?"

I batted her hand away in annoyance. "Ma, really? I help with dishes, and suddenly I'm sick?"

"You've literally faked your death at the dinner table in order to get out of doing dishes." Izzy pointed out. "Twice."

"It was a joke!" I said defensively as I balanced the plates on each other.

"It wasn't funny," Mom deadpanned. "You sure you're—"

"Great! Just trying to stop being an asshole, thanks for nothing." I quickly left the table and put all the dishes in the sink.

"You forgot mine," Annie said in a small voice from behind me.

Every single nerve ending came alive. With rage. With lust, if I was being completely honest. With hatred at myself, at her, at Claire.

I could see her small frame reflected in the kitchen window. The lights above her created an almost halo effect through the inky darkness of night. And I started to wash the dishes because I couldn't compartmentalize my feelings anymore.

Maybe that was why I was numb, my body so fucking confused right along with my heart that we were in a purgatory of sorts.

Great.

"You can just set it on the counter," I finally said, careful not to say anything hateful, wondering why I couldn't help myself to the point that it was painful to keep my mouth shut. "I'll get to it in a bit."

She still hadn't left.

With a loud sigh, I placed the plate on the counter, then very slowly turned around and crossed my arms. "Something tells me you have a question."

Her blue eyes were huge, her lips trembled a bit as she crossed her arms like she was uncomfortable with me seeing so much skin when I'd seen her naked.

Being inside her for a few brief moments where I felt like I was cheating on my soul mate, basically was...

She trained her eyes on my shoes then. "Are we going to be safe at the university?"

My eyebrows shot up. "That's your question?"

I immediately deflated like a popped balloon. She didn't want to fight me? And I wasn't making her cry. We were having a normal conversation.

I hated it.

She nodded her head, her short hair grazing her chin. "Yeah."

It was just us in that immaculate kitchen, with its fancy white granite countertops and state-of-the-art appliances.

"A question for a question..." I said instead.

Her head jerked up. "Okay?"

"Are you afraid of me?"

She gulped. "Sometimes."

"At least you're honest." I scratched the back of my head. "Look, I'm not in a good headspace right now, but that doesn't mean I wouldn't give my life for yours. Does that answer your question?"

She blinked a few times like she wasn't sure what to say and then a slow nod of her head as she whispered, "Yes. Thank you."

"For what?"

"For answering."

"You're thanking me for having a normal conversation?" I asked dumbfounded.

"Well, you tend to yell at me a lot, so yeah, I'm thanking you for not threatening me, yelling, calling me names, or making fun of my tears." Her smile was sad as she turned on her heel.

Before I could stop myself, I reached for her hand and jerked her body back against mine.

She went completely still in my arms. "Since we're so good at conversations now..." I whispered in her ear, my arms bracing her against me. My forearms pressed against her breasts. "He's not good for you."

"Wh-who?"

"Tank," I said his name like a curse. "He's in this just like the rest of us are, only he's more dangerous because he's playing games with both sides. This is the only warning I'm going to give you—find someone safe."

"Safe," she repeated. "Safe sounds boring. Are you suggesting I find some nice accountant to settle down with? Maybe a teacher? Or a vet, they do save animals." She struggled in my arms, and I was clearly a sick bastard because I liked her fight, would probably orgasm on the spot if she drew blood with her fingernails digging into my arms. Already my zipper was having a hell of a time containing me.

"Perfect choices. All of them," I agreed. "Just not Tank."

"I like Tank."

"Tank's a tool," I snapped. "Besides, you know he serial dated like hell when you were gone. Something tells me you had a small fantasy that he maybe waited before sticking his dick into whatever hot girl looked his way—trust me when I say he's a player."

"And what? A tiger recognizes similar stripes? Is that it?" She struggled more. "Let me go."

"I'm actually quite comfortable." I held her harder, then heard someone walking down the hall into the kitchen, so chose that opportunity to shove her into the pantry and close the door. Flicking the light on and facing her.

"Ash." Her eyes were frenzied. "Please, no, I can't, I can't do small spaces, please." She started clawing at my chest.

Frowning, I pulled her roughly against me and ran my hands down her hair to her hips, holding her there. "It's just a pantry, Annie, and it's just me."

She shuddered. "It's small. It's dark."

I flicked on the light and pulled slightly away. "The only difference between the dark and the light is one small switch. The things in the dark still exist in the light, Annie. You just can't see them—but believe me, they're there."

Her eyes darted to mine. "Was that supposed to make me feel better?"

"No." I found myself smiling. "Not really. I'm not the one they go to for a pep talk."

"Somehow, I believe you." She looked around wildly, her gaze landing on anything and everything but me. "Can you let me go now? Please?"

"Always so fucking polite." I ran my tongue along my bottom lip. Why did her mouth look so good? And why was I even thinking about it?

Remembering the way she'd tasted.

Or the greedy way she rode my leg last year, like her body was begging for it.

"Stop looking at me like that." She jerked away from me, but I still had my arms pinned around her.

My brain told me to let her go and that I was being an ass, but my body was frozen in place like it had been so long since I'd had human contact that it was starved. Already addicted.

"Promise me." I lowered my head so I could look directly into her eyes, get at her level. "Promise me you'll think about what I said. I know it doesn't seem like it, but I'm actually looking out for you this time. It's not fun, you know…"

"What's not?"

"Getting your heart obliterated," I said through clenched teeth.

She let out a choked laugh. "Believe me, I know."

Anger built up like a volcano inside. "The hell? You were

fucking someone in Italy? Who? Who'd you spread your legs for? Tell me now—"

She slapped me so hard my ears rang. Guess there was a first for everything, son of a bitch!

I yawned and stretched my jaw. "That hurt."

"All you do is hurt!" She struggled against me. "And for your information, I didn't spread for anyone in Italy! The only guy I've ever even been close to sleeping with kicked me out of his bed while screaming like it was my fault. So excuse me for slapping you, but most days I want to do more than slap you. You're a bully. A jerk. An asshole with a silver spoon shoved so far up his ass that you can't even see how your words affect the people around you. Don't even get me started about your actions. Do yourself and everyone else who knows you a favor, Ash. Grow up." My arms dangled at my sides as she finally shoved away from me, opening the pantry door to see Maksim standing there with a sloppy grin on his face as he sipped his wine.

"Oh, ladies first." He moved out of the way as she stormed off, grinning the entire time. He waited until she was out of earshot and then. "That was brutal, my balls were tingling, and she wasn't even talking about me."

"Shut up." I shoved at him. "How much did you hear?"

"Only the interesting parts." He shrugged, his perfect golden blond locks falling across his forehead. Damn, I hated him sometimes. "I never thought I'd see the day when Little Miss Perfect lost her temper on you."

"It's new."

"I wonder why you get under her skin…"

"Probably because she hates me."

"Huh…" Maksim scratched his head. "Well then, good

thing Tank has a hard-on for her, huh? Besides, she's too good for you."

"Can you leave now?"

"Nah, I'm good, bro. I'm good. By the way, you might want to take care of that before going back into the kitchen." He pointed down.

"Wha—" I looked down, and sure enough, you'd think I'd been in the friggin pantry masturbating next to the Cheerios.

"No judgment, bro, you do you. If small dark places next to the rice make you horny, I'm all for it, but something tells me it's a feisty little straight-A student that's causing that reaction as much as you hate to admit—"

I gritted my teeth. "Leave."

"Oh right, right, um, do you need like lotion or something? I think there's some coconut oil in there. I heard great things—"

"Son of a bitch, Maksim. Do you ever shut up?"

He winked. "Never."

"You slept with my sister."

His smile immediately fell. "What's that, Junior? Yup." He cupped his ear. "Sorry, bro, gotta go." He darted away from me so fast I had no hope of catching him, and of course, he did this at about the same time King arrived for the party. He took one look at me, then the pantry, then me as a slow smile curved his lips.

Without warning, he took out his phone and snapped a picture.

"KING!" I bellowed, fists at my sides.

"Shhhh, wouldn't want your mom running in here worried for her poor little boy only to see he's finally turned into a man, and Maksim's right about the coconut oil, trust me, bro."

I squeezed my eyes shut as he patted me lightly on the

shoulder and strolled into the dining room.

I had a hell of a time walking back to the pool house.

And the minute I reached for myself, I had guilt.

So much fucking guilt.

Claire was my last.

Which meant the minute I touched someone else, had sex with someone else, she would be erased, or at least it felt that way.

So I lay there, uncomfortable as hell, and tried to let the sadness take away whatever the hell was wrong with my body.

Unfortunately, when I closed my eyes, all I saw was Annie's face.

And my hate grew in that moment to epic proportions.

Fuck turning over a new leaf—this was all her fault.

And I was going to destroy her.

Starting with Tank.

Ending with me.

A cruel smile passed my lips as the anger left; suddenly, I had a plan, one that guaranteed revenge.

And for the first time in over a year, I exhaled a sigh of relief, a sigh of cruelty, a sigh of purpose.

After all, sometimes destroying someone is equal to fixing yourself, right?

This wouldn't end in bloodshed after all—no, it would end with tears.

Hers.

And I'd finally have my revenge.

"Don't worry, Claire… I'll take care of her, the only way I know how."

CHAPTER
Six

I fall asleep in the full and certain hope that my slumber shall not be broken; And though I be all-forgetting, Yet shall I shall not be forgotten, But continue that life in the thoughts and deeds of those I loved. —Samuel Butler

Chase

"Come in." I squeezed my eyes shut then rubbed them with my fingertips before the door to my office swung open. Footsteps sounded.

Fourteen of them.

He was wearing boots, size twelve—no, thirteen.

His breathing was even, but there was a certain taste of agitation in the air like he didn't want to be here but knew he had no other choice.

"Update me." I crossed my bulky arms. I'd been hitting the gym more now. I had no other choice. Ash was bulking up, fuck he was a mini-me in every way that I hated.

I wouldn't wish his pain on anyone.

And I knew firsthand what it was like to lose someone you loved, only to find out later that they weren't who you thought they were.

Claire, in this instance at least, wasn't a rat.

No, she'd been worse.

Weak.

"I can't do it anymore." She hung her head in her hands. The green chair she was sitting in may as well be a confessional as she laid down all her sins at my feet—the feet of her soon to be father-in-law. *"I love him. I do, but this life? You have to help me convince him. Please!"*

I weighed my words, took my time as I tapped my red pen against the black folder in front of me.

Annie Smith.

Smith, my ass.

How did Phoenix even survive with the weight of these secrets on his soul?

Sex?

Alcohol?

The man didn't even seem to have a vice—and I was pretty sure I'd have multiple vices at this point; I was already side-eyeing the brandy on my liquor cart.

But I needed to be sober for this conversation, unfortunately.

Slowly, I stood to my feet, adjusted my patriotic as fuck red tie, and walked over to the empty green chair next to Claire's.

I would need to be careful.

After all, when dealing with weak individuals, you weren't allowed to come on too strong; no, you had to come from behind, pretend to be a friend even though they'd just shown all their cards as foe.

My son.

My fucking son deserved better than that.

Even if he loved her.

He deserved a Queen.

Not someone I could so easily use as a pawn.

I sat, crossed my legs, and put a hand on her thigh. "You realize that by coming to me, you've already lost?"

She sniffled and then wiped her nose. "I—I did something unforgivable."

I squeezed my eyes shut and waited for the gauntlet to slice through my head, my heart because I knew before she even said it—she would ask me to keep this from my son.

At all costs.

And I would want nothing more than to tell him.

Because as much as he drove me crazy—he was my only son. And I knew as he grew in age, he would become my best friend, my confidant, my everything. And her secret would destroy what solid ground I had with him.

I felt it in my soul.

"What did you do?" I whispered. "And how can I undo it? Because you aren't sitting in my office, making it so I had to cancel multiple appointments because you guys got in a fight."

She lifted her head, her lower lip trembling. "I lied."

"About?"

"Something horrible." She looked away as tears streamed down her cheeks. "And now I'm stuck."

"Why did you lie, Claire? What drove you to be anything but honest with the man who has shown you nothing but love and honesty?"

She looked down at her hands as she wrung the tissue over and over again. "A lie, no matter how big or small, is still wrong, and

I did it because I thought he would change his mind. I thought maybe if—if he believed me, he'd walk."

And there it was.

The gauntlet sliced.

The head rolled.

The soul died.

I kept my emotions neutral. "Walk? From what?"

"This." She sniffled again and finally looked at me. "I can't do it, Chase, I can barely stomach it. I thought if I just pretended that I'd eventually turn into this, this monster of my own making, but instead, it gets harder and harder, and he—" She cursed. "He likes it. No, he loves it. He loves this life. He loves... killing."

"Is this your way of saying you want our enemies alive?"

"No!" Her head jerked up. "It's just... I know he would never hurt me, but sometimes in his sleep he says random names, he taunts them, and then he kills, it's like a sport to Ash—you've made him this monster, and I can't help but see blood every time I see his face. It's going to destroy him unless we leave. Chase, we have to leave."

They weren't going anywhere.

"The only out clause for my son is death, Claire..." I waited, tilting my head as goosebumps seemed to rise and scatter over her flesh and her eyes seemed to flicker away like she was trying to keep all her secrets inside but struggling with the quantity of them. I made a mental note to talk to Nikolai later. "For you... it would need to be the same."

"I understand."

The chair creaked as I shifted my position and leaned in. "You would die before living this life, Claire. Is that what you're saying?"

"I would die before letting this life destroy him." She clenched her teeth. "I would die for him to live, to truly live."

I cursed under my breath. "You were never strong enough."

"Don't you think I know that?" she screamed as she finally grew enough balls to fully face me, her expression tight. "I know what I'm capable of; I also know what he's capable of. I can't bring him back from this, Chase. I can't. I don't know how. My love is as strong as my fear, and that's not fair to him. It's not fair to us! Or anyone. If he goes off the deep end, I don't think I'll ever get him back, and I don't deserve that. I don't deserve a madman killer with so much blood on his hands he laughs in his sleep in order to take away the pain."

I leaned in, my free hand cupping her face. "So. Fucking. Weak."

She jerked her face away. "I've made up my mind."

"And you'll die for it," I whispered. "There is no resurrection story here, Claire."

"You know what's sad?" She shook her head. "Is I know what this will do to him. And still… I truly believe I'm saving his life."

"No." I sighed. "You're ruining it. You will be the final nail in the coffin, Claire. You're afraid of the monster he'll become? Well, congratulations. You've just created him." I stood. "My assistant will see you out. We'll be in touch."

She nodded wordlessly and rose to her feet, then she slowly walked toward the door, head held high like a fucking pageant queen.

I would kill her if it would save him.

Instead, she was going to kill herself.

How the hell did I let this happen?

Where he saw strength, I'd always seen weakness.

And now I knew the truth.

We'd trusted her too soon.

Never again.

"Claire?" I called after her. "Take a few days to decide."

"It's decided."

I expelled a sigh. "I was afraid you'd say that." I walked back around to my desk and sat, folding my hands in front of my face as I spoke. "I'm extremely disappointed in you."

She lowered her head as my assistant opened the door to escort her out. "You'll see, Chase. You'll see."

Funny. I already did.

And if my son didn't love her so damn much—I would have put a bullet between her eyes the minute she opened her fucking mouth.

"Chase?" Tank said my name as he took a seat in that same green chair. "Did you hear anything I just said?"

"Some of it," I lied. "Just repeat the important parts. I have a busy day ahead of me."

He snorted out a laugh as he crossed his denim-clad legs and leaned back in the chair like he had all the time in the world.

I shook my head. "Your black beanie looks ridiculous. Take it off, you aren't in Pearl Jam."

He frowned. "Who?"

"God, I hate Millennials."

"I'm a Z—"

"Yeah, don't really care." I waved him off. "Speak."

The chair groaned as he leaned forward. I had to hand it to Ash. With all his anger, he needed more and more sparring partners, and he'd made Tank into… well, an actual Tank. In the last year, he'd put on thirty pounds of muscle. Impressive, even for one of our associates.

It was another reason I let him stick around; he was like a walking talking body shield for my family.

"The check-in went fine…" He sighed. "Nothing strange to report on that front." He shifted uncomfortably again in the chair like he had more information. "Are you sure it's best we do things this way?"

"Trust me," I said quickly. "If I saw another path, I'd take it."

"But—"

"It's not up for discussion."

He nodded. "Understood."

"And the other situation?"

"Why do I need to do this again? I mean, I semi-get that you're trying to drive Ash into action, but if the whole moving in thing didn't work, how the hell do you think this is going to work?"

I grinned. "I know my son."

"Yeah, I know him too. He's scary as fuck, and last night he looked ready to filet me while still breathing. I'm lucky to be alive, Chase, and— What the hell, man? Stop smiling like it amuses you!"

I chuckled. "It actually does. He kept eyeing the one allowed steak knife. Phoenix and I bet a thousand bucks that he was going to jump the table."

"Awesome, gambling with my life, thanks. I'm so glad my boss thinks it's funny that I almost died during dinner."

Snorting, I waved him off. "Don't be so dramatic—it was during dessert where he got really testy."

Tank shook his head. "You're all insane."

"Thank you." I moved the black folders around on my desk and pulled out Annie's. "She seems to be thriving."

"Thanks to your black credit card, I think any college girl would be thriving—did you see the shopping trip bills?"

I didn't even blink. "I'm a billionaire; ask me if I care."

"I'm a billionaire," he mimicked in my voice, then winced. "Please don't kill me."

"I entertain the thought on a daily basis."

"Good talk." He groaned and wiped his hands down his face. "I already told the other bosses. I'm working on this whole bomb angle, but I've come up with nothing; the only lead goes back to her."

I grabbed a pencil and started to tap. "Her as in…"

"Last time I said her name, you yelled and then broke a baseball bat over your knees, so I'm just going to say *her*."

"She's dead." I pointed out. "And the bat was old."

He held up his hands. "Whatever you say. And I know she's dead, but her contacts clearly aren't. The FBI believes that they're using all of this white horse business as a scare tactic, and if they kill someone in the process awesome, it's all smokescreens, a distraction in order to do something big."

I thought about it for a minute then spoke. "I agree, but they're also only targeting the second generation. Why?"

"I have a theory." Tank lowered his voice. "You wiped out the second generation of the De Lange Family and then somehow sprouted a conscience out of your ass and saved the remaining kids. What if this is their way of doing the same to you guys? They don't have the same resources but think about it. What would hurt you the most?"

I closed my eyes. "Losing our children."

"Exactly."

"Keep digging." I stood. "And this conversation never leaves the room."

"I remember," he grumbled and then shot up to his feet like they were on fire and stalked out of the room, leaving me to again wonder how Phoenix did this.

So many secrets.

So many lies.

So little time until the dominoes fell.

I just hoped to God my son was strong enough to bear it.

CHAPTER
Seven

The night has a thousand eyes. And the day but one;
Yet the light of the bright world dies. With the dying
sun. The mind has a thousand eyes. And the heart but
one: Yet the light of a whole life dies. When love is
done. —Francis Bourdillon

Annie

One Week Later, September

"I hate him, I hate him, I hate him, I hate him." I chanted this all through my morning routine as I put on my Eagle Elite Uniform—short navy skirt, knee-high socks, white blouse, and navy jacket.

I'd had zero sleep thanks to my encounter with Ash, and when I did close my eyes, I had nightmares of being locked in a cupboard—something he wouldn't have known actually triggered me but telling him that would be like telling a kidnapper your address.

He'd use it against me.

And I'd cry myself to sleep like I used to.

Ugh.

I grabbed my satchel and hurried down the stairs, nearly bumping into Ash as he held out a plate full of eggs, bacon, and toast.

With a wink, he leaned in and whispered, "Gluten-free."

My eyes narrowed. "You on pills again?"

He scowled. "Can't I make our houseguest breakfast?"

I sniffed the plate. "Did you poison it?"

"Please." He rolled his eyes. "If I wanted to poison you, I'd use the—"

"The scary needle dart, already had this convo several times with multiple people I don't need a recap."

His eyes flickered to my mouth as he said. "Actually, I was going to go with the whole tasteless powder in your OJ, but the needle works too. All good options, all good options." He handed me the plate then reached for a glass filled to the brim with OJ. "Thirsty?"

I shook my head. "I like you better angry at least then I know what to expect. When you're happy, I think you're either high or ready to kill me."

"That's confusing." He frowned. "So when I'm mean you feel safer, when I'm nice you're waiting for the other shoe to drop?"

My stomach growled as I eyed the plate in my hands. "M-maybe."

"Annie." He put his hands on my shoulders. "Just eat the damn peace offering."

"I don't trust any offering from you." My stomach rumbled again. I was so starving that I was ready to eat the plate along with the food.

One of Ash's eyebrows arched as he reached for the bacon and held it in front of my mouth. "Bite it, or I'll bite you."

"That's—"

He shoved the bacon in my mouth the minute my lips parted. It was crispy and hot against my tongue. How did I not know he cooked? Oh right, because he'd only ever kissed me, almost had sex with me, yelled at me, and then traumatized me.

I literally knew nothing else about him other than he had anger issues and liked to kill God's creatures.

"So?" He rocked back on his feet, his smile triumphant. "How's it taste?"

I chewed and then shrugged. "Not sure yet." I opened my mouth and pointed.

He actually smiled, not a smug I'm going to terrorize you later smile, but one that felt genuine, that had warmth spreading from my head all the way down to my toes as he moved closer, the plate still between us, grabbed another piece and held it in front of my mouth.

I leaned in and bit down, only to have him replace his fingers with his mouth as he tugged the bacon toward him.

One more centimeter, and we'd be kissing.

It was another mind game.

A trick.

But it was also bacon, so I held on for dear life.

Never thought I'd be playing chicken with Ash in the kitchen using bacon as our weapon, but then again, the mafia was a strange, *strange* world, so why not?

He inched his mouth forward, his eyes locked on mine in amusement like he knew I was starting to sweat.

I gave a hard tug with my teeth and his lips pressed against mine briefly before I jerked my head away, taking most of the bacon with me in triumph.

"Winner, winner, bacon dinner?" He didn't take his eyes off my mouth.

I kept chewing. "Are you sure you're not on something?"

He snorted and rolled his eyes, taking the plate with him and setting it on the breakfast bar.

I will not stare at his ass in those trousers.

I will not stare at his biceps in that ridiculous Eagle Elite sweater vest.

I will not imagine eating bacon off his eight pack.

"Why are your eyes closed?" Ash asked a few seconds later.

I quickly opened them. "No reason, just doing... math."

"You're not *in* math." His lips pressed together in an amused smile. "Try again."

"I was thinking."

"Extremely hard," he pointed out as he grabbed the orange juice and handed it to me.

I took it and then frowned as I looked down into the cup. "You're sure it's not poisoned?"

He took the glass with a curse, downed half the juice, and then handed it back to me. "Happy?"

"No." I took a few sips of juice and set it on the counter by the plate. "Because now your germs are all over my OJ."

"Germs?" Both eyebrows shot up. "That ship has fucking sailed, little girl... or have you forgotten that night in the pool? My tongue was so far down your throat it was almost between your thighs."

"Ewwwwww." Izzy's voice sounded in the kitchen. "Why do I have the worst timing ever?"

"Oh please." Ash flipped her off. "It's not like you and

Maksim were playing solitaire all those times he stayed over—he's lucky he isn't walking with a limp and only half his dick."

Her eyes flickered with anger and then sadness as she stared him down and then went over to the fridge, pulling out the milk.

I almost asked her if she was okay.

Or if she wanted to talk.

But last time I even mentioned him, she threatened me, so maybe she just needed time?

God knows I needed at least a year to recover from Ash, and now I felt like I was back at square one. I half expected him to nudge me in the arm and then mess up my hair.

What was with him?

I quickly glanced back at him.

His smile was gone.

Expression blank. "What?"

"I don't trust you."

His smirk was drop-dead gorgeous spreading across his face like a cruel promise. "Good. You probably shouldn't."

Frowning, I walked past him only to have him grab my arm again and drag me toward the door.

"Bye, Iz!"

"See ya!"

I dug my heels in the ground, but it was no use. "What are you doing? Let me go!"

"You have class, I have class, we're saving the environment, get in." He gave me a little shove toward his BMW i8; I nearly got taken out by the suicide door as it stretched vertically dangerously close to my head.

I was too busy gaping at the door to realize that he was already in the car waiting for me to get in with an annoyed look. "You need to eye fuck the car any longer, or can we go?"

I shot him a nasty look and ducked inside the car, careful not to flash him. My skirt was a bit too short for a sports car.

When I thought it was safe enough to plop down on the leather seat, I did just that, causing my skirt to fly up and my butt to kiss the leather. So basically, it felt like I was almost naked against the seat.

Hopefully, Ash didn't notice.

It wasn't like he paid attention to me much anyway, and I was just waiting for this cease-fire to end—I mean, it was Ash; he'd fight the wind if he could. Any reason to yell, to draw his sword, the King of Eagle Elite was grumpy and mean. Trusting him would be my own stupid fault.

It would be the final nail in my coffin.

Utter obliteration of what was left of my heart.

He cranked up the music so loud it would be impossible to have a normal conversation—not that I was complaining—and he weaved in and out of traffic so fast my stomach started to roll.

I hated it.

Hated him.

This was a game, wasn't it?

He was nice.

And then, aloof.

What was he going to be like at University?

Would he give me a ride back home?

All the things that stressed me out as we finally pulled up to the black iron gate that led to Eagle Elite. It slowly creaked open, and Ash finally turned down whatever heavy metal music he'd been listening to and slowed the car to the twenty-five mile an hour speed limit as we crept closer to campus.

"Rules," he said without looking at me.

I frowned but kept my eyes straight ahead. "I'm listening…"

"I'll take you to and from class every day. I'm going to need to search your bag morning, noon, and night."

I clenched my teeth. "What? Now I'm a spy?"

"This is how I protect you and everyone else, Annie, so pay attention." He turned the car into one of the front spots near the registration building and cut the engine. "Rule number two, or is it three?"

I sighed in agitation. "Three."

"Just making sure you're paying attention." His voice held no humor, only a cold detachment that hadn't been there this morning when he made me breakfast. Why had he been so nice? And why was he mean now? "No guys that haven't been vetted, I don't really care who you let see you naked as long as I have a background check on them, but if I find out that you've been with Tank in any way romantically, you'll be punished."

"Punished," I repeated. "Who says you get any say in who I date? You're not my dad, you're not even family—"

He held up his hand.

I hated that I immediately responded to it like I'd been trained to submit to the jackass just like all the other associates.

"Fine, if you want something with Tank, then it's your heart that's going to be broken. In fact…" He chuckled under his breath. "Wow, right on time."

"What?" I stole a glance at Ash, but he was looking straight ahead.

Frowning, I followed the direction of his gaze and nearly threw up.

It was Tank, and he was making out with some random girl with long red hair, her hands clung to the lapels of his jacket, and he looked ready to swallow her whole.

"Wasn't he just flirting with you last night?" Ash just had to ask.

"We're friends." I ignored the swell of emotion and betrayal in my throat as I forced a smile at Ash. "Any more rules, or can I go to class now?"

"Last rule." His grin was cruel. "At home, I'll tolerate you—but here? You don't look at me in the eyes, you don't approach me, you don't hang out with me. Here we're enemies. Got it?"

"Fine." My voice was shaky.

"Oh, and Annie?" Ash unbuckled my seatbelt and leaned over the console. "I need you to understand one thing…" His fingers trailed my jawline delicately; I was too pissed and terrified to pull away. "Break any of my rules… and I will fucking destroy you."

How could a man so beautiful be so cruel?

"I hate you," I whispered.

"Finally, something we can agree on." He pulled back. "Now get the hell out of my car."

He didn't have to tell me twice as I opened the stupid fancy door and attempted to get out without flashing anyone. I stomped through the parking lot past Tank, who probably wouldn't notice anyway since he was too busy swallowing some random girl's face, and made my way to the Science building.

And that was how it started.

My first semester back at Eagle Elite, I was already trying to keep the tears in as I ducked my head and tried to do anything not to be noticed.

It worked for about three minutes, and then I heard Tank calling out my name. I gripped my satchel with my fingertips, pulling it higher on my shoulder, and kept on walking.

Because he knew.

He knew he was my rock.

He knew I liked him.

And I'd just seen him kissing another girl—devouring her. And I'd stupidly told myself that coming back to Chicago wouldn't be so bad as long as I had one friend.

Just. One.

"Hey, wait up." Tank grabbed my hand and turned me around.

With a sigh, I waited as his fingers left my shoulder, pulling away a bit at the jacket uniform. "What?"

"He being an ass to you?" Tank actually grinned; his lips were wet from her kiss, his stance casual like he'd just been ordering fries at McDonald's.

Why was I constantly surrounded by blind idiots?

Men who were mean by accident?

I would prefer the ones who were mean on purpose.

Then again, that was half and half with Ash, but with Tank? I expected more. I came back expecting at least this close friendship that we used to have, a safety net that I so desperately needed.

Instead.

I came home to a pawn.

A man who would do everything and anything to keep the mafia safe, to keep himself safe, to make sure his secrets were safe.

It reminded me of the first time I met him when he made me promises he clearly was having trouble keeping.

"No," I lied but answered his question. "He's just being himself."

Tank snorted, then wiped his sleeve across his mouth.

I followed the direction with my eyes then looked away in disappointment. "Who is she?"

Next to me, I could feel him still. "What? Bianca?" He let out a snort. "She was a distraction, a cover, nothing more."

"Mmm…" I nodded. "A cover so that what? Nobody suspects you of being FBI?"

In an instant, he was all rage, cupping his hand over my mouth, his eyes wild. "Are you fucking crazy?"

I did not recognize this man.

I did not recognize the wild green eyes.

The pale face.

The way his mouth pulled back into a tight line.

And in that moment, I realized he was theirs.

No longer mine.

Owned.

Gently he pulled his fingers back. "Sorry, I just, I can't blow my cover, can't let the office know how far— I have to choose soon, Annie, just like you, and I still don't know what the hell I'm doing."

"You let yourself fall," I answered simply. "Like the rest of us. We saw. We took. We fell, and now we're all trying to figure out what falling actually means."

His green eyes narrowed. "You'd tell me if you weren't okay, right?"

No. Not anymore. "Yeah. Of course." I shrugged. "I gotta head to class, but I'll see you later…"

"Annie." He reached for me again, his smile kind now, sexy, compelling as he pulled back then crossed his bulky arms. "We should hang out this week."

"Sure. Yeah." Over Ash's dead body. "I don't want to be late."

I walked away from his easy smile.

I walked away from Ash's angry stare.

I walked into class and pulled out a chair.

I sat and took notes, not remembering what class I was even in.

And never, in all my life, even as an orphan, felt so alone.

CHAPTER
Eight

"Everything comes to us that belongs to us if we create the capacity to receive it." —Rabindranath Tagore

Annie

October

"Get out," Ash barked.

I was so used to it by now that I was basically a robot. He'd make me breakfast in the morning all smiles, he'd give me maybe fifteen minutes of reprieve where I was able to actually look into what seemed like his soul, and then he'd close me out.

Like he was rewarding me for eating.

Only to punish me for surviving him.

I learned early on that he liked being provoked almost as much as he liked me being submissive, so I just simply...

Stopped.

I stopped fighting.

I stopped talking.

I stopped existing.

After all, I was the reason he had wanted to die last year; I was the reason he almost had.

I was the reason for everything.

The cause.

It didn't matter that I had my own reasons.

That I was a victim.

Because he was too busy taking over that entire role for himself, not allowing anyone else the chance to even grasp at the last remaining pieces that said that life wasn't fair—for either of us.

I guess my only saving grace with him was that he was nice to me in the mornings only to be completely cold at school.

I reached for the car door handle and hesitated, then looked over my shoulder with a sigh. "I get it, you know."

He gripped the steering wheel, staring straight ahead. "You get what?"

His jaw was sculpted into perfection, his full lips pressed together in a firm line as his chin jutted out, his whiskey-colored hair fell across his brow.

It hurt to stare at him.

Someone so beautifully mean.

"You hate me. I get it. I get that you have a part to play at the house and a part to play at college—you don't have to punish me to remind me. I get it. I know that after eggs and orange juice, I march my ass to the car of your choosing. I know that I get in and let you turn on whatever music you want. I know that the minute you park the car, the expectation is for me to get out, for you not to be seen with me and for me to hurry and get on with my day so I can get on with my life, so I can be the good little orphan who graduates and moves on. I get it. I've gotten it since I was nine, Ash. You reminding me only sets the remaining pieces of hope in my soul to burn. And I don't know if I can do that for another year. So please, just... when you park, could you say nothing?"

He was quiet.

His head bowed a bit, maybe in shame, maybe in submission, and then he pressed the unlock button on the door and rasped, "Be safe."

As much of an ass he was.

He always told me to be safe.

As if I mattered.

As if my safety was his top priority.

And I'd had it.

"Don't," I pleaded, my throat thick. "Don't ask me to be safe when the most convenient thing for you right now would be to lay down in front of your car and squeeze my eyes shut as you put it into drive—"

"Stop!" He had my wrist in his hand before I could escape, his chest heaved, and then he was pulling me, jerking harder, until I was nearly halfway across the console.

Hand shaking, he released me. I was too afraid to move. His blue eyes flashed as he reached out and touched my cheek with his right hand, then his left.

In all my life, I'd never felt revered.

But in that moment, I was somehow his.

Owned by the look on his face.

By the clench in his jaw and the trembling of his fingertips as he held me captive and whispered. "I don't know how."

"How?" I repeated, throat dry.

"To be a friend to the one person I blame for taking

everything I've ever held close in my life, and yet I know I should. I want to, but then I see you, and I see—" His voice cracked. "I see her. I see those last moments."

I leaned in. "Her last moments?"

"Protect Annie," he whispered. "Protect Annie."

"Wait, what?" My voice shook.

He pulled away. His hands dropped, his stone-cold face was back. "You'll be late for lab, Annie. Run along."

Run. Along?

Seriously?

"Sometimes I hate you," I said under my breath.

He just let out a dark chuckle and whispered back. "Good, that makes two of us."

CHAPTER
Nine

"Life hurts a lot more than death." —Anonymous

Ash

November

I made her breakfast.

I watched her eat.

I smiled as much as I could, even though I knew I was spiraling again without any reason why.

My brain told me it was because Annie reminded me of Claire.

But my heart?

My fucking heart told me it was because we weren't so sure anymore because we were starting to question, starting to wonder, starting to do so many things that made me want to project my anger onto the only object I had.

She drank her orange juice. A drop slid down her chin

before she blushed and wiped it away with her napkin.

"You ready?" I barked.

Hell, she'd been back for nearly two months, and I still couldn't get over the way she looked at me—sometimes like I was a monster, sometimes like she wanted to pull me close, hug me tight, and scare the monster into submission, revealing the broken man beneath the surface to afraid to hope anymore.

Annie jumped to her feet and then glared. "Yup."

She'd been doing that a lot more.

The glaring.

I told myself it was unacceptable.

And then, during the day, I felt my body responding to her defiance, to the way she now lifted her chin at me like she was ready for a fight. I loved it more than I would ever admit.

Just like the way I admired her ability to stay in my company and not strangle me alive.

"Come on." I grabbed my key fob for the Tesla and nearly jogged out to the car, not even opening her door.

I had one class; she had two. It only made sense that I took her every Friday.

I ignored the way my heart beat a little bit faster as she buckled her seat belt and, like always, set her satchel between her feet, then adjusted the collar of her jacket like it was out of place when we both knew it wasn't, just a way for her to keep her hands busy, so she didn't punch me in the face, most likely.

And I realized then that I was lingering, that I was watching, calculating, memorizing.

Such a dangerous thing to do—concentrating on your downfall.

I started the car.

We rode in silence as always.

And I parked. "Pick you up after class."

"Thank you."

I nearly groaned.

It was the fucking thank you that got me.

Every. Single. Time.

Because I knew I didn't deserve it. I knew I was in over my head with this constant need for revenge, for her to feel my pain, right along with this natural need to protect her from every bad thing in this world.

It was like I was playing both hero and villain, and it was exhausting.

"Yeah," I said. "Same spot."

"Great." Her smile was forced.

My chest hurt.

With anger.

Words left unsaid.

Pain.

So much pain because when Annie smiled, I saw Claire's last few breaths, asking me to do the one thing I couldn't even stomach.

Take care of her friend.

Watch over Annie.

And so I did both.

I did what Claire asked.

And I got my revenge at the same time.

So why did I feel guilty?

Sick?

She hesitated at the door and then looked over her shoulder and damned me with the sad look on her face. "I really do appreciate it, Ash. I know you'd rather drown, but thank you—for breakfast and for the ride."

She was out before I could say anything more.

The door clicked shut, blanketing me in damning silence, and then my fucking phone went off. Heaving a sigh, I wiped my hands down my face. Why was it getting harder and harder to get revenge on someone who actually deserved it? And why did her words hurt?

With a curse, I picked up my phone and felt the blood drain from my face. I'd been driven to distraction by her—that was a problem—I'd put this plan into effect over a month ago.

Out of anger.

Out of necessity.

And now it was too late.

"Shit, shit, shit!" I slammed my hand against the steering wheel because, in all my failures, this would be my worst. I'd been upset.

Could anyone blame me?

I'd wanted to hurt her.

I'd wanted to embarrass her.

Take her heart and stomp on it, then kiss it better and fuck with her head.

And because I was still so messed up.

I'd forgotten my own damn plan.

I'd fallen.

Bit by bit.

Maybe it started with the stupid bacon.

With the way her eyes lit up over the things that should have been handed to her the day she was born, the moment she first smiled.

I forgot.

And as I lifted my head, my eyes greedily searching the campus as she stopped and looked down at her phone, I knew.

I only had one choice.

One.

And I had to take it.

Or Claire would haunt me the rest of my life, and I'd want to die even more.

Fuck, I'd fallen so deep into despair I hadn't even seen how wrong I'd been, how horrible. And I'd been so pissed that even having someone tell me would have done nothing.

"You're not mine anymore," I choked out to Claire, to whatever spirit I felt that followed me. "You're gone… so that means I'm no longer yours."

I could have sworn I heard her say. "Go."

CHAPTER
Ten

"The bitterest tears shed over graves are for words left unsaid and deeds left undone." —Harriet Beecher Stowe

Annie

December

December sucked.

Really, that was all there was to it.

I got out of the car every stupid day. I walked to my classes, I went through the motions like every student did, I gave Ash a wide berth and was thankful for Izzy when I did see her or even Serena on campus for her remaining final class, but other than that.

I was alone.

And for some reason, it made me feel destitute. I lived in the home of one of the wealthiest families in the US, and still, I found myself...

Jealous.

It all started during lunch yesterday. I went to the rich kid cafeteria because of who basically owned me. I watched people eat organic everything from pasta to soups to salads to bread that wasn't even bread anymore, and when I couldn't stomach all the faces openly staring at me, I went to the Quick Bite Grill in search of a hamburger only to have even more eyes staring at me as if I didn't belong there either.

And that was the problem.

I was Cinderella but in the wrong story.

I wasn't a slave.

I wasn't a princess either.

I was a charity case who had no place at Eagle Elite, and yet it was my only ticket to a life where I no longer had to worry about any of these things anymore.

I decided if I could just survive my lunch hour, I could survive anything, even if it included violence—what with the way students stared at me, all calculated, judging, from what I wore to how I did my hair, and it didn't matter if I was in the earlier lunch with the richer kids or with the later lunch with the scholarship kids, I had no place.

Then again, I'd never had a place.

But this last year, at one point, I'd felt like I did.

When Serena and Junior took Tank and me in, when they told us we had a choice when they decided to train the rest of the De Lange kids despite their parentage, when they looked at me like I was more than my blood.

I finally had hope.

But now, it was as if everything was forgotten.

As if they realized I wasn't De Lange.

I was a nobody.

Not worth training, only worth protecting because of who

I had been to Tank, and even then, all he'd said was, she's with me, like some horrible gang movie where I went where he went.

And still, was I even with him?

Um no, I was with the enemy.

Just thinking about Ash had me fuming.

Hot all over.

Angry.

"Until the stars fall," Ash had whispered, instead of the sky but why? And why was I so damn fixated?

I shoved the phrase from my head and stared straight ahead, lifting a cold fry to my mouth only to drop it and get rid of the rest of my lunch in the scholarship kids' section.

When I left the building, he was there.

Because, of course, he was everywhere.

"Ready?" Ash had said yesterday without looking up.

"Yeah." I gripped my backpack tighter.

"Shit." He dropped his arm and showed me his phone. "Could you at least try to be more discreet?"

"What?" I was the epitome of discreet; nobody cared because nobody looked in my direction with anything but pity to fill the lonely void I carried.

There was a pic on Twitter of me smiling at Tank.

And then smiling at the TA in my bio class, the hashtag read "#sluttytriangle," as if I was leading them both on.

Tears had burned the back of my eyes. "I hate social media."

Ash snorted out a laugh. "Careful, there's truth to everything, isn't there?"

I had said nothing.

Instead, I went home.

I did my homework.

And at the end of the day, when everyone was sleeping.

I cried for the girl I used to be.

Then cried for the one I had to become.

And finally cried for the one I wished I could be, a future where I was someone stronger.

A future.

With someone like the person I hated the most.

Yet swore to my mom to trust.

An Abandonato whose heart wasn't even his to give.

Ash.

Mine.

But never to be claimed.

Damned.

And wallowing in it like he wanted it more than life. I shook the thoughts of yesterday away. This morning I'd had a plan.

Gratitude.

Maybe if I started thanking him rather than reacting or just plain ignoring, he would see that I wasn't the monster he made me out to be.

It had been worth a shot, and by the look on Ash's face this morning, he'd been so stunned that it was as though I'd just pulled out a gun and announced I knew how to use it.

I smiled a bit and gripped my bag tighter.

Maybe today would be the day where things changed for us, for me.

The wind picked up around my hair, setting a cold chill deep in my bones as I tried to pull my jacket tighter around my body.

I was about maybe thirty feet from the parking lot when I noticed people pointing at me, laughing, then looking back down at their phones.

Mine was in my bag, so I stopped walking and quickly grabbed it to see if there was a tweet or something on the Eagle Elite social media account. Nobody knew who controlled it, only that we didn't want to get on that person's bad side. Then again, I'd already been an unlucky victim, so fingers crossed I wasn't continually pissing off the rich kids.

I nearly dropped my phone onto the cement. It was a picture of me, all right.

And the tweet beneath it read. "Back from Italy, rumor has it she was sent away because she was pregnant... but don't believe our word for it, ask the guy she tried to hook up with, none other than Ash Abandonato. I'll be your daddy."

My hands shook as I read the tweet over and over again; more and more people crowded around me until I couldn't breathe.

"Annie!" Izzy's voice was the only clear thing I could focus on, and then Serena started yelling at people to move before she stabbed them.

If they were on this side of campus.

They'd seen it and were pulling in the troops.

Which meant rumors were spreading like... well, apparently my slutty legs.

I fell to my knees on the concrete, phone still in the palm of my hand as the two girls circled me and protected me from the rest of the students.

"Breathe." Izzy rubbed my back. "It's going to be okay. We had Ash call Sergio; he hacked the system and deleted the tweet; it's already gone."

"The damage is already done," I whispered hoarsely. "Who would say that about me? I'm not even... I haven't even..." I couldn't get the words out or the reason why they hurt so much in the first place.

Like someone knew the truth.

And wanted to air out the dirty laundry.

Who would be so cruel? And how did they know where to hit me the hardest? The worst part was that I had slept with him.

And I'd wanted that moment for just me.

Between us.

Because it was already so damn hard sharing it with her ghost.

"You're a whore just like your mother!" Daddy spat out the word whore so often now I responded better to it than my own name. "You were supposed to be a boy, you know that?" He took another swig of beer. "She just had to get pregnant with a girl and ruin all my fucking plans!" He threw the beer bottle at my feet then grabbed my wrist, squeezing it so hard that I heard a crunch, felt blinding pain as I swayed toward him. "Wish you would have never been born, worst idea I'd had—trying to fight my way to the top. Worthless…" At my scream, he released me.

Mama ran toward me only to be stopped by Daddy. "Leave her alone to think about what she did—what you both did."

"Stop this!" Mama whimpered. "I only did what you asked me to do."

"You bitch!" Daddy's hand came flying, slapping mama in the face so hard that Mama fell to the ground. "I asked you to get pregnant with the next heir, and you gave me a fucking girl!"

"I can't control—"

"You should have figured out a way! Or at least tried again!"

"Having a child nearly killed me the first time," Mama whispered, cupping her cheek.

Daddy just snarled out another foul curse. "Good, maybe this time you'll die."

It was the last fight they had before Hell's fury broke loose over us. Before I was covered in blood that wasn't mine. Before strange men came barging into my house, guns blazing.

I held my brown bear close to my chest as screams filled the air. And then I prayed they'd take me too as I closed my eyes and wished for it all to go away.

To finally be free.

"Hey, don't pass out on us yet," Serena whispered in my ear. "Can you get up?"

I nodded slowly as a hush fell over the group of students circling me, ready to throw insults at me like perfectly sharpened arrows.

I'd always been on the outside looking in.

Only because the inside was deadly, and once you were in—there was no escape, was there?

I saw his combat boots first, black, most likely designer, as he stepped forward into the circle.

A tear slid down my cheek as I looked up into Ash's cold eyes. I couldn't tear my gaze from his, was afraid if I did, he'd laugh at me, or maybe worse.

This was, after all, his Kingdom. His world.

The students? His loyal subjects.

Me? A mere slave.

He crouched down on his haunches, his chiseled face completely unreadable, full lips pressed together while whiskey-colored hair tousled across his forehead. Why were the pretty ones always the most angry?

"What did I say about crying?" he asked, but before I could answer, he reached across the space between us and used his thumb to wipe away the tears still rolling down my cheeks. He then used that same hand to grip my chin and force me to look at him. "Ignore them."

"Wh-what?"

"I said ignore them," he whispered. "Your tears are worth more than all of their lives combined." He moved his hand, and then he was reaching for my waist, pulling me to my feet.

I was so shocked he was actually helping that I was light-headed as he intertwined his fingers with mine. The crowd parted. People refused to look directly at Ash and me, choosing to look down at their phones and furiously text or pretend that they weren't bullying and walk off.

My palm was sweaty against his. He squeezed my hand tight like he was taking possession, and I was petrified that he was seconds away from shoving me up against one of the old building's brick walls and threatening me again.

When we reached the science building, I tried to pull away, but he just gripped my hand tighter as people watched in fascination at us, probably trying to figure out why the campus King had an orphan dangling off his arm.

He opened the door to the building pulling me in after him, and then continued walking at a purposeful pace until we reached Human Anatomy.

The hall was filled with around a hundred and fifty students as he brought me directly to the front and stood.

The professor glanced up, paled, and then grabbed his empty coffee cup and left out the side door; the click of it shutting was equal to a gunshot as everyone froze and stared at Ash.

"Human Anatomy and Physiology." Ash dropped my hand and leaned against the desk while I watched in horror as every single student stared at us. I was paralyzed with fear of what he would do, fear of what they would do, I didn't know if I could sit down in a chair or if I should stay up there with him, and the minute I turned to take a step, Ash grabbed my arm again as if to say, stay.

Shit.

Tears welled in my eyes as he started pacing in front of the class.

"I've always found the human body interesting." He reached behind him and pulled out an ugly looking dagger with a serrated edge. "Take our ability to handle pain as an example. Did you know that the human brain doesn't feel pain?" He tossed the knife in the air. "In fact, surgeons don't even need to put patients under when they operate on the brain because no pain receptors exist in the brain tissue. So if I were to take this knife—" He grinned. "—and make tiny, itty, bitty cuts inside your skull, you'd smile at me like we were on a fucking picnic." He walked toward one of the students sitting in the front. "Don't believe me?"

"No, I mean y-yes, yes I believe you," he stuttered.

"I do like experiments." Ash grinned. "What? No volunteers? I'm disappointed." He walked back toward me. "Tell you what… I'll pay for the first volunteer's entire college tuition—all they have to do is step up as a volunteer. It's not hard, right? You just get out of your seat, and I get to play Adult Operation. The rest of the students learn a bit about the brain, I get to show the rest of the world how idiotic all the students here are by cracking open someone's brain and seeing cobwebs and Snapchat, and Annie over here, well, she gets that pound of flesh she deserves after that tweet went out this morning."

Gasps were heard around the room, and people started murmuring.

"Hmmm." Ash shrugged and leaned against the professor's desk. "I guess since we have no volunteers, I'll just start picking them at random, only this time I can promise pain. You see, I gave you guys an out. Nobody took it, so to collect the pound of flesh she deserves…" He pointed the knife at me. "I'll just be taking a few ounces from each of you. I'll stop when she's satisfied and when the floor's covered in blood. Don't think I won't do it." He thumbed the knife and moved back to the student directly in front of him. "Your hand, please."

Shaking, he slowly held out his hand. Ash lifted the blade.

"STOP!" I yelled, unable to keep the horror out of my voice. "I'll volunteer, I'll do it."

The blade hovered over the kid's hand as he puked on the guy sitting next to him and then passed out.

Ash dropped his hand and glanced over his shoulder with a wink. "You had me worried there for a minute."

"Wh-what?"

"That, dear students, is your lesson of the day." Ash walked back toward me and wrapped an arm around me. "You don't pick on the weak ones; they're usually the first to take the fall for all of you because they're secretly the strongest ones in the group. Besides, it just makes you look like a fucking jackass. If you want to pick on someone, pick on me. That at least makes it a fair fight." He grinned. "For at least the first few seconds while I let you think you have the upper hand." He sighed. "If I see any more bullying, any more tweets, even a hint of hate. I'll stop at each class and collect." He abruptly pulled away and slid the jagged knife across his palm. "My oath."

People looked ready to cry. One girl was rocking in her desk while another was hurriedly packing up her bag.

"All right." He smiled wide. "Class dismissed, our professor was feeling under the weather, be sure to volunteer for the Fall Thanksgiving Drive."

I was so stunned I didn't even remember walking back toward his car.

Or how I even got my seatbelt buckled.

All I could say as he drove down the road was, "Why?"

It was quiet for a few minutes before he whispered, "Only I get to be the reason for your tears. Not them. Never them."

I had no idea that for the next two months, Ash and I would be at odds, that he'd make breakfast, take me to school, he'd be as polite as possible.

But that he was more bodyguard than friend.

Angry around the edges.

Unrecognizable.

And I was still the same.

Going through the motions.

Empty.

CHAPTER
Eleven

"The fear of death follows from the fear of life. A man who lives life fully is prepared to die at any time." — Mark Twain

Ash

"Could you try not to hit me in the junk next time?" King dodged my next hit. Sweat poured down his recently tatted chest.

"No promises." I sneered as I threw another punch.

I'd driven Annie back to the house and instantly bolted from the car, my brain a whirlwind of emotions from anger to revenge, lust, sadness. It was like every single human emotion possible had chosen this day to dump on me, fucking with my brain and my heart.

I expected her to follow me down into the basement and was a little disappointed when she didn't. But I kept going. I knew at least one of my cousins would be waiting to spar—it was an unwritten rule, either go to my house or Nixon's and expect blood. Thankfully King was only too happy to jump into the ring—though he lost his shit-eating grin after I took out all my rage on his body.

"Hope that doesn't get infected," I said, landing another punch across his face.

"Son of a bitch, Ash, who the hell pissed you off today?" He held up both hands; the white tape was stained with wide streaks of crimson at this point.

"I get next," Junior said from the side of the ring.

I barked out a laugh. "No, Tank's next."

Tank glared up at me. "No, Tank's good. Thanks, though."

"Pussy," I spat just as the girls walked in. Annie was hanging in the back with Izzy and Kartini while Serena was making an angry beeline toward Junior. Ah, the entertainment never did end with those two.

King nodded his head toward the girls. "Come on, they like it when we get all bloody and dirty."

"Ew, that's your cousin," I pointed out.

"Okay, there's first cousins… and second cousins—"

"Fuck, is he quoting Mean Girls again?" This from Junior, who still didn't realize his very angry girlfriend was standing right behind him, arms crossed, nostrils flaring.

Both King and I immediately stopped fighting and watched in rapt fascination as Junior slowly hung his head, cursing under his breath. "She's behind me, isn't she?"

"YES." Serena gave him a shove. "*SHE* IS!"

Annie's eyes widened as she took in the scene. Already Serena was beating on Junior's back, then sideswiped him with a clever Jiu-Jitsu move that had me slow clapping in encouragement. I mean, it was a great takedown; it needed to be acknowledged.

He went sailing to the floor and onto his back, guarding his face with his hands as he yelled. "I thought you would be happy!"

"DO." Swat. "I." Punch. "Look." Ohhhhh hell. I winced as she grabbed his balls. "HAPPY TO YOU?"

"No. Yes." Junior winced in pain, his teeth clenched. "Just tell me the right answer before I lose my ability to have children."

"YOU FILMED US!" she screeched in a horrified voice that had my own balls trembling in fear. I wouldn't put it past her to just castrate him right then and there.

"Oh shit." King burst out laughing as he crossed his arms and leaned against the ring. "This is better than TV."

Maksim stopped training with a few of the De Lange orphans in the corner and walked over, arms crossed while they stayed where they were as if moving too close to Serena would suddenly make them just as guilty as Junior.

Smart guys.

All five of them were petrified of Serena. Then again, they were only eighteen. Hell, I knew thirty-year-olds who refused to look her directly in the eyes lest they lose their dicks.

"I can explain!" Junior yelled again, then flipped in a classic move and managed to throw his weight toward her then flip her onto her back.

"Full mount. Very nice." King whispered under his breath.

Junior pinned her. "Look, you looked really hot, you are hot... What am I saying right now—"

"He's so dead." I laughed out loud, and the feeling felt so foreign that I almost stopped laughing altogether. How long had it been since I didn't think twice about laughing? As if I wasn't honoring her memory by having a good time? Being miserable, staying miserable meant that I remembered her, right?

"And I didn't know we were going to have sex, all right?"

"WHEN DO WE NOT HAVE SEX?"

"That's actually a very valid point." Maksim just had to chime in.

"Maksim!" Junior yelled as Serena bucked underneath him. "Not now, man!"

Maksim held up his hands, and I could tell the little shit was seconds away from making it worse.

"Well?" Serena seethed.

"Fuck, I hate all of you sometimes." Junior kept her pinned and then, in a very low whisper, confessed, "I was going to propose."

She went completely still beneath him. "Wait... what?"

"I wanted it to be just us." Junior's eyes searched hers. "That's why I had the camera set up; I wanted you to have it on video. It's not like I set you up. And again, you're sexy, I couldn't help myself."

"Maybe you guys just delete that part of the proposal video," I suggested with a shrug. Sounded reasonable to me. "I can't imagine Nixon wanting to watch you get his daughter naked before asking for her hand..."

Maksim snickered. "He'd probably just chop off his hand to make things even."

Junior scowled. "I would have deleted it, except I got distracted by this one." Junior put more weight on Serena as she struggled to get free. "And then we fell asleep, and I knew she had an appointment with her mom and—"

"You idiot!" Serena tried bucking her hips again. "You don't have to do anything special. All I want is you!"

"Classic hot girl falls for stupid guy." Maksim sighed. "I'm here for it."

"Go anywhere else, Maksim. Really ANYWHERE else," Junior called from his position on the floor and then slowly started to let Serena up.

She mauled him again and started searching his pockets. "Where's the ring? You didn't change your mind, did you? Junior, hello?" She shoved him again and again as she moved her hands all over his body in a way that looked almost painful.

"You, uh…" I laughed. "You sure about this, bro? She's a bit of a handful."

Junior just winked at me. "I got big hands."

"Yeah, you do." Serena smiled.

I just shook my head because they were idiots, both of them idiots that deserved each other, idiots that I loved.

The pain in my chest intensified.

It wasn't from the fighting.

It was jealousy.

Jealousy that they had the ending I should have had.

The happy one where you fuck as much as you fight.

Claire hadn't ever pushed me. No, it always felt more like manipulation.

"We're pregnant," she said in a hush. "We need to think about the baby's future, Ash, not just ours. I mean, can you really see us raising a child in this environment?"

I immediately tensed. "What the hell's wrong with being raised like this? I had everything as a child. I wanted for nothing. I had family. I had friends. I grew up with my best friends. What the fuck, Claire?"

She scowled and looked down at her hands. "You say that now, but would you really raise your son or daughter up in this life?"

"My dad did it, my uncles did it, why not us?" I reached for her hand only to have her jerk it away and rub it. "What? Now you're pissed? You know I've got you; I won't let anything happen to you."

"I know." Her smile seemed forced. "Come on, let's get to class." She stopped walking. "Actually, I was going to run some errands, but I can do them later. Can I borrow your car, like later this week?"

I tossed her the spare key fob. "Just let me know when and try not to wreck it."

She smiled and then walked back up to me and kissed me soundly on the mouth. "I probably won't go until later this week, but I'll text you."

"Send a nude along with that text, will ya?"

She laughed and pulled me in for a hug. "We'll get through it, right?"

"We get through everything, Claire. We'll get through this."

"I love you, you know. I do." She clung to me tightly.

"And I love you." But even as I said the words, they tasted bitter in my mouth, like she didn't understand the depth of my love.

And she never would.

I wanted to break my body in half so she could see how much of my heart she owned. It seemed no matter what I said, she wouldn't ever get it.

I just wish my words were enough.

My actions enough.

Everything I did, I did for her, in order to keep her safe.

And on days like this, I felt like a fucking failure because it still wasn't enough for her to feel like I could be a good father, was it? It still wasn't fucking enough.

"Marry me." Junior's words interrupted my trip down depressing-as-hell memory lane.

"YES!" Serena jumped into the air and then jumped onto him as he swung her around. "But the ring?"

Junior just sighed, pressing his forehead against hers. "It's in my car; let's go."

They ran up the stairs as Serena sang out, "Champagne in twenty, bitches."

"Why twenty?" King scratched his head.

"Because the rest of the fifteen minutes is going to be spent with Serena, most likely on her knees servicing her king." I shrugged and then started walking out of the ring.

Wanting to be alone.

And hating that no matter what—I always felt like I was.

CHAPTER
Twelve

"The song is ended but the melody lingers on." —
Irving Berlin

Annie

I was still traumatized from my horrible week—and every ride home with Ash had been some of the most awkward and tense experiences of my life. Then again, he had most of my tense experiences in the ball of his fist, so I shouldn't be that surprised. I couldn't read him. At University, he seemed almost playful and protective, if that made any sense, instead of scary as hell. Though, when it came down to it...

I'd liked it.

Who was I kidding?

I'd loved the fact that out of everyone on campus—it was enemy number one who decided to play hero. It gave me a glimpse of hope that maybe Ash wasn't such a horrible person after all. Maybe deep down, he did have a heart; he just hadn't known how to fix what was broken, so every time he tried to use it—it hurt.

I could justify so many moments with him after that rescue.

After he threatened everyone in class.

And after he basically took ownership of my tears as if they were his and his alone. Did it make me sick that I liked it? That if I had to cry, I wanted it to be over him? Like a baptism of pain and longing all at once?

Every time we pulled into the garage, he'd grip the steering wheel until his knuckles were white. Then he'd turn to me, open his mouth, and shut it again like he was trying to silence himself before he said something he'd regret.

Which seemed to be his MO lately when we were alone.

He always left me there, waiting, with my seatbelt still strapped and my chest still heavy from the trauma since that fateful day.

What sort of person did it make me, that I would have done anything, sold my soul for him to reach across that console and squeeze my hand.

I just wanted someone to tell me it was going to be okay.

For someone to see me.

Actually, see me.

Not as the reason the love of his life was gone, but as my own person. God, it would feel so good to have that. Maybe that was why I liked Tank, but I would be lying to myself loving a man like Tank, wouldn't I?

He was more friend than lover.

Savior.

Safe.

I deserved safe, damn it! So why was I attracted to broken and deranged?

And why was I on the verge of tears—all because I just needed to be seen, to maybe have a hug, or a pat on the back, to be told that eventually, it would be okay, maybe not now, no now it was painful, but one day it wouldn't be.

I swiped the tear on my cheek and grabbed my bag, then slowly got out of a car that cost more than the average house in Chicago.

I went from the garage to the kitchen and decided to make some food. Thankful that nobody was in there to watch me.

I lived there, but I still felt weird eating their food, like the orphan caught stuffing their faces in the pantry for fear they wouldn't get fed again. I couldn't help it; when you have a past like mine, you learn to look over your shoulder in dread for the next time you take a misstep, and it seems that the only thing I was good at.

Was offending people.

Ash included.

Heart heavy, I looked around the corner again and quickly opened the fridge door, my chest tight, wondering how long I had before someone barged into the kitchen and judged me for taking some lunch meat and cheese.

I knew it was stupid.

In my gut, I knew if I just said something to Chase, he'd probably build me a kitchen, he was so extravagant, but I wanted to still be treated like everyone else.

Like Ash.

Which left me in the position of feeling like a thief in need of an after school snack.

I grabbed the mayo, some sliced cheese, and lunch meat, then went over to the bread box and tugged out some sourdough.

I had my sandwich done in under a minute, crumbs cleaned from the counter, all traces of what I'd done gone, just as Phoenix rounded the corner.

Anyone but the scary one.

I had trouble looking him in the eyes most days. His were piercing, filled with secrets that I was convinced he'd sell to the highest bidder if he didn't have a loving wife and son.

"You see Chase?" He leaned against the door frame, his massive build taking up over half of it as he ran a hand over his closely buzzed dark hair. Tattoos peeked out from his blue suit jacket. He never wore a tie, and more often than not, weirdly matched Andrei, the Sinacore boss, as if they'd decided to use the same personal shopper when everyone knew they'd rather be shot than be seen shopping.

The sandwich was dry in my throat as I swallowed, then croaked out. "N-no, I just got back, though. Um, Ash is probably sparring, though. Downstairs."

With shaking hands, I hid the sandwich behind my back like a thief out of total habit, hating that I was afraid for the other shoe to drop.

Phoenix's eyes softened as he slowly made his way past the door and toward the breakfast bar. "I used to hate color."

"I'm sorry, what?" Why was he still here?

"Eating color," he clarified, jerking his head at the hidden sandwich. "Didn't think I deserved anything that tasted good. I was bad, you know. The worst of all the bosses. Sometimes I still think about it, about how I punished myself because I didn't deserve better, because I was so used to the darkness I forgot the light even existed."

Tears welled in my eyes. "I'm not punishing myself if that's what you think."

"No," he whispered. "I don't think you're punishing yourself. I do, however, think you're afraid to hope, and sometimes I think that's worse than self-punishment because at least one you can control, the other..." His words trailed off as his face took on an inscrutable expression.

"I'm okay," I found myself saying. "Chase and Luc are great."

"Of course they are." His smile was sad. "I wasn't talking about Chase and Luc, though..." He took another tentative step toward me. "It's okay to sit, Annie. It's okay to sit and to grab a plate. Nobody's going to take it away from you." He reached out and brushed the side of my face; a crumb came back on his fingertip then fell to the floor.

Embarrassment washed over me as I looked away.

"Ash's favorite fruit snacks are on the bottom shelf hidden behind the maple syrup." He pointed out. "Do me a favor and eat every last one. Little shit deserves it. And next time you make a fucking sandwich, I want it to be too big to eat. I want you to get so stuffed that you have to throw half of it away— and I want you to know you deserve every last bite."

"Why are you—" My voice caught. "It's fine, I don't mind—"

"*I* do. Chase would. You're under our protection now, Annie, no matter what... You're in this, you get that, right? And we protect our own, even when we aren't blood."

I nodded, not trusting my voice.

"Bottom shelf." He winked and then walked over to the cupboard, grabbed a plate, and handed it to me. "Take your time."

He had no way of knowing.

It was the first time I'd eaten something after classes that wasn't rushed, including eating at Eagle Elite.

It was the first time I felt like it was okay to enjoy something, to sit and think about my day without wanting to cry tears of frustration, fear, and pain.

I took the white plate, set my sandwich on it, then slowly went to the barstool, and pulled one out.

"Better." Phoenix nodded. "Let Chase know I stopped by if you see him. And Annie?"

"Yes." I paused with the sandwich halfway to my mouth.

Phoenix's lips curled into a knowing smile. "Give him fucking hell. He deserves it."

"Who?" I played dumb.

"Forget about the fruit snacks, and I'll be very disappointed."

I found myself smiling. "I swear to steal every last one."

He barked out a laugh. "Sure you aren't a De Lange?"

"Positive," I answered easily.

Because I wasn't.

I was much, much, worse.

According to my dad, the devil had sired me.

I averted my eyes and took a bite as Phoenix gave me his back and left the kitchen.

I finished my sandwich in silence, put my dish in the dishwasher, then walked past the pantry only to backtrack, open the door, and move the maple syrup.

A smile spread across my face as I grabbed the box and dumped the remaining five fruit snack packages into my hands, leaving the empty box for him to find.

Satisfaction coursed through me.

It was a small thing.

Petty really.

But it would make Ash react.

And for some reason, I felt alive again, like maybe the world wasn't against me, maybe I could hope a little bit more.

I went to my room to stash the fruit snacks and had every intention of doing homework when I heard Serena's voice as she basically yelled to herself in passing my bedroom door.

Silently, I followed her as she stomped down the hall and then took the door to the left, leading to the home gym in the basement.

Curiosity piqued, I watched an entire drama unfold as Junior and Serena fought. My skin got hot as he threw her on her back.

What did that feel like?

To be so dominated?

Protected?

Memories of that night assaulted me.

"Beg me." Ash gripped my wrists so tight that pain started radiating down my arms, but I loved it, craved more as his body poised over mine, ready to take me. Primed.

"Please, Ash, please!" My voice was a harsh whisper as he thrust into me, filling, owning, commanding.

The world had never felt more perfect.

"You're mine." His mouth moved down my neck.

"Yours."

"Until the stars fall," he vowed.

A tear slid down my cheek colliding with the pillow. "Until the stars fall, Ash. Until they fall..."

My head jerked up when suddenly Ash was stomping away from the ring, his face pale, mouth in a taut straight line like the world had pissed him off again.

He didn't even see me until he was right in front of me.

He stopped.

I lifted my head.

"Innocent little Annie coming down here to spar?" he sneered.

Innocent little Annie was seconds away from kneeing him in the junk. Instead, I pasted a bland smile on my face. "I don't think I'd last five seconds."

He snorted out a laugh. "Make that one second."

"You should teach her." Maksim suddenly appeared, earning a giant *stay the hell away from us* scowl from Ash. "What? She's in this whether she likes it or not, and it's your ass if she gets hurt."

"Why's it my ass?"

Maksim pointed up.

Ash groaned. "Because God says so?"

"Bro." Maksim shook his head in disappointment. "No, because she's under your roof, ergo under your protection. Simple math."

"Sometimes I wonder if you're too smart to even do simple math," Ash grumbled and took a look at me, then another, a closer one, like an idea was forming.

I remembered Phoenix's talk.

And then I remembered the fruit snacks and stupidly gave Ash a knowing smile.

His eyes dropped to my mouth.

Maksim cleared his throat. "Soooooo, what do you say, Ash?"

"Huh?" He shook his head.

"Sparring." Maksim did a few jabs with his hands. "Making sure she knows how to fend off predators..." He grinned at Ash. "You being the predator in this scenario."

"Got that, thanks," he barked.

"It's okay…" I offered lamely. "It looks like Ash already got his ass beat today…"

I had no clue where that came from.

Maybe the blood on the corner of his mouth.

Or the fire in his eyes.

"The hell did you just say?" Ash moved so fast I nearly fell back on my own ass; we were chest to chest.

"Just that…" I licked my lips. "…you're probably tired after losing all those rounds."

"What the fuck makes you think I lost, little girl?"

"Blood." My voice shook. "Doesn't that mean you lost if he gets that many hits in, plus your right eye's already bruising, and is that a cut on your—'

"That's it." He grabbed my wrist and spun me around until I was nearly jogging with him back to the ring.

King's eyebrows shot up to his hairline as he shared a look with Maksim, who was already jumping from foot to foot in anticipation.

Great, so they wanted me dead?

Then again, I did have a secret.

I smiled to myself.

"What? That excited to get the shit beat out of you?" Ash sneered.

"Your dad would murder you," I pointed out.

He shrugged and held open the ring for me to step in. "Shoes off."

I kicked off my boots; I was still in my skirt and blouse. I shrugged out of my jacket and stood in the middle of the mat while Ash started to circle me.

We had everyone's attention.

The gym was completely silent except for Ash's footsteps as

he circled me like a caged animal.

"Annie." King jumped in the ring and moved behind me. "Get your guard up, like this." He held up my hands in front of my face while Ash glared. "Good, good, now dominant foot first, you're going to want to jab and block, jab, block."

He tried showing me while Ash waited with the patience of a frayed shoestring.

"Let her learn her lesson, King," Ash grated out.

"Don't kill her, man," King said under his breath as he got out of the ring and joined Maksim, Tank, and the other recruits.

I didn't look in Tank's direction.

I could already feel his disapproval, which just made me want to stay in that ring all the more.

I kept my hands up to block my face and nearly fell on my ass when Ash threw a right hook. I blocked it, but my palms stung from the effort.

Was he seriously going to fight me?

Satan himself?

Everything I learned in Italy came back full force as he swiped my feet and sent me directly onto my back, my skirt hiked up past my thighs showing off my black underwear and way too much skin for my liking.

Thankfully, it was the distraction I needed as Ash's eyes flickered to my thighs. I kicked out, hooking both of his feet and sending him sailing onto his back, then I used my momentum to flip over and get an armbar.

Teeth clenched, I pulled back until I heard something pop.

Ash tapped against my arm.

"Did she just…" King burst out laughing. "Holy shit! Did she just submit you?"

"Element of surprise," I said, releasing Ash.

He didn't move.

"Leave," he said in a lethal tone.

I started to move, but with one hand, he flipped his weight and pinned me to the mat. "Not you."

"Ash, she was just defending—"

"Maksim, if you want to live to see your next birthday… I'd go. Close the door."

When I glanced to my left, Tank had both hands clenched into fists; it took both Maksim and King shoving him toward the door to get him to leave with the recruits shuffling after him.

And then, with finality, it shut with a resounding boom resonating through the basement.

"Talk." Ash gritted his teeth, keeping most of his weight against my pelvis so I couldn't move, could barely breathe.

"Italy." I squeezed out some air. "I learned some self-defense."

"Who taught you?"

Oh no.

"One of your cousins…" I licked my lips. "Enzo or something…"

"FUCKING ENZO TOUCHED YOU?"

I squeezed my eyes shut so I couldn't see the rage on his face as I nodded my head. "He said I was…"

"He. Said. What."

"He said…" I chewed my lower lip. "…that I was too pretty not to know how to defend myself against jackasses." I slowly turned and locked eyes with him and added. "Guess it worked."

"Touché." He ground out. "But he lied…"

I was on a cliff.

Ready to get pushed.

I braced for it.

For the words.

You're not pretty.

I welcomed them because it was an easier blow to take. No surprises that way, just truths.

"I know." I held his gaze.

"You have no fucking clue what I was going to say." Ash's voice was hoarse. "And Enzo was wrong because there's no chance in hell he was giving you lessons for your protection—more for any chance to get close to you, to touch you, to see your eyes light up like they are right now. To be the center of that fucking stare that haunts my dreams, finishes my nightmares."

I gasped.

He lowered his head, his lips pressed against my ear as he whispered. "I would never lie to you."

"Wh-what?" I could count my heartbeats, feel them banging against my chest.

"You are, and always have been… very pretty." I was weightless then as he slowly moved away from me and stood, then held out his hand.

I took it.

And Ash Abandonato, fallen angel half the time, devil the rest, held up his hands and whispered. "Again."

CHAPTER
Thirteen

"You must not shut the night inside you but endlessly in light the dark immerse— A tiny lamp has gone out in my tent, I bless the flame that warms the universe."
—Author Unknown

Chase

The Past: A Week Before Claire's Death

"They really are the worst at sneaking around," I said under my breath as Junior ran up the stairs with Serena in tow. They didn't even see us sitting at the table in the dark, drinking wine, thinking dark thoughts, blood still caking our fingertips.

Phoenix shrugged. "I thought you were gonna deal with it."

"This is me dealing with it." I lifted my wine glass to him and drank deep. The wine was bitter on my tongue. Hell, these days, everything felt bitter.

In a hoarde of cousins and fucking De Langes, around fifteen people ran up the stairs and down the hall toward the movie room. It was nice to see them at least making an attempt at being normal.

I sighed again as Ash lingered in the back, his eyebrows etched together in concern as Claire shook her head and then rose and kissed him on the cheek, holding her hand there.

I ground my teeth.

Ash stared down at her like she was his heaven.

And I couldn't help but wonder if he realized she would eventually become his hell.

"He loves her," Phoenix whispered. "Beyond all reason. Desperately."

"He does." I sighed as a weight settled on my shoulders.

The small quiet girl, Annie, came up behind them. Neither of them even noticed her existence as she tugged at her cardigan, trying to cover the bruises we all knew were there.

Why else would we be covered in blood after hearing about what she'd dealt with? Ash and Junior killed her adoptive parents—and we killed the rest of the monsters, the associates, involved. It was an easy in-and-out job.

At least we continued to protect her and to protect the rest of the De Lange orphans; we did what we had to.

We killed those who would use them against us.

And would keep that secret to our grave.

Annie walked by Ash and Claire.

Ash glanced at her, his eyes lingering on her longer than I'd seen him look at any other female since Claire.

The hell?

Frowning, I sharpened my focus on Ash.

Did he... like her?

Was he attracted to her?

Claire gave his hand a tug and then smiled at Annie, a

genuine smile, one that was full of happiness and protection.

Annie shook her head and made her way into the kitchen only to see us both sitting at the table, looking like a horror movie gone wrong or perhaps a horror movie gone right?

Depended on who was alive or dead, I supposed.

"Hi." She was a few feet away from us and waved like we were across the street playing friendly neighbor.

Phoenix smirked and looked away. She was small, quiet, unassuming—she was also a victim, and I wondered if it would be my son or me who would fight for her vengeance one day?

"Are you enjoying yourself tonight, Annie?" I asked.

She gulped, her eyes drinking in all the blood most likely still covering my face. "Y-yeah."

"Halloween costume." Phoenix coughed. "Fake blood."

I almost choked on my laugh as Annie nodded slowly as if to say, *"Your secret's safe with me... besides, I like living."*

I'd never seen a human being grab a bottle of water from the fridge faster than that girl, and then she sprinted down the hall, nearly colliding with Ash in the process.

He gave her an annoyed look.

She hung her head.

And Claire?

She was staring straight ahead at the wall like it held secrets.

Heavy is the crown.

It seemed that was all I'd been thinking.

"Have you decided?" Phoenix asked what I'd been thinking—what we'd all been thinking since that day.

"I can't make that decision. It's not my choice. It never was. Let him love her. Let him watch her resentment destroy him from the inside out. That's my decision."

"Blood in, no out." Phoenix poured more wine.

"To the day we both get out of the mafia—our funerals." I clinked my glass against his as a shroud of sadness draped over us until I felt like I was choking with it.

For the first time in a very long time—I wished for a different life for my son—because maybe then he'd have the happy ending he deserved rather than the smokescreen of perfection.

Ash deserved someone strong.

He deserved someone who wouldn't ask him to change who he was.

Even if he was a killer, it was his choice to be made, to follow in my footsteps, and I hated anyone who made him feel like it was wrong—to want to be like your father and to already surpass him in so many ways—in all the ways that counted.

"You know…" Phoenix followed my line of sight. "…I can always talk with her or tell Nikolai to call. She'll listen to her uncle."

I released a humorless chuckle. "She won't even listen to the man she loves. What makes you think she'd listen to her uncle? The same one who kills for sport with one hand while holding a Nobel prize in the other?"

Phoenix choked out a laugh. "Sorry, it amuses me every fucking time."

"Same."

"Besides, Nikolai can be very convincing…"

I snorted and looked back up at my son's hurt expression. "Fuck it, give him a call; I don't need to know the details, just that he gets the point across to her in a way that I clearly didn't."

"Consider it done." Phoenix's grin was menacing. Hell, I

almost felt sorry for Nikolai now.

Some of the sadness dissipated.

And to think it was Phoenix, the man who used to be enemy number one back in college, who was sitting with me in the dark... bloody, beaten, drinking wine and offering to fix what I couldn't.

Yeah, God was probably having a laugh over that one.

CHAPTER
Fourteen

"They say you die twice. Once when you stop breathing, and a second time, a bit later on, when somebody says your name for the last time." —Banksy

Ash

"Ma!" A swat landed on the back of my head after I attempted to grab one of the breadsticks she'd made from scratch. "That hurt!"

"Manners!" She jabbed a wooden spoon at me. The same one that she used to smack my ass with when I used to lie to her about finishing my vegetables. It wasn't like it was a hard smack; I was just more terrified of it than I was anything else for some reason. Now just seeing it had me holding my hands up in surrender.

Dad chuckled.

I shot him a glare.

Got a middle finger back.

Then watched in horror as he picked up a breadstick and took a huge bite.

"How is that fair?" I asked the table.

Ma just grinned and kissed him on the head. "He's worked hard today."

"Yeah, son." His grin made me want to hurl. "I worked real hard today." Note that he said this as he was grabbing Ma's ass.

"Not at the dinner table!" I nearly shrieked as Izzy walked in, sighed, and then blindly tried to find a chair while covering her eyes. Thank God the baby of our family, Ariel, was at a friend's house, nobody needed that sort of trauma.

"What did we say about censorship?" I grumbled to myself.

Annie came in next, took one look at them, blushed, and quickly pulled out a chair.

Damn girl blushed at anything and everything like she was some virgin who'd never seen a dick before.

And mine just chose an inopportune moment to remind me and my brain that she had, in fact, seen mine, touched mine, that I'd been inside her, that I'd nearly gotten off on her. Used her as a way to make the pain go away, only to discover that she made it worse.

She always did.

Was it her smile?

Her fear of me?

Her presence?

No clue.

But it seemed after sparring for a bit tonight, after teaching her more of the basics, we had some sort of white flag waving between us.

Already I knew she had been hurt after the tweets that had gone out. Add that to my basically threatening the entire school, and it had been a long day.

And with Mom and Dad flirting over the pasta.

It promised to be an even longer night.

"So." Ma held out her hands. "Who wants to pray?"

"Pretty sure you two shouldn't," I grumbled. "What with you fornicating all over the place."

Annie flinched in her chair. Why the hell was I noticing every single thing she did? Like I was hyperaware of each reaction, each movement when all I wanted was revenge.

Pain.

Blood.

"Married," Dad annoyingly pointed out, shaking me out of my dark thoughts as I pulled my head out of my ass and tried to focus on the plan ahead, which did not include thinking about how close Annie had been when we trained, the way her breaths came out in short little gasps from those parted full lips.

I adjusted myself under the table like I was in junior high and then looked up, only to see my dad giving me a knowing smile. "Been a long time since you've been to confession—you pray."

Son of a—

Was it wrong to pray with a hard-on?

Because I was pretty sure that was in the Bible somewhere: *thou shall not think of sex and thank God for food at the same time.*

"Sure," I grated out and bowed my head. "Dear God, thank you for our health, our family, and our food. Amen."

I quickly grabbed my fork, so I was doing something with my hand other than thinking about rubbing one out beneath the dinner rolls and shot a glare toward my dad, who seemed to be purposefully taking eons to reach for the pasta and hand the dish to me.

When I reached for a roll, he passed the basket the opposite direction like a complete savage and then eyed Annie with a smirk. "Heard you were sparring today."

She grabbed a roll and was about to bite into it; I licked my lips in anticipation and then verbally slapped myself for staring at her mouth.

Again.

"Yeah." She relaxed her shoulders. "Well, someone has to teach your son a lesson."

My mom, aka Judas, raised her wine glass into the air and said, "Cheers."

Izzy followed.

Dad grinned.

"Cool, everyone's against me. Thanks, guys," I grumbled under my breath, suddenly not even hungry anymore.

"So, Annie," Mom piped up. "How were classes today?"

My fingers curled around my wine glass as I watched Annie's short intake of breath, the way her eyes darted down to her empty plate like it would have all the answers.

With an annoyed sigh—more with myself than her that I couldn't seem to stop staring at her or thinking about touching her, I spoke up. "Some asshat started spreading rumors about Annie this week via the university's Twitter account."

Mom gasped while Dad dropped his fork onto his plate.

I'd seen that look of rage before.

Actually enjoyed that it was clearly pointed at someone else other than me since Dad could be fucking terrifying.

The table was silent. "I hope you took care of the fucker."

Guilt gnawed in the middle of my chest so viciously I had

the sudden urge to rub it away with my fingers as I chugged the rest of my wine and shrugged. "I took care of it."

"Any body count?"

Annie made a choking noise.

I grinned. "Not this time, unfortunately."

"How disappointing. Is my son losing his touch?" Dad's eyebrows shot up as he reached for his wine, the dark tattoos on his fingertips moving with the motion.

I glanced away, my eyes zeroing in on Annie. "What do you think, Annie? Am I losing my touch?"

She squirmed in her seat while Izzy looked between us with a shit-eating grin on her face.

She was always too perceptive.

I could only hope this time she'd just stay out of my shit.

"Yeah, Annie..." She licked her lips. Well, there went that wish. "How is Ash's touch?"

I kicked Izzy under the table while Mom tilted her head at me as if questioning why the fuck I was touching the poor innocent girl living under their roof.

If she only knew I was balls deep last year in the shallow end while my dad watched.

Okay, creepy thought.

Dad cleared his throat. "Well, I'm glad things are okay—you are okay, right, Annie? You don't need me to follow up? I would hate for your sophomore year at Eagle Elite to be anything but positive?"

I snorted. "Yeah, that's just what she needs, Dad. A US Senator known to be involved in the mafia just strolling onto campus, guns blazing. Besides, you know it pisses Mom off when the fangirls start taking pictures."

"Didn't a student faint last year?" Izzy asked damn well

knowing the answer since we refused to let dad forget about his popularity.

"No, no." I waved my hand in the air. "That was the year before. Last year a girl went topless and painted her chest with *'Mr. Senator,'* then asked him to fu—"

"Enough of story time," Mom said through clenched teeth. "And watch your language, Ash."

"I've always wondered," I teased. "When you're asked to watch your language, does it mean to like literally watch it, because that's impossible to do since speaking isn't writing and—" Mom held up her hand, silencing me in the process. I just grinned and shoveled some food onto my plate.

Dad chuckled under his breath as the tension dissipated, and I tried like hell not to bring my attention back to Annie by focusing on getting as much food into my mouth as fast as possible so I could wash her off my body.

Wash off the sweat from our sparring and pray it would wash off the temptation as well.

"Someone's hungry," Izzy observed under her breath. "What did you and Annie do down there, hmm brother? You show up all sweaty, she's out of breath, and now—" She shoved the fork into her mouth and bit down, pulling it out slowly. "Extremely." Chew. "Extremely." Chew. "Hungry."

Annie's fork clattered to her plate.

"It's just food, Iz, you should know since you refuse to let any of it touch on your plate. God forbid your broccoli mates with your mashed potatoes and poisons you."

Dad laughed. "Just like your mom, all prim and proper…"

"NOPE!" Iz covered her ears. "Can we please have one family dinner where sex isn't mentioned? It's traumatic and damaging to my young mind!"

"You know what else is damaging to your young mind? Maksim." I grinned.

Dad let out a growl. "You two hanging out again?"

"Yeah, you two 'studying'?" I made air quotes.

Izzy appeared ready to murder me.

"Well." I stood and grabbed my plate. "Since you've got dishes all covered, sister, I'll just be going to wash the sweat from working out off my body. Oh, and Dad, my advice, chop the tree in the north yard."

"IZZY EUSTICE ABANDONATO!"

"And there it is." I snapped my fingers. "Middle named by Scary Dad. Have a good night, sis." I winked as she shot to her feet, reaching behind her and pulling out a knife from the waist of her jeans.

Mom reached for her wine with a dramatic sigh. "Put the knife down, Iz."

I made a face at Iz once I was behind Dad and then strolled out of the room and into the cool night air.

I was about halfway to the pool house when footsteps sounded behind me. I hung my head. "Iz, if you're planning on sneaking up on me, do it better!"

But when I turned, it wasn't Izzy.

It was Annie.

Slightly out of breath.

Her cheeks flushed as her eyes met mine. "I figured my chances of survival increased if I followed rather than stayed."

"Me? Safer?" I flashed her an angry grin. "Not a chance." I took a step toward her. "Did you forget our little… bargain?"

"B-bargain?"

"We aren't necessarily… friends." I tilted my head. "And yet you keep acting like that's still on the table despite what I say."

"But—" Her eyebrows drew together as her forehead furrowed in confusion, and then she sucked in a deep breath and steeled her expression. "I don't need to be your friend to stay safe from Izzy wielding a knife, and I sure as hell don't need a friend to learn how to defend myself. I'm not inviting myself into your stupid pool house because I want to eat popcorn and brush your hair." She shifted her weight on her feet. "It's not that."

"Then what the hell is it?"

"I'm lonely!" she yelled and then covered her mouth with her hands like she'd just admitted to kicking puppies.

And something in my chest cracked.

Because I knew that look.

I knew that feeling.

I'd been lonely for the last year.

Existing but refusing to enjoy my actual existence.

Waking up every day, wondering when things would begin to feel different. Lying to my friends that I was okay, lying to my family that I wasn't still in severe pain, my heart in need of triage.

So lonely?

I understood loneliness probably as much as I understood rage.

If rage was my soulmate.

Loneliness was my heart.

"Come on," I barked. "Can't have my dad seeing us argue by the pool again; he'll just push me in and try to drown me."

She gasped.

"I'm kidding, Annie." I stomped toward the house and pulled open the door. "After you."

She moved around awkwardly, wringing her hands in

front of her as I grabbed the Apple TV remote, and tossed it to her. "Watch whatever, drink whatever, but if you touch my fruit snacks, I'm going to end you." I started running up the stairs, only to stop and look back. "And if you even think about turning on Hallmark or some shit where they're all in a small town, and someone owns a damn goat farm, there will be blood."

I left her gaping after me.

And hated myself a little bit more as I stripped in my bedroom, made my way into the bathroom, turned on the hot shower, and remembered the last time I was in there with her.

Naked breasts sliding down my back.

Legs wrapped around my waist.

Hot mouths with velvet tongues tasting and retreating.

I leaned my forehead against the tile wall and reached for myself. I imagined Claire. Her lips, her smile, even her laugh.

And slammed my free hand against the tile over and over again when each time, Annie's face took her place.

The guilt resurfaced.

The need for revenge.

But this time, I didn't stop.

I gripped myself.

My lust and anger boiling out of control, spilling over into the chasm where my heart used to be one.

And with one damned whisper, uttered her name. "Annie."

CHAPTER
Fifteen

"Life is constant uncertainty. The only certainty is death." —Sadhguru

Ash

I watched her sulk. The only difference was, this time, it was my job to be as physically close as possible, so nobody gave her shit. Only I'd run off to grab a coffee and decided that not a lot could happen across the lawn; besides, it had all been part of the plan, right? Count her tears, measure them against her, strike with finality.

Instead, I was intrigued.

And if completely honest, pissed at myself for my own damn mistake this last week, and chicken shit for not admitting it.

She wasn't the same girl she had been last year, and it bothered me that she was stronger than I was used to.

I meant what I'd said.

She was alone here on campus. I wanted her to experience what that felt like, the utter abandonment of everyone and everything you loved, the security, the knowledge, but instead, I was watching her.

And she smiled.

Over a fucking donut.

Minutes ago, she'd been the weak sniffing creature I came to expect before she left for Italy, and then she'd straightened her shoulders, marched to the cafe next to where I picked her up on weekdays, ordered a donut, and was in the process of making it her bitch.

I was about to join her when Tank beat me to it.

He sat next to her.

He made her smile.

Which just reminded me that all I did was make her cry.

He made her laugh.

I made her scream.

Good. Bad. Did it even matter anymore?

All the choices I'd made that led us up to this point, where I had her where I wanted her, seemed irrelevant as she bit into that donut, as she chatted with him, put her hand on him.

Touched his skin while using her mouth to communicate what I wanted all along.

Her words.

Her mouth.

Her truths.

Before I knew what I was doing, my legs were taking me over to where they sat.

"Hey," I interrupted, shoving my hands into the pockets of my jeans. I hadn't had class today; no I'd insisted I could do recon all day along with the babysitting duty she knew nothing about. "You ready?"

Tank eyed me up and down, his green eyes calculating. He wanted to punch me in the dick so bad, but he knew I was his boss; I owned him. So instead, he stood, shook my fucking hand, then gave her a curt nod and simply walked off.

Fuck I loved my job sometimes.

Her face fell right along with the donut; I caught the pastry just in time. "You don't want any more?"

"What?" Her eyes seemed unfocused, blurry. "Oh." She looked at her hands. "Sorry, you're right, that's such a waste; I could probably salvage the rest for breakfast or a snack mid-day or—"

"Are we not feeding you enough?" I snapped, not meaning to gain the attention of the people next to us, all of them frozen in place, ready to piss their pants at any minute.

I snapped my fingers.

Both couples moved from their booths.

The tinkling of the bell over the door as it opened and closed and the steaming of milk behind the counter were our only musical companions as I stared her down. "So?"

Annie looked away and swallowed. "It's great. Your house, I guess my house, for now, I didn't mean it like that. Your parents are extremely generous."

"They are."

"But..." She lifted her shoulder. "Sometimes it's hard not to go backward, to default, you know?"

Oh, I knew. Defaulting was what I did. Emotionally. Physically. Even spiritually. "So you default with your food?"

Her lush lips curved into a smile. "I don't mean to. I just... I know this sounds dumb, but—" She turned and gazed out the window, a look of wonder on her face. "I have exactly one good memory of my dad before I was fostered out, adopted by a new family. He took me to some local donut shop, and he let me pick out anything I wanted. He apologized for being… mean, and he was, don't get me wrong." A shudder traveled through her. "So mean. It was my last happy memory of him as if he was trying to make amends for the yelling, for the fear with Mom and me. The stupid donut gave me hope, and then…" Her hands started to shake as she grabbed a napkin.

"And then…?" I prompted. Almost afraid to know her truth when earlier I would have killed for it, slit throats, taken souls.

"And then," she continued, "a man walked in with a gun. My dad blocked me. The gun went off. The donut went flying. I hid under the table. Then a hand with a glove on it reached out and grabbed my hair, pulling. I just remember it hurting so bad. I followed him, and he said I was his new daughter. My dad said something like, not this way, and the man let me go. Later that night, though, he came again, this time with more men. He said he would make things right, that I was his now. I had no idea what he was talking about at the time."

"And now?" I asked. "What about now?"

"A pawn," she simply said. "In a very dangerous game I didn't know the rules to. He's gone now; you made sure of that." She rubbed her arms where a few pale scars remained. "My bruises are gone. But sometimes, I still felt them lingering. And sometimes… I wish I could still see them to know I survived them."

I cursed. "I would kill him again for you."

I tried to keep the rage at bay, remembering the bruises I'd see on her arms last year and the way I lost my shit, killing her adoptive dad without so much as blinking. It's like he knew I was coming for him too, me and Junior, as we stormed the house with Tank, showing the De Lange associates we'd recruited just how dirty we got when someone threatened our own.

A sad smile played at the corners of her lip, and she said softly, "I know you would."

"Annie?"

"Yeah?" She finally locked eyes with me.

"We should get home… so Mom doesn't worry."

A quick swipe at her cheeks and she smiled and stood. "Right, sorry, yeah, so your mom doesn't worry."

I grabbed her phone, ignoring her protests, and clicked through the tweets that had spread so many horrible rumors about us, my expression tense. "This won't last forever; it's just because I'm me and you…" I eyed her up and down. "You're you."

She flinched as if slapped but nodded her head like a good girl.

Like a girl who did what she needed to in order to survive when all she wanted was to be the girl that was held so she could do more than that.

So she could thrive.

CHAPTER
Sixteen

"The truth that I have been seeking—this truth is death. Yet death is also a seeker. Forever seeking me. So—we have met at last. And I am prepared. I am at peace."— Bruce Lee

Chase

The Past: Six Months After Claire's Funeral

My son was my life.

My kids were my soul; they balanced me. Focused me.

They made the blood staining my hands worth it. Nobody had ever told me that it was easier to kill than to parent.

Easier to shoot someone first, ask questions later, than watch my son as his heart broke outside of his chest over and over again.

He was stumbling back into the kitchen, slightly drunk, but at least he wasn't wailing.

The wailing is what got me.

What got me those nights after Annie left.

When he said Claire had visited… said goodbye to him as if she was an angel in heaven, when I compared her more to a succubus who took over souls. I couldn't help it.

I wasn't a selfish little shit anymore.

So when my son hurt… I hurt. When he cried… I cried. When he felt like killing something, I wanted to provide the volunteers.

Annie had called earlier and said she was doing good, and I knew it was the smartest thing I could have done. Give them space. Because even though I saw what they couldn't, they would destroy whatever good pieces that still existed before either of them stopped hurting.

So sending her away was a kindness when I knew it hurt Ash more than he'd admit, bothered him that he was hurt by it more than he'd ever say out loud.

Because he was my son.

I still remembered hating Luc.

Despising her light.

Because it reminded me that I was in the dark, rocking in a corner, holding a bottle of Jack, and screaming until my voice was hoarse, just begging God to answer my pleas.

To kill me too.

"Ash." I leaned forward as he came into the kitchen, dropped his key fob and wallet onto the counter, and then jerkily pulled out a chair. "Good night?"

Dirt covered his shoes.

His hands shook as he ran fingertips through his overly long whiskey-colored hair. A smudge of mud had attached itself to the right side of his cheek, and I knew the answer before he even said it.

He'd lied again.

Said he was going to hang out with Junior.

"You go to her grave again?" I asked.

"Yeah," he croaked. "The flowers Dad, they were gone, so I just figured, I figured." His lips pressed into a thin line. "I failed her in life, I failed her so fucking bad, and I can't even keep fucking flowers on her grave?"

Could he hear the sound of my heart breaking right along with his as my breathing slowed to a near stop? Throat burning, I tried to swallow back the anger that was so often intertwined with the sadness.

I reached for him and pulled him into my arms, not caring that he was fighting me, beating at my back, yelling at me to let him go.

I held him, and I repeated his truth over and over again. "You're good, Ash. You're so good. You're an incredible son. Friend. Brother. You are enough in this life and in the next, flowers or no flowers. You're no failure."

"I am." His voice cracked. "I can't feel her anymore. I can't feel her, and then I keep having dreams about our fights, about the times in the end when I questioned her loyalty. I did that. I pushed her."

I sighed. I didn't have the answers. But I had my son.

So I held him.

"I feel guilty when it doesn't hurt as much as it did." He shuddered. "And then I hate myself for slicing open the wounds that already tried to heal, only to bleed again, only to feel again because of the guilt."

"Moving on." I sighed. "Sometimes means allowing those wounds to heal for good, Ash. And if you can't do that, then you'll always be stuck in this place, where it's your best friend's birthday, and you're falling asleep by yourself on Claire's grave." I pushed him a bit then. "It's not the flowers that keep bothering you, is it Ash?"

A solitary tear rolled down his cheek as he looked away. "What?"

"You know you need to move on, and I think part of you sees glimpses of what that may feel like, returning to your new normal. You're afraid."

Ash pulled away from me and stood. "I don't know how to do life anymore, it's like someone stole part of what made me work these last few years, and now I just feel so fucking lost."

"Sometimes being lost... is the only way to be found," Phoenix said from the door.

I hadn't even heard him walk in.

Junior poked his head out from behind his dad and then in two steps had Ash in his arms.

On his birthday, he wasn't partying with his friends; he wasn't buying new cars or jet-setting around the world.

Because I'd like to think we at least didn't fuck up as parents, that at the end of the day, we may be justified killers.

But we love just as much as we hate.

And we protect our own.

Phoenix locked eyes with me and then slapped Ash on the back. "I'm going to tell you what I told your dad so many years ago when he was ready to burn down his own house."

I snorted out a laugh.

Phoenix began, "You have. You love. You lose. And then you live—the universe gives you no other choice but to wipe your tears, take a breath, and manage one small step and then another. One day 'all you can do' turns into what saves your soul." He walked over to the table and grabbed a bottle of wine. "Now why don't you go get cleaned up so Junior can at least see where he lands the good hits."

Ash's head jerked to attention. "You came to spar? On your birthday? Where's Serena?"

"Sexually satisfied back in my room—sorry dads—at least Nixon isn't here. I mean, can you even imagine—"

A throat cleared.

Junior hung his head. "Just walked through the door, didn't he?"

"Yes," Nixon said in a lethal voice. "He did."

"Right." Junior hesitated and then started sprinting down the hallway; Ash hurried after him with a choked laugh.

And I knew one day, it would be all right.

One day I wouldn't hate myself for my part in this.

One day I would tell him the story of loss, love, redemption.

One day he would know his truth.

That day, however, was not today, not with her blood still staining his hands, not with the dirt from her grave marring his body.

One day.

When his heart was full.

When he could handle it.

I'd sit him down.

I glanced back down at my phone again and sent a quick text to Annie. "Sorry I had to hang up so soon—let them teach you some self-defense, and if you don't start shopping, I'm going to start randomly shipping you clothes—and I'm a shit shopper."

She texted back right away.

> Annie: Okay. I'll let him teach me. And I'll go shopping again, it's just hard.

> Chase: Life is hard. Let my money make it easier.
> Besides, you're going to need armor when you get
> home.
>
> Annie: Armor?

I smiled at the phone.

"You ready for our meeting?" Nixon wrapped his knuckles against the table. "Or do you need to sext your wife in the next room some more?"

"Nah, not my wife, Annie just won't spend any Abandonato money."

Nixon whistled. "Can't have that."

"Exactly." I grinned. "Besides, she's going to need to feel as healed on the outside as she does on the inside."

Nixon nodded in understanding while Phoenix pulled out a chair and started pouring wine into his glass. "Does she know?"

"Nope," I said quickly. "I think she's lying to herself as much as my son is, were we ever this stupid?"

Nixon shot me a glare. "You were, or should I say are?"

"Who's stupid?" Tex piped up after he walked into the kitchen, followed by Sergio, Dante, and Andrei.

"You are." Andrei patted him on the back.

Tex reached for his gun.

Everyone started arguing.

And I typed a reply but decided not to send the text. Just in case it scared her.

So I stared at the cursor and grinned.

> Chase: Love is war. Get ready to battle.

CHAPTER
Seventeen

"No one ever told me that grief felt so much like fear."
—CS Lewis

Annie

I shoved my hands into my coat pocket as I made my way across campus to the usual meeting spot for Ash.

For exactly one week, we'd been at this weird standstill where Ash drove me to class, basically shadowed me, and growled at anyone who approached, trained me whenever I showed up at the ring. And then let me watch TV in the guest house while he showered or did laundry.

Sometimes Junior and Serena would pop over; other times, it was just Maksim and King, which usually ended in all of us watching some sort of horrible reality TV show because, in their words, Ash deserved a bit of torture since they couldn't beat him in the ring.

Twice they tried to nominate him for The Bachelor.

And twice Ash threatened to leave them in tubs of ice with their kidneys' missing; whatever that meant, sometimes I didn't understand their sick senses of humor, other times I knew it was probably best I didn't try.

Ever since admitting my loneliness, it was like he assumed that if he just put people around me, it would be the same thing.

But it wasn't.

I was just as lonely and just as terrified of admitting to him, telling him I missed laughing with Claire, missed the only true friend I'd ever had.

Because bringing her up was like killing her all over again.

At least that was what it felt like for me.

I wondered if he understood that her death affected me too, in ways I knew I would never come back from. So wanting to cry? To scream into the night air about the unfairness of the world? I felt it too. I felt all of it. Because I'd finally had someone who clicked with me, who made me feel safe, who told me she'd protect me even when it wasn't her job or her business.

She'd taken one look at the bruises on my arms, expression hardening, and told me that she knew a guy. Obviously, she was talking about Ash, but I kept telling her to keep it to herself. I didn't trust him, not yet. And not when I saw the way he could turn from loyal boyfriend to ruthless killer in a heartbeat.

With a sigh, I leaned against the tree and pulled my jacket tight around me as I waited for Ash to show up.

Already he was a few minutes late, completely unlike him, which always unnerved me. Because I'd already lost Claire. I wouldn't survive if I lost the monster that remained because somehow—he'd turned into a protector, an evil anti-hero friend.

My stomach dropped.

What if something happened to Ash?

What if he died not knowing how much he was truly loved? Cared for? But how did you tell someone who used his anger as a shield to keep everyone out—that all you'd ever wanted was to be let in?

My teeth started chattering as my eyes searched the grassy area then the parking lot for him.

It was Friday, and I was feeling sorry for myself. Everyone around me seemed to have plans, and yet my plan was hanging out in the house of someone who probably didn't even want me there because I was just that desperate for human connection.

"Hey, stranger." Tank's voice sounded from behind me. I jumped a foot then smiled as he opened his massive arms wide like he used to before we came to this school, before the mafia took over our lives, before... when it was just us.

With a grin, I threw myself into his arms, loving the smell of his spicy cologne, and I pressed my face to his chest.

It was the first time he'd actually touched me—he'd been so distant, following all of Ash's rules to a T.

Then again, that was Tank.

A rule follower.

That was one of the reasons we got along so well. We liked coloring inside the lines and were horrified when people did the opposite—on purpose.

Kind of like Ash...

I tried to hide the sadness in my face when Tank pulled back, hands still on my shoulders. "You doing okay? Ash still being a jackass?"

My stomach clenched. "That's just him being himself."

Tank barked out a laugh. "If that ain't the truth." He

looked around him like he was either embarrassed to be seen with me or worried Ash was going to pop out from behind a tree with a gun and say, gotcha!

It was awkward.

Why was it awkward?

Why were tears stinging the back of my eyes? Where was my friend?

"So I was thinking…" Tank licked his full lips and smirked. "We should hang out, my class got canceled, and you're done for the day, right?"

My heart leaped in my chest. "Wait, really?"

"Shit, Annie." He hung his head. "Honestly, I've been the worst friend, I probably don't deserve the time of day, but things have been… difficult, not just with Ash and the rest of the De Lange kids, but at… work."

I frowned. "What's going on?"

His smile was tight. "Nothing I can't handle. I just… thought I had more time, you know?"

"Time for what?"

"Don't worry about it." I hated that smile, the one on his face that said drop it, that he wouldn't tell me unless he was getting tortured, which meant no matter how close we were, there would always be a line he wouldn't cross.

He'd say it was to protect me.

But I'd had enough with everyone's protection at this point.

"Sorry," I apologized for literally no reason and smiled. "I'd love to hang out; I'm sorry you've been stressed."

His face lit up. "Really? Just like that? You'll forgive me?"

I rocked back on my heels and laughed. "I don't recall you asking for forgiveness, but you'll be one step closer if you have skittles."

"Please." He snorted. "I always have skittles; they are one of the four food groups." he held up his hand for a high five.

I moved to hit it only to have him raise it higher and higher; he busted out laughing and then flicked me on the nose. "Still the same old Annie even though you cut your hair."

My heart sank. "Yeah, still the same old Annie."

If he knew me, truly knew me, he'd know that wasn't a compliment, but I was desperate to hang out, to escape, to do anything except feel like a charity case.

"Annie." Ash's voice barked out my name like a curse. "The hell are you doing?"

I jerked around in confusion as he stalked toward me, looking more angry Roman god than senior in college.

"I was waiting for you?"

He gritted his teeth. "Tank."

"Ash." Tank crossed his arms.

The tension was thick.

Students clearly noticed as they started giving us and the tree a wide berth as if there was going to be a fight between the guys.

"Let's go." Ash reached for my arm.

I stepped back. "Actually, Tank invited me over to hang out for a bit."

Ash's eyebrows shot up his forehead. "I'm sorry, can you repeat that? Because it sounds like you said Tank here asked to hang out with you."

Tank glared. "Because I did, dipshit. It's a free country, and she needs a friend, and lucky her, I'm standing right here."

"She has me," Ash proclaimed, sounding like a mini-dictator.

I snorted out a laugh before I could stop myself and then

covered my mouth with my shaking hands and muttered, "Sorry."

"It wasn't a joke." Ash eyed me up and down.

Tank started to chuckle. "Could have fooled me... Anyway, I'll drop her off around dinner. Annie, let's go—"

"Yes, let's," Ash interrupted with a terrifying smile. "She's under my family's protection, which means, where she goes, I go, so what are we doing?"

My jaw dropped. Was he seriously inviting himself?

Tank clenched his teeth, eyes wild. "You think I can't protect her?"

"The way I could?" Ash let out a snort. "Not a chance in hell. Get back to me when you've killed your own cousin in cold blood for uttering the word 'no,' and then we can talk."

A chill ran down my spine.

Tank was quiet, and then. "Fine. You can come."

"I wasn't asking, but thanks for your permission anyway," Ash muttered. "I'll follow you."

"I'm sure you will."

"Come on, Annie." Ash tugged me again. "Apparently, you have a play date."

I jerked away from him. "Actually, I think I'm going to ride with someone who doesn't treat me like a toddler."

His blue eyes flashed. "Annie, I was kidding."

"It wasn't funny." Tears filled my eyes.

He opened his mouth, but I turned away. Whatever he had to say, I didn't want to hear. It was like he couldn't help but use his words as weapons, constantly firing them at my face and then my heart for good measure.

I took a step and accidentally collided with a student who obviously wasn't paying attention as he ran into me. My bag fell to the ground, my two books, kindle, and headphones all fell out, scattering over the concrete.

"Watch where the hell you're going!" Ash shouted.

I thought he was talking to me.

And then he surged from behind me, grabbing the student by his collar and shoving him into the grass. He was on him in a flash, his fist coming back before colliding with the guy's jaw. Blood spurted as I heard a crack. Ash shook the guy, then slammed his head back into the grass, again and again, only to hit him in the cheek.

"Son of a bitch!" Tank grabbed Ash from behind, but Ash threw his head back, hitting him in the chin, causing him to stumble backward.

More students circled us.

And then King and Maksim were running into the circle. Thank God they had class today too. A flash of blond hair was all I saw as Maksim leaped into action, grabbing Ash, while King went to the other side and broke them apart, not that the other guy was putting on a good fight.

He looked seconds away from passing out and needing medical care as his eyes rolled to the back of his head.

"Go!" King shoved Ash's chest. "Tank, get him out of here. Annie, you good?"

I gave him a jerky nod, not trusting my voice as Maksim slowly went to his knees and gathered all my things, shoving them back into my bag, his blue eyes locked on mine. He reminded me of an angel with his fair looks and strong jaw.

"You sure you're okay?"

"I will be. I'm headed to Tank's," I whispered, grabbing my bag from him.

He kept holding onto it. "So was he pissed about you

hanging out with Tank or the fact that that idiot ran into you?"

"The guy trust me."

"Mmmm." Maksim let go of the bag. "Sometimes I wonder, Annie, if you'll ever see yourself the way Ash sees you."

I rolled my eyes. "Like the charity case?"

"Hah!" He stood and helped me to my feet. "Nah, like the cold drink of water after years of wandering in the desert. Sometimes I think he's just afraid it's all a mirage and that the minute he reaches out to drink—it will disappear."

"Is there a lesson in there somewhere?" I found myself smiling.

He just winked. "I'm sure there is, then again, what do I know? I'm only nineteen..."

"You're literally a genius, but okay." I smiled. "Thank you for the rescue and for helping me with my bag."

"Hey, I helped too." King was dusting off his uniform; his golden tipped mess of curls chaotically thrown around his head, his eyes bright like his blood was pumping through his veins, ready for a fight.

"Thanks, King." I grinned.

"Hey, what are friends for?"

Oh great, now they were going to think I was crazy as I swiped a tear from under my eye and looked away.

Suddenly I had two giant, lethal guys surrounding me and then pulling me in for a group hug.

"Annie sandwich!" Maksim announced.

I didn't wonder if Ash saw.

I didn't even care anymore.

I just sat there and let them both hug me, two of the most good looking guys on campus and quite possibly in existence— who was I kidding? Every single one of the mafia guys could be models.

Girls would die to be the Annie sandwich for that reason alone.

But they said friends.

And I knew they meant it.

"Hey," Maksim whispered so only King and I could hear. "Give him time, all right?"

I didn't argue.

I just shuddered and murmured, "Okay."

And then they were gone.

I turned on my heel and started making my way toward Tank. Ash was nearby kicking the crap out of a tree stump, blood caked on his knuckles.

"You ready?" I gulped, trying not to look too much in Ash's direction.

"Yeah," Tank barked out. "Let's go."

Before I could say anything, he grabbed me by the arm as if trying to protect me from Ash.

"But what about—"

"If he really feels the need to come, he'll get his stupid ass in the car and follow," Tank said through gritted teeth.

He didn't give me a chance to ask Ash if he was okay.

Because while he was angry.

He never once just physically attacked a person for not watching where they were going, and even more so, it was like the old Ash was back, ready to strike at whoever and whatever blinked at him wrong.

And because I was a sucker for punishment—I needed to know why.

CHAPTER
Eighteen

"To the well-organized mind, death is just the next adventure."— JK Rowling

Ash

I slammed my car door and stomped into the house. Irritation twined like hot barbed wire around every nerve ending. I'd lost control over something so dumb, fucking blinded by how angry I'd been as if that one random stranger was the reason for it all.

I waved off the associates in suits at Sergio's. I'd grown up around them all, and they knew to always let me in. Besides, she was in there with Tank.

Mine.

Something raged inside me, like a beast rattling its cage, desperate to get free. Part of me knew why I was upset.

And refused to even acknowledge it.

Because I knew what I would do at midnight tonight.

Just like I knew what I'd done last year, only months after her death.

"Ash, heard you got in a fight…" Sergio didn't even look up from his cell phone. "Wanna talk about it—"

My answer was to growl.

He just chuckled like my anger and intolerance amused him. "Guess not."

"They in the theater room?" I clenched my fists so tight that I probably broke some of the scabs already forming on my knuckles.

Keep it together.

It's just Annie.

Annie and Tank.

Fucking Annie.

"Sounds like it," he said dryly as more laughter bounced down the hall, attacking my ears with a cruel vengeance.

What the hell was he saying getting her to laugh like that? So free and open? Without a care in the world?

And why was jealousy raging through me like a fucking canon at the idea of her responding to him in a way I'd felt so damn guilty for wanting for so long.

Long before she left for Italy.

His chuckle grew louder as I stomped my way down the hall and into the large theater room.

The lights were low like Tank was seconds away from asking her to make out before fumbling through what would be the worst feel up in human history.

I mean, one could only hope, right?

Because the last guy to touch her was me.

Right?

Right?

Shit, had she hooked up with anyone in Italy? Why was I choosing now to focus on all the things I didn't know when the one thing I did was like a movie that refused to pause playing before me.

They were sitting in the top reclining love seat next to the large wooden bar Sergio had flown in from Europe.

Something was on the screen, but I refused to focus on it.

No, my focus was solely on Tank's hand as it inched closer to hers.

And the arm that was seconds away from no longer being attached as he scooted his massive body even closer, his forehead nearly touching hers as she smiled up at him.

Hell no.

"Hey!" I barked out and then, like a complete monster, moved through the air at record speed and jumped between them where there really wasn't a seat but enough space that I almost ended up in Tank's lap.

He wasn't amused.

Annie gave me a funny look. "You, um… doing better?"

"Perfect. Wonderful. Actual unicorns stampeded out of my ass on the way here as I drove under a double rainbow and waved at a leprechaun."

Behind me, Tank sighed heavily.

"So what are we watching? Where's the popcorn?" I shoved Tank's arm back and then moved my arms to surround both seats.

"I'll go." Annie hopped to her feet, clearly eager to get away from me. Not that I blamed her. I had just pummeled a guy near to death and needed three guys to get me off him.

All because he'd touched her then had the audacity to be clueless about it.

"Second drawer in the pantry," Tank called after her.

"I remember!" She grinned over her shoulder, damn near skipping out the door.

The minute she was gone, I shoved away from Tank and stood. "She *remembers?*"

After a heavy sigh, he took a breath and stood. "Look, I get that you're angry at the world, but we're friends, you know, people who enjoy each other's company, hang out, endure small talk about the weather during awkward moments only to stay up until midnight sharing secrets just because we can…" His eyes got all wistful making me want to choke him.

"I'm seriously tempted to punch you in the face right now," I deadpanned. "But I think the fact that you're sharing secrets until midnight with people is punishment enough." I twisted my face into a grimace. "The hell, man? Are you painting each other's fingernails too?"

"Jealous?" He crossed his arms, and I could have sworn his chest puffed out like he was actually proud.

Yes. "No, not even a little bit."

Whatever, I could share secrets.

Maybe.

But then I'd have to kill her, right?

"Sure. Okay." He wasn't buying it. Hell, I wasn't even buying it.

Tank glanced behind him then faced me again, all brawn, with his dark hair and chiseled jaw clenched like he was thinking of biting something off, preferably a fight with me, which sounded better by the second. "Look, honest moment, I know you're suffering still. Hell, it's like you want the world to pay attention to your pain, but I'm sick and tired of this manipulative shit!"

"Excuse me?" I asked. "Are you seriously calling me out right now?"

"Yes." He threw his hands up. "It's like you want to be both sinner and saint, protector, and persecutor. Pick one already and stop messing with her head. Don't be nice to her only to rip her a new one every time she smiles, and it makes you fucking sad. It's not fair to her, and it sure as hell isn't fair to every single family member and friend who've stood by your miserable side while you self-destruct."

Anger flared to life at the truth of his words. "You son of a bitch!"

I wasn't used to being called out.

To being talked down to.

To not being revered in every way that mattered.

I was king, after all. Or had I already fallen off that throne by my own hand? By hers?

"I'm serious, Ash. I like her, actually *like* her! I don't just want to be her friend, I want—"

"Yeah, I know exactly what you want. The answer is no. You don't get to have her, ever!"

"You aren't her dad!" he shouted.

"She's under my protection!" I jabbed my thumb into my chest. "Mine."

"Oh? And how's that going for her so far? What with a bomb getting sent to your house, her getting sent away to Italy for a year, or how about the constant bullying on social media. You can't do shit unless you're using your fists or your words, and I'm tired, we're *all* fucking tired, Ash!"

His words hit home.

Too close.

Too close until midnight.

Too close until the dirt.

Too close.

My vision tunneled as I screamed, "Fine! You want Sunday school pussy wrapped around your cock, be my guest!"

The sound of something crashing against the floor semi-jolted me out of my angry stupor, the haze lifting slowly, painfully.

And there she was. Just standing there. Eyes wide, popcorn all over the floor, hands shaking. Staring.

It was empty, that stare.

Like I'd taken the last pieces of her that were good and swallowed them up into my bad, taken them away because how dare she be happy when she was still here?

And Claire wasn't.

How dare I still want her? When I knew what she'd done.

How dare she make me think back on all the times I'd doubted Claire only to come up with several reasons we'd been struggling.

It was all there.

In her stare.

It was there every time she smiled at me. Every time she rolled her eyes and fought back, it was there. Every time I woke up in a cold sweat only to rush to Annie's room to make sure she was okay, still alive, breathing.

And now it was gone.

Replaced with a chilling emptiness that made me want to crash to my knees and crawl toward her, beg the universe to give them back.

God, give it back!

"Go," Annie said. Her voice didn't waver. Tears didn't fill her eyes. There was no reaction other than emptiness.

"I'm lonely!" she'd screamed at me, her pain palpable.

And I'd wanted to scream back so desperately, "Me too! God, me too!

Instead, I'd offered her what? A place to watch TV? Snacks?

My own cousins, so she didn't feel so alone when I knew it didn't do shit when you were hurting and surrounded by people, that if anything, it made it worse.

"Annie." My voice cracked. "I was upset. I didn't mean—"

"What else is new?" she said in a hollow voice. "Ash Abandonato upset again. You'd think I'd be used to it by now." She lifted her shoulder like it didn't matter anymore.

Like I didn't matter.

I may as well be invisible.

"Claire—" I stopped myself.

Holy fuck.

Annie's head whipped up. "What the hell did you just call me?"

"It slipped, I'm sorry. I didn't—I'm sorry... Fuck!" I ran my hands through my hair and moved toward her.

"I'm not her," Annie whispered. "I'm sorry, Ash, but I'll never be her."

She sidestepped me and walked right into Tank's arms.

And I let her.

I let her because he was what she needed.

I let her because it would be selfish to demand her attention, to force her heart when everything in my soul bubbled to the surface then crashed like a wave over me, damaging, destroying, killing.

I didn't look back.

I didn't want to see the look of anger on Tank's face or the one of horror on hers. I walked away.

And I kept walking.

To my car.

Then from my car to my house.

Then to my mom's greenhouse, to the flowers I'd planted the day of Claire's death.

I mindlessly dug through the dirt.

Then I cut.

And cut some more.

I didn't wipe off my hands as I gripped the flowers and laid them in the bucket.

And then I went back to get some more.

Losing myself in the mindless feel of the soil beneath my fingertips and the stems of the flowers as I collected.

Maybe this was my life now.

There was no in between the grief and the healing.

There was only this empty feeling in my soul and sickness in my chest.

All that was left of me.

Were the pieces nobody wanted.

And the ones I desperately needed someone to put back together because I no longer knew how to do it on my own.

And I lacked the heart and energy to even fucking try.

If I was really being honest, I'd admit the only person brave enough had been the one I'd just accidentally called my dead girlfriend.

And now, she was lost to me too.

It was better for her.

Better for everyone.

CHAPTER
Nineteen

"Grief is not a disorder, sign, a disease, or sign of weakness; it is an emotional, physical, and spiritual entity, the price you pay for love, the only cure for love, is to grieve." —Earl Grollman

Annie

I was livid.

So hurt that I was done.

And I burned to tell him exactly that.

So when Tank had dropped me off after offering to shoot him in the face, I'd slammed the door and marched toward the pool house.

Because how dare he!

The bastard called me by her name!

And it brought back everything he didn't even know.

How I thought I was trying to save him, give him the closure he needed—the love he needed!

"So stupid," I muttered to myself.

I was seriously an idiot.

Ash was never going to change.

Sure, he looked perfectly fine to most of his family, but deep down, he was dark, rotten, cursed. And I wanted no part of it because already he was bringing me down with him.

God, and I'd basically begged him to be my friend that night!

So. Stupid.

I wanted to smack myself as I marched into the guest house, throwing open the door, ready to wage a war against him.

I nearly tripped over a lamp in the dark.

And then I noticed the dirt on the floor, dirty footsteps? *What the heck?*

The footsteps led around a throw pillow that had seen better days if the dagger sticking into its center was any indication. I kept following the steps into the dark kitchen. The only light was the one above the cooktop, and even that was faint.

Ash was sitting in front of it, a bottle of whiskey in his dirty hands. God, it looked like he'd dug up a grave.

My stomach clenched.

He wouldn't, right?

His eyes were clear.

The bottle was full.

But he looked—so lost I didn't know what to do.

"Go," he rasped. "It's better this way."

Why? Why did he always make my heart twist like I was abandoning him when he was never mine to begin with?

I chewed my bottom lip.

Cursed him to hell about a million times, then promised myself this was it. I'd sit next to him. I'd refrain from strangling him to death. And I'd at the very least be another body in that sad, depressing kitchen, as he sat covered in dirt.

"I think—" My knees cracked as I sat down next to him, careful not to sit in a pile of dirt, and curious why he was clutching flowers in his right hand with a death grip while he had whiskey in the other. "—that the Sunday school teacher better stay since clearly, her unruly student can't even keep his hands out of the dirt."

He visibly tensed. "I'm sorry."

"You're always sorry," I fired back.

"It's a habit."

"A really, really shitty one," I pointed out.

"That, we can agree on," he answered.

Silence blanketed us, and then I just had to know. "Were you burying a body or digging one up?"

His head lolled forward a bit in what I could only guess was extreme exhaustion as he blew out a breath and whispered, "Neither, actually."

I frowned. "Then why all the dirt?"

"I was digging up flowers, with my bare hands, mind you, no time for tools, I had to feel the soil—it's what I do every time—I have to feel the life slip between my fingertips, I have to let it remind me, you know?"

My heart sunk. "Ash... why were you doing that? Is this a new hobby?"

He frowned. "Real shitty hobby for a hitman, am I right?"

"No. Maybe it grounds you. Get it? Ground? Dirt?" I elbowed him.

He sighed. "You shouldn't be here; I just hurt you. I know that. You know that. Eventually, the world will know that, because I can't stop, Annie. I can't fucking stop."

"Maybe it's because you need someone to hate. And…" I couldn't believe the words coming out of my mouth, but I said them anyway. "Maybe I'm that person. Maybe I'm the one you need to hate to get through this. I'm not saying I enjoy my role in your life, but if it helps, I can do it. I'm strong enough. I know that now."

He lifted his head and turned it, his blue eyes flashing with something other than anger; he leaned in, setting the whiskey down, he touched my face with a dirty finger. "That's the saddest thing I think I've ever heard."

"I've heard sadder." I gulped.

He shook his head. "It shouldn't be you. It's like butchering the perfect white lamb when there's a shitty tiger close by."

"Who's the tiger, then?" I asked.

"Tank. I'll kill him." He shrugged, and then a ghost of a smile appeared across his face. "I'm kidding, you know."

"Glad you clarified." My voice cracked.

He dropped his hand. "You should come."

"Come?" I shook my head and then looked around. "Are you planning a scavenger hunt or something?"

His laugh was full of pain, but it was still a laugh. "God, I wish. That sounds so much better." Slowly, he moved to his feet then offered me his hand. "Come on."

I didn't want to trust him.

But something in his eyes said I was the only one who could go wherever he was going and that this moment would pass by and if I didn't take his hand, regardless of all the times he's hurt me—I would regret it for the rest of my life.

So I trusted.

Again.

I put my heart in his hands.

Again.

My safety.

My sanity.

Our palms touched. He didn't let go. He squeezed my hand, and then we were walking out of the kitchen, out of the back yard across his property.

"You own all this?" I asked.

It was pitch black, nearly impossible to see. He still clutched the flowers in his right hand and walked as if he knew the path by heart as we made our way across a well-kept field and then into a small, wooded area that seemed magical, possibly man-made.

We passed an old white chapel.

"I was going to marry her there."

I let out a gasp, tears welling in my eyes as a path appeared; it was lit with lights as if planned.

"She wanted to get married at night with jars of lightning bugs; I thought it was complete bullshit. I mean, a man can only go so far, but she begged me. We didn't have a church outside the city…" We finally passed the church, and I noticed a plaque in front of it. "Claire's Chapel."

My breath caught as a tear slid down my cheek. "You dedicated it to her?"

He stopped and stared up at it. "Nah." He sighed. "I built it."

Had I been walking, I would have tripped. "You? Like with your hands?"

"No, with my big toe and gusto." He cracked a sad smile toward the chapel like it held memories too sacred for me to ask about. "Yeah me."

"I didn't even know." Embarrassingly, my voice caught. "I

mean, I had no clue you even knew how to use a hammer!"

I suppressed an eye-roll. Seriously? That was what I went with?

"I know how to screw too," he snapped quickly and then sobered. "Sorry, I'm not sure where that came from."

I elbowed him playfully. "Maybe the old Ash is tired of being sad and needed to get a good one-liner in there."

His lips twitched. "Yeah." He hung his head. "Maybe." He sighed like the old Ash was never coming back, twisting my heart in his grip. "Come on."

We kept walking in silence.

I noticed little jars lining the pathway; they were a bit dirty, worn, as if they were set out for something… for some*one*.

"I stopped lighting them when you left for Italy," he whispered almost under his breath. "I said goodbye to her then, or so I thought, you know?" He frowned as if wondering why he was telling me all of this. "I'm not crazy, I felt her, I just needed the closure, and then I realized that there was so much more I hadn't dealt with, memories I had chosen to forget because it made her death less holy, less… just less. When someone dies, you want to remember the good, only the good, because the bad just tarnishes the memory, and that seems like such a fucking cruel way to remember a person you loved, by even once focusing on the fact that they were human—she was, though, very human."

"Aren't we all?"

He chewed his bottom lip and glanced over at me. "Honestly? Sometimes I think you're more angel."

My lips parted on a gasp. "Wh-what?"

He shrugged. "I think it's what I both hate and love the most about you. Your ability to be good even when things are so fucking bad. I used to think I hated you—now I think all this time, I've just been jealous."

I didn't know what to say to that. I stared at him as a wave of emotions crossed his handsome face, and then we were walking again.

There was a small clearing.

And then.

Just feet from where they were to be married.

Claire's grave.

I swiped at my cheeks, and before I could stop myself, I fell to my knees on the dirt in front of it.

Her grave marker was huge.

In the shape of an angel.

Immaculate in its glory as it towered over us mere mortals. He'd literally immortalized her, made her a goddess with the gorgeous headstone and the words encrypted on the rock.

"Until the sky falls," I whispered. Using the right phrase, the one they used to use, not the one he'd said to me, the one that I kept as ours. The one I'd take to my grave too

I had no idea how much I missed her until that moment.

Until I burst into gut-wrenching sobs, the headstone a blur as I pressed my hands against the grass, almost bowing in reverence.

"She'd been my friend," I cried. "My protector." Another sob. "She said she'd save me!"

Ash's arms were there before I could stop him, pulling me against him as we both collapsed against the grass. He braced me.

He held me.

And he let me be weak.

Something I didn't realize I'd needed, not just in that

moment… but since her death.

I never got to mourn, did I?

I was too worried about Ash.

Too terrified of the bruises on my arms and returning to the life that had given them to me.

Petrified of my own shadow.

Trusting no one but myself and Tank.

I couldn't stop the tears. "I hope you're at rest, Claire." My voice shook. "I'm so sorry you felt you had to protect me from my family, that you took the car that day when it should have been me. Oh, God." I covered my face with my hands, my fingertips wet from the tears. "It would have been better had it been me."

"No," Ash said firmly behind me. "No, Annie."

"Yes! I ruined everything. I ruined—"

He turned me in his arms and pulled my hands from my face, the dirt from his fingertips mixing with my tears. "Annie, look at me."

He pried my hands down, and I stared into crystal blue eyes, eyes I could drown in. Eyes that could hate. Eyes that could love.

His smile was sad as his voice cracked. "It was an accident. It was not your fault, do you hear me? It wasn't your fault." He shook his head. "If anything, it's mine, for using you as a way to grieve, for being weak when I should have been strong enough. You didn't do this. The fucked up world did this. You don't get to take credit for something so sinister."

"But I—"

He covered my mouth with a dirty hand. "Everyone lets go in their own way. Don't walk down my path—it's a lonely one, full of sadness and selfishness. Take the fork in the road, the one that's harder—the one that ends in closure, in forgiveness."

I shuddered. "And what about you?"

His smile was sad. "I'm a guy. It might take me longer."

"Because you're slower?" I asked in confusion.

He pushed my hair out of my face. "More like stubborn… and stupid, thinking that by sheer will I can fix this when I've known I was damned all along."

He had set the flowers down on the ground.

Wordlessly he reached for them and then, as if having second thoughts, handed them to me. "Go ahead."

"What?"

His smile was sad. "It would have been her birthday tomorrow. She died weeks before. I planted flowers in the greenhouse, nurtured them, watered them, taking perfect care of them for this moment only to realize it's not mine. Maybe it never was."

"Are you sure?" I sniffled.

"Now?" He nodded. "I'm positive."

With shaking hands, I took the beautiful daisies and laid them to rest on her gravestone. They looked so bright and alive against the dark colors, so wrong for someone so young.

"It reminds me of a song…" I sighed. "If I die young…" I sighed. "I don't have a bed of roses or satin, but…" I reached for the clasp of my ever-present pearls and very carefully took them off. "My mom gave these to me before she was mur— before she died…" I slowly laid them to rest next to the flowers. "Better than satin?"

Ash's throat bobbed as he nodded, his voice hoarse. "Better than the way they used to bury the kings and queens of old…"

"She's happy, right?" I sniffled.

His arms tightened as he whispered in my ear, his lips

touching my skin briefly. "Of course... because she's free."

I don't remember falling asleep against him, only the fact that hours later, I was lying across Ash on the couch. He still had dirt caked to his fingertips, and I'm sure I looked like a mess.

But I stayed.

I stayed with him on her birthday.

I allowed myself those moments of peace against his solid chest.

And when I thought of her looking down on us... I smiled.

"Until the sky falls..." I whispered.

"Until the sky falls," Ash whispered in a rough voice pulling me tighter against him.

He wasn't mine.

Would probably never be.

But at least, for a few brief hours, we saw our friend find peace. We had real closure.

And just like clockwork, rain started to pour as if the earth wept with us. *Until the sky falls—or maybe until the rain cleanses.* Whichever came first.

Eyelids heavy, I drifted off to sleep.

CHAPTER
Twenty

"Life asked Death, why do people love me but hate you? Death responded, because you are a beautiful lie, and I am a painful truth." —Author Unknown

Ash

For the first time in a year—I wanted to wake up. My eyes were fuzzy as I blinked down at the girl in my arms.

Necklace gone.

Left on the grave of her friend, my Claire.

The one prized possession it seemed she had was left on the grave of the dead, and I felt like shit all over again.

In hundreds of lifetimes, I would never make up for the pain, the anger, the shit I was still dealing with, and trying to project onto the precious person in my arms.

And even then, the guilt came full force because I liked it.

I liked the gentle weight of her body pressed against me, the way her lips parted as she frowned in her sleep.

I loved the way her hair spread across my dirty white shirt.

The way she still had dirt smudges on her cheek from my fingertips, stained there by her tears.

Mine.

The word refused to leave as I squeezed her closer against me and then noticed how dirty my entire body was and how I was ruining her clothes, not to mention mine and the couch.

Begrudgingly, I eased myself up and put a pillow under her head, pulled an afghan over her small body and then, stared.

Just stared at her small form.

I had no clue what I was waiting for.

I wanted to wake her up so bad.

To ask if she was okay.

To say thank you for not giving up on me when I deserved it.

I'd shown her my pain.

I had bled my emotions all over the place, my soul cried out, and hers answered, so a simple thank you seemed ridiculously elementary.

Damn, if Claire could see me now, she'd probably kick my ass and then tell me I was *being* an ass.

I gave my head a shake and then started walking away, only to backpedal, lean down over Annie and press a kiss to her forehead.

My lips lingered.

And then hovered close to the corner of her lips, and without thinking, without letting the hatred or the sadness seep in, I kissed the side of her mouth.

I tasted.

I healed.

I was somehow reborn for just a few seconds, like her touch let the light in, destroying some of the darkness I'd kept so close for so many reasons.

Nobody ever said healing was easy.

It was painful.

Hard.

I welcomed the grief more than the healing because it somehow still kept her alive; even though I knew it was wrong, my heart screamed that it was right, that if we just kept remembering, getting angry, fighting, that her spirit would remain.

But she was gone, wasn't she?

Gone.

I lowered my head and wished she could see me now.

How far I'd fallen and failed.

And how much I'd needed someone to take my hand and tell me it was going to be okay, one day, not now, maybe not for a while.

Annie was that person.

The one person I didn't want help from but needed it the most from.

Life never played fair, did it?

And death, death just laughed in our face.

"Stay," I whispered to Annie like she could hear me, and then I made my way slowly up the stairs to wash the tears and dirt off of me. The last thing I needed was to scare the girl, even more, a few days before Christmas.

For the first time in, I couldn't even count how long, my smile was still sad but hopeful as it led me up the stairs and into the shower.

Memories of her in there with me weren't as painful or full of guilt as before.

Everyone grieves differently. Maybe I did mine wrong,

maybe there is no right way other than to just feel the pain and let it out, but I was different that morning. Like I'd somehow been healed without even knowing how really broken I was.

I took my time, washing the grime off my body, the tears, the anger, the dirt. I wanted to be clean.

And it occurred to me.

I cared.

I finally cared.

It wasn't about keeping up pretenses; it was about actually wanting to feel like myself again as I washed and washed, then finally shut off the water and grabbed a towel running it down the length of my body and pausing on my right leg. Frowning, I paused, the scar wasn't deep, and even though my memories were fuzzy, I knew that this one always carried more weight than the rest of my scars—because even though I didn't remember much, I remembered that it had been caused by my own hand. Somehow Claire had been there. She'd stopped me. I'd wanted to follow her so desperately, and then her hand touched mine, she begged me to stay, or at least that's what it felt like. With a shudder, I shoved the weak memories away and focused on the present. On getting dry. On going back downstairs.

I brushed my teeth, smiled in the mirror, and felt almost like an alien in my own body as I shook the remaining water from my hair, and ran my hands through its thickness.

Muscles flexed, and I realized I was skinnier.

How did that happen?

How?

I still had more muscle over most guys, but I wasn't me.

Fuck.

I hung my head and then wrapped the towel around my waist and went into my room, searching for a pair of jeans and a shirt.

I grabbed an older worn pair that had seen better days and a white long-sleeve shirt, then grabbed a gray beanie and threw on my brown combat boots. I added my Rolex, wallet and realized my phone was downstairs with a sleeping Annie.

Trying to be as quiet as possible, I made my way down the creaky stairs only to see that the couch was empty.

Had I taken that long?

Frowning, I jogged down the stairs. "Annie?"

A sick feeling built in my stomach as I searched the kitchen, living room, spare room downstairs, laundry. "Where the hell is she?"

I quickly called her, holding the phone to my ear only to have it go to voice mail.

And all of a sudden, I was there again.

Getting news of Claire's death.

Watching Breaker, my best friend take his car over the side of the bridge this last year.

Helpless to stop the people I loved from dying.

I wanted to go back.

Back into that place that was safe.

Where my grief told me it was okay to burn the world when I was hurting.

But then I saw the blanket I'd put on her.

She was fine.

Right?

Because the universe wasn't that cruel.

Right?

Right?

Trying not to panic, I grabbed my keys and jogged across the yard into the main house. Maybe she was eating breakfast?

The kitchen was bare except for my dad, who was reading the newspaper like he was actually fucking normal.

"Son." He didn't look up.

I wanted to strangle him. Instead kept my face impassive. "Yo."

He slowly lowered the paper giving me an amused look with his bright blue eyes. "Did you just... 'yo' me?"

"Yes." I inwardly cringed. "No... Hey, have you seen Annie?"

He gave me the longest sigh in the history of sighs. "And if I have?"

And strangling my own father... back on the table. "Just... curious?" Or worried, so ridiculously worried there was a sword jabbed into the exact spot where my heart should be.

"Mmmmm." He turned a page, then another, picked up his phone and sent off a text and then, "Oh." Finally. "She wanted to borrow a car to go run some errand, so I loaned her the Jeep. She refused the Lambo and all the rest of—"

"SHIT!" I yelled, and then I was out of there, sprinting toward my car, getting in, and using my Find My Friends app, tapping it angrily to get her location.

She was somewhere downtown.

I zoomed in.

Not good enough.

My engine didn't roar to life, but I'd like to imagine it did as I told the car to dial Sergio and waited.

"Yo." He laughed.

"Shit, how is my dad always this against me?" I gripped the steering wheel with ferocity. Damn, was he a teen? Just texting everyone he knew that I'd said "yo" and laughed behind my back?

"He was literally texting me... probably mid-conversation."

I groaned, and there it was. "Fine, just tell me where Annie is?"

"It might cost you."

"I'm good for it."

"Babysitting—"

"Kartini is old enough to watch herself." I left out the part about her partying ways recently for good reason. I wanted to LIVE.

He sighed. "Fine, babysitting at a distance."

"Done. I'll kill anyone who touches her."

"Wow, even better." He chuckled. "Give me a minute, we have trackers on everyone... wanna know the nickname for her?"

"No." I grit my teeth. "Not really."

"Bunny," he said, obviously not listening. "You know because you're like the stupid wild animal that just realized he needs to chase."

I clenched my teeth. "LOCATION."

More maniacal laughter from my uncle. "She's at a jeweler downtown, off second, sending her location now, but don't worry, looks like King's right—"

I hung up.

He could yell later.

What the hell was she doing without protection?

A gun?

Especially after last night?

The car refused to go as fast as I needed it to. Minutes later, I was pulling into a parking spot next to the store.

The red Jeep was parked out front. Thank God.

Seconds after I turned off the engine, she was walking out with a small white bag and a smile on her face.

I saw nothing but that face.

Showing me she was okay.

Making me angry because I hadn't thought she was.

"The FUCK!" I bellowed, rushing over to her, grabbing her by the arms, causing the package to fall to the ground. "Why did you leave? Why?"

Her body trembled a bit. "I was getting a surprise... for you."

My entire body deflated as every ounce of adrenaline surged through my blood. "Annie..."

"I wanted to surprise you." Her small smile nearly killed me.

"Fuck." I lowered my head and then pulled her into my arms. "I thought— I don't know what I thought, maybe I thought too much, but you're safe? Right? You're okay." Suddenly I pulled back, cupping her face as if to inspect for blood when a throat cleared behind me.

I didn't let her go.

But I knew that throat clear.

"Junior." I gulped, refusing to turn around. "You also doing some shopping?"

"Smart girl asked us to go with her," a female voice said.

Shit. "Serena."

"Ding ding ding!" She laughed.

"Is he okay? He looks rough, man." Maksim's voice.

"I know, I think he's a vampire now; he's up at night and sleeps during the day," King said wistfully, then sighed. "lost to us..."

With a growl, I looked over my shoulder. "Really? All of you are shopping at the exact same time?"

King grinned. "Well, my *FRIEND*—" He made sure to say it loud just in case the deaf couldn't hear. "—Annie, the one you're holding, knew it was probably best to go out with company so she texted and we all met her down here." He lifted a black bag and shook it. "Got myself a sick pair of briefs. Wanna see?"

I pulled my hands away from her face and cleared my throat. "I was um… showering…"

Junior started to slow clap. "Awww, little buddy, I've never been so proud, so hygiene is important to you? And to think this last year, I thought it was just this annoying thing you had to do in order to keep people in your company without killing them dead? My mistake."

Serena snorted out a laugh behind her hand.

I glared. "Very funny."

King just shrugged. "I mean… if it's true, is it really funny?"

"Do you really want to die?" Maksim said under his breath.

I shook my head and looked around the group. "So what? Are we Christmas shopping?"

"Yup!" Junior grabbed Serena's hand. "There's peppermint mocha, shit tons of coupons, and enough Santa to make you want to kill yourself, welcome to the fold!"

I turned to Annie and offered my arm. "I guess I have no other choice."

Her face lit up. "Guess not. But thanks for the rescue anyway."

"Always," I whispered. "I'll always rescue you."

She stumbled and then clung to me.

I'd like to think it was because of me, not just the words.

But after three more hours of shopping, I truly did want to kill myself.

King had the right idea as he pulled out a flask and dumped the entire thing into his Starbucks coffee.

"A thousand bucks for that coffee," I offered.

"Two thousand," Maksim countered.

"Four!" Junior's voice was desperate. "There was a Hallmark store, it had… cards."

We all groaned.

"And then, and then it was like, Family. Singing…. Joy…" More groans.

"Take it!" King shoved his drink toward him. "For your sacrifice, sir."

"It was so scary…" Junior shuddered.

"Should we kill someone to make it better?" I offered.

"That Santa over there with the perpetual joy looks ripe." Maksim joked, earning a horrified look from a passing child.

"Kidding!" Maksim laughed. "So sorry, I meant, killing him with joy!"

The kid clearly wasn't buying it and burst into tears as his harried mother shot us a "mom glare" and rushed her child past.

"Aw shit, three years in a row? Really Maks?" Junior stood. "We had to pay off the fucking mall Santa for scaring the children last year!"

"NOT my fault!" Maksim said and then shrugged. "They should come tougher."

"They're KIDS." Junior rolled his eyes. "Okay, we gotta get the girls before we have to buy our way out of community service."

We all stood and went in search of Serena and Annie, who

were apparently trying to see how many couches they could test at Pottery Barn.

"Gotta go!" Junior picked up Serena while I snatched Annie and shook my head.

"But—"

"No arguing." I grinned. "Mafia life."

She rolled her eyes, then wrapped her arms around my neck.

It felt like heaven.

"Big bad mafia life?" She grinned.

"One hundred percent," I answered. Why was I so breathless? Why did I want to take her back to that couch and kiss my way down her neck counting the ways I could make her scream?

"Mm. Okay. Sure." She squealed and held on tight.

And I stored the memory of her smile in my heart.

In a place I hadn't dared open for over a year.

Sacred.

Holy.

Shared.

With someone who knew my pain.

Shopping was over. I had Annie hand King the keys to the Jeep so he could drive it back.

Our ride home was silent other than the Christmas music Annie demanded we play as if she wasn't afraid of me anymore.

I wanted to hate it.

But I loved it.

Loved her smile.

And her genuine joy.

I parked my car near the front entrance of the garage, and grabbed her few bags, proud that she was finally spending money that my dad had given her. I'd heard she refused for a while, so even though she only had like two bags, it was nice.

Really nice.

"Want these up in your room?" I asked.

Her eyes darted away. "Um, no… actually… they're not mine."

"Okay…'" I said slowly. "So do we need to wrap them for someone."

She shook her head no. "They just go under the tree."

"We have a tree already?"

"Fingers crossed." She laughed. "Your dad was supposed to go cut one down with Izzy in your mini-forest out there while we were gone."

I laughed. "Then it's going to be a very sad Charlie Brown tree that needs lots of love and has a few scattered patches of branches, damn Izzy."

"I LOVE CHARLIE BROWN."

I let out a sigh. "Of course you do." I held out my hand. "Come on." When she didn't do anything, I leaned in and whispered, "You take it—my hand."

"Oh." She blushed. "Sorry, yeah… sorry."

"Forgetting things." I winked. "It tends to happen in my presence."

She tripped. "Was that a joke?"

I frowned and then shrugged. "Maybe?"

"Aww, look at you, Ash Abandonato, all grown up…"

"Awww, look at you," I mimicked. "Annie Smith… being all brave."

She smiled back at me. "I missed this."

"What?"

She hesitated, her eyes going sad before she said, "You."

A knife to the heart would have hurt less.

"I'm sorry—"

"Annie!" The door to my own house burst open. "I missed you!" Tank pulled her in for a hug, glaring at me over her shoulder.

Deserved.

I let him.

Because now I knew.

I would fight for whatever I got.

Even if it just meant friendship.

She laughed as he kissed her cheek.

Or maybe I'd kill him... The night was young!

"Come on!" someone yelled. "Time to eat and open early Friendsmas presents!"

"Shit!" I wanted to bang my head against the counter. "I totally forgot."

It was Annie who pulled herself away from Tank, took my hand, locked eyes with me, and whispered. "We have you... Gift received."

So simple.

Pure.

She had no idea that for the next hour, all I could focus on was the gift I would give her.

And I hoped to God she would take it.

Scream it.

Remember it.

Claim it.

Knowing—I'd never deserve it.

CHAPTER
Twenty-One

"The trouble is you think you have time." —Buddha

Annie

The last twenty-four hours had been... horrifying. Then restorative, in a way, I didn't realize I needed.

Shopping had been therapeutic that morning, and now that things were... as normal as possible between Ash and me, I wasn't really sure how to act.

Everyone was going over to Nixon's for the Friendsmas get together; I was nervous in my own house let alone another.

Was it because of the way Ash was suddenly looking at me? It was as if he'd finally climbed the ginormous wall he'd put between us and decided he liked things better on the other side.

I knew how to treat Ash when he was cruel.

What I didn't know how to do, was handle him when he

was nice, sweet, when he smiled, or when he reached for my hand.

I was suddenly in way over my head. I almost preferred the mean because at least then, my heart wasn't in any danger of falling all over itself. Already, I'd been half in love with him even while I hated him.

Now?

Now?

I wanted to slap myself across the face and then give myself a shake for good measure. It was Ash.

Ash!

He still had so much to work through, and after last night, I knew we were friends, but that was it.

So what if I woke up in his arms a few times last night and just stared? Or if today I couldn't stop thinking about the warmth of his body as our legs intertwined on the leather?

I cleared my throat and reached for another plate as I helped Izzy set one of the three tables. Since everyone was here, all the bosses, all the wives, kids, and some associates, we had close to seventy people in the house, and as much as I loved the noise, the laughter, I found myself constantly wanting to draw into myself because I wasn't a part of this.

And I would have killed to be.

I mean, I was there.

Present.

But this wasn't my future.

And I didn't want to be one of those people who whined about where they were or where they were going. I just—felt sad.

And sometimes, it was okay to grieve what you wished you had while still having hope for a future that might one day look similar.

"Annie?" Luc, with her jet black cropped hair and crystal blue eyes, put a hand on my shoulder. "Can you go let Ash know that dinner's almost ready at Nixon's and we're all riding together?"

It would be the first time I saw him since we were all out shopping. Why was I freaking out over something so stupid?

"Sure." I licked my lips and then ran back up to my room to grab the present I'd gotten for him. Granted, I'd gotten it using his dad's money, but still, after last night, I figured Chase would be one hundred percent okay with my choice.

In all honesty, he probably wouldn't even see the small amount I spent compared to the near billions they had.

With the little white bag secure, I made my way down the stairs through the back entrance, tracing my steps all the way around the pool toward the guest house.

The door was open, so either he was welcoming in the chilly Chicago air, or he was getting ready to come to the main house.

I stepped inside. "Ash?"

"What?" His voice was muffled.

I frowned. "It's, um…" I raised my voice. "Time for dinner at Nixon's!"

"Does that make you my dinner bell?"

I hesitated, a smile tugging at my lips. "Maybe?"

"Do I get to eat you too?"

I felt my entire body flush. "Um, pretty sure that plain Annie isn't on the menu, but I'm sure I can find you a turkey leg."

And silence.

With a sigh, I made my way up the stairs and poked my head inside his room. "Ash?"

"Almost ready." He made his way out of the bathroom in nothing but skin-tight black briefs that left nothing to the imagination, strutting his way around his room with a white T-shirt hanging loosely across his muscled body.

Tattoo's swirled down his arms, wrapping his tan skin like a Christmas present.

Mouth dry, I looked away. "I can wait downstairs."

"Not like you haven't seen me naked before, Annie., he said casual enough that I glanced up only to have him send me a devastating wink. "Or do you need reminders of those two times?"

Three.

It was three.

I let out a breath like I was annoyed. "Trust me, you're hard to forget when you're being all forceful and grumpy."

"Ohhhhh, so I forced your tongue down my throat?" His chuckle was warm. "Good to know." He grabbed a pair of jeans that I liked but was literally taking longer than the entire dinner took to make.

Sighing in frustration, I marched over to his closet and walked in, searching for one of his tighter long-sleeve shirts.

"You're driving me crazy," I mumbled. "Wear this." I pulled the shirt from the hanger and turned, slamming directly into his warmth as he steadied me. The shirt was sandwiched between us along with his present.

His eyes locked onto mine with an intensity that was frankly terrifying.

I gulped and then somehow managed to free the shirt enough to wave it between us like a flag of surrender. "Here."

He took the shirt, his fingers brushing against mine as he pulled it over his head and asked. "What's with the bag?"

"Oh!" I couldn't contain my excitement as I thrust it in his face. "It's for you! I just didn't want to give it to you at Nixons." I explained. "In front of everyone. You know, just in case…" I gulped. "In case…" Ugh, could I sound at least a bit more eloquent. "Ignore me; just open it before they send a search party."

His eyes never left mine as he took the bag from my fingertips and peeked inside. How anyone had hands that sexy was beyond me, but one of them reaching into the bag and pulling out the small white box was enough to send my heart racing.

Frowning, he set the bag down on the carpeting then clicked open the white velvet box.

His eyes flickered down.

And then he tensed.

"You hate it." I was horrified as I reached for the box. "I'm so sorry I just thought—"

He jerked away from me.

Tears stung my eyes.

Damn it!

"It's too soon. I'm sorry, Ash, really. I just thought if you had them close to your heart, on you, you know, that you wouldn't feel so alone…"

Hands shaking, he pulled the long vintage necklace from the box; it was on a silver chain. Dangling from the end was an old key, and inscribed in it were Claire's initials and then "my angel," for whatever baby they would have had.

He gripped it in his hand.

"Ash, really—"

He crushed his body against mine in a hug so tight that I was afraid I was going to pass out from lack of oxygen.

I wrapped my arms around his waist as he held me tight.

And my stupid heart beat excitedly against my ribs.

Friends.

We were *friends*.

"Thank you," he whispered, pulling his head back and kissing me on the cheek so softly I wondered if I imagined it.

An electrical surge pulsed between us as we entered another stare down, but she was still there, between us, in that necklace, so I took a step back because this wasn't my moment—ours.

Maybe we'd never have one of those, but at least Ash would have her, pressed against his heart for eternity, and maybe I'd get lucky enough to sometimes be able to hold his hand.

Once.

Twice.

I took a deep breath and stepped far away from him. "You're welcome." He was still staring at me, so I rocked back on my heels and nodded toward the door with a smile. "We should probably go."

I was maybe a foot from his bedroom door when he called after me. "Don't you want to know what your gift is?"

I froze, afraid to turn around. "My gift?"

"Your gift," he confirmed.

"I-I'm sure it's going to be great," I said lamely.

"Great?" Amusement laced the word. "You'll have to let me know once you have it…"

His palm met the small of my back; I could feel the heat pouring out of his skin as he pulled me against his front and then whispered in my ear. "I'm going to make you wait until after dinner, more fun that way, with you wondering what could be so great…" He chuckled. "Your word, not mine."

I shivered and then joked to break the tension. "You better not have gotten me pearls…"

He froze. "How did you know?"

I let out a gasp. "Oh my gosh, I'm so sorry!" I turned in his arms only to see him cracking a smile. Then I smacked him. "That's mean!"

"I'm mean." He shrugged. "That never really changed. You know that, right?"

"Maybe I like you mean." I shrugged and looked away.

"I'm beginning to think you wouldn't know what to do with nice, Annie…"

"Tank's nice," I said defensively.

"He is…" Ash agreed. "But who's the one holding you alone in his room?"

I chewed my lower lip. "The mean one."

His forehead touched mine. "Correct."

"Ash!" Izzy yelled. "Annie! Get your asses over here! It's time for food. Junior texted and already tried to steal the turkey leg, King hit him, a knife that should have been confiscated wasn't, mashed potatoes went everywhere, Trace is super pissed, and Nixon looks ready to set King on fire. So if you want food, I'd hurry."

"Coming!" I yelled when Ash didn't answer.

I could have sworn I heard Ash say "you will be" under his breath.

My imagination, of course.

Because it was Ash.

And I was me.

CHAPTER
Twenty-Two

"The trouble with quotes about death is 99.9% of them are made by people who are still alive." —Joshua Burns

Ash

"PUT THE KNIFE DOWN!" Dad roared, pointing his drumstick at King, who continued to wave the knife in Dad's general direction while people made bets.

Money exchanged hands over what was supposed to be a peaceful moment, then again, when had our family dinners ever been peaceful.

I slapped a fifty into Junior's hand on my left. "Dad takes poor Tom's drumstick very seriously."

"Normally, I'd agree with you." Junior sipped his wine as King lunged forward with his knife in Dad's face. "But he's getting scrappier."

"Atta boy." Tex clapped and leaned back in his chair while Mo smacked him across the chest. "What?"

Nixon and Sergio were already trying to find all the dark meat, using the distraction for their own holiday purposes.

And when I thought that Dad really would fillet King alive, someone pulled the turkey leg from his hand and took a huge bite out of it.

Tex burst out laughing. "And my other boy!"

Valerian sure did know how to make an entrance as he took another bite, swiped his mouth, and then handed it back to my very purple-faced dad.

The best part was that since Valerian was the Petrov boss, my dad could do nothing, and we all knew that after this last year when my dad went at Valerian with a steak knife—repeatedly—for marrying my sister—well, he probably deserved it.

I mean, a fucking serrated steak knife?

No thanks.

"Happy Holidays." Valerian grinned.

Chase jumped to his feet only to have Violet, hug him, completely disarming what looked like attempted murder.

"Nice to see you," Junior called out to Valerian.

"Yeah." His green eyes lit up. "Sorry, we were late." He tugged at the collar of his jacket.

Lipstick… correction, my sister's lipstick was stained across his neck like a fucking stamp.

"My. Sister," I grumbled.

Valerian winked. "Yeah, she is…"

"Son of a—" I jumped to my feet only to get shoved back down by Junior.

From across the table, Maksim cackled.

The other two tables were reserved for the younger cousins and associates, and by the looks of it, we were the entertainment for the night.

Of course, we were.

Chaos ensued, and something close to contentment washed over me as I watched my family fight and eat, fight some more, then pull out weapons that were supposed to be in the delegated weapon bucket at the door.

Seated next to me, Annie was quiet.

But smiling.

The necklace she'd given me dangled beneath my shirt, pressed against my skin. I'd wanted to kiss her then.

More than I'd wanted anything in a really long time.

But it felt… wrong.

Maybe because the necklace was about Claire while the gesture was all Annie, and I was having trouble sorting the two.

I slid my hand under the table and squeezed her thigh in what I thought was reassurance.

Instead, she jumped a foot, banging her knees against the table, and gaining the attention of every single adult and cousin, including an amused looking King who was chewing, mouth open, with a shit-eating grin on his face. "Got jumping spiders over there?"

"Got flies in there?" I nodded toward his mouth.

Mo, his mom, and my aunt smacked him on the back of the head. "Manners!"

"Oww!" King rubbed the spot and shot me a dirty look. "Manners don't count when man eat meat." He pounded his chest and ripped into it again.

"So civilized, my son." Tex released a sigh.

Valerian and Violet grabbed their seats and started piling food onto their plates, and my palm was still pressed against Annie's thigh.

I should have pulled it back.

But it was warm there.

Her skin.

She was in a short sweater dress, which meant I had nothing but smooth skin to touch, and I found that the more I touched, the more I wanted.

And it was such a foreign concept after so much shit that I just wanted to be selfish and keep that moment—her skin, for myself.

She jumped again, but this time I wasn't the culprit. Nope, that was all Tank as he cursed next to her and jerked another glass of wine away from Kartini—girl was turning into a handful, and he'd just been nominated as babysitter. Sergio and Val were worried; ergo, Tank got the job of being full-time sin watcher.

Shit, I almost felt sorry for the poor guy.

Almost.

I smiled and took another sip of wine with my free hand and looked up to see my dad staring me down with a look of pure joy on his face.

My eyes narrowed. "Hey, Scary Dad, what's with the creepy smile?"

He scoffed. "I'm never creepy, always sexy."

"Sure, sure." Mom patted him on the arm.

"It's okay Chase, not everyone can be as sexy as yours truly." Dante interrupted, earning a few sighs from that side of the table.

Back in the day, he apparently turned all the wives' heads, my mom included.

I shuddered.

Old people were so weird.

"A toast," Dad said, standing and shocking the hell out of me. When there was that much food involved, he rarely came up for air. "To our children…"

All the bosses and associates stood. "Hear, hear!"

Dad locked eyes with me and said, "Good to have you back, son."

Stunned stupid, I could only stare back and give him a small nod as everyone sat down and continued eating.

My heart hammered against my chest as I realized the gravity of what he'd just said as if I'd been the prodigal and was now finally home.

And as that warmth spread through my chest, down my arms, to the hand that was touching Annie—I realized.

I hadn't been home in a fucking long time.

Not like this.

No, it had been over a year since I felt this contentment.

The hurt was still there.

The pain.

The burning question of why?

But the rage was more of a slow fire than a furnace I wanted to jump into, and while my friends and family were always there to help…

I had one girl in particular who deserved more than the hatred I'd spewed her way.

And I had every fucking intention of making sure she knew it.

"Speaking of scary smiles," Junior said under his breath. "The one you're sporting right now looks absolutely terrifying—whose death are you imagining?"

I shrugged. "I guess it's sort of like death then getting reborn, depends on how you look at it—and how you…" I looked down at my hand on her thigh. "...execute."

Annie was busy talking to Kartini.

But Junior followed my gaze and smirked. "She's either going to kill you or kill you. I find myself looking forward to dessert more and more."

I shot him a cocky grin. "Me too, me too."

The rest of dinner was a blur of eating, chaos, violence, and the random gun draw between Phoenix and Andrei, which ended with a very intense draw over the stuffing that had everyone holding their breath, mainly because any sort of body part in the food was frowned upon.

I let myself hope as all of the older cousins made their way to the theater room where we usually hung out. Sparring was completely out of the question since everyone was undergoing a turkey coma. The younger kids went to the basement to watch their own movie that didn't have bad words, and all the parents knew at this point that we refused to censor what we watched—it was the mafia, I mean, really, what's the point?

Junior and Serena jumped on the love sac in the bottom corner of the room that was shrouded in almost as much darkness as the couch on the other side. The one I commandeered.

Tank started walking toward me.

I gave him a look that said walk away.

His jaw clenched, and then he was going in the opposite direction toward the single-seat theater loungers.

Valerian and Val surrounded King and Maksim, Kartini and Izzy huddled in the corner, most likely talking shit about Tank because they could.

The lights flickered overhead.

And then they were completely off.

"The hell?" I jumped to my feet.

"Chill." Dante's voice sounded from the hall. "We tripped a breaker with all that turkey making—give it a few minutes."

And then he was gone.

"Ummm." I would recognize the panic in Annie's voice anywhere.

I quickly turned on the flashlight on my cell and searched for her; she was standing just inside the room, equal distance from Tank and me.

We both moved at the same time that she did as she made her way down the stairs and toward me as if she hadn't even seen Tank, but when he stopped right next to her as she faced me, I could see the guilt there as she hung her head and then flashed a smile up at him. "I'll just sit down here."

"Annie—"

"Tank." She crossed her arms.

He shook his head vehemently. "I don't get it. I'm never going to fucking get why girls love being treated like shit, more than the queens they are." He zeroed his focus in on me. "And yeah, I know you want to slit my throat, but you don't deserve her, Ash. You're toxic; you'll always be toxic and cruel. She deserves better."

"Like you?" I snorted.

"Pissing match, party of two," Junior coughed. "We can aaallll hear you."

"Good, then you can all see the beginning of this so that I can say told you so when it ends like shit!" Tank threw up his hands. "He's going to break you, Annie. Just don't expect me to be waiting to pick up the pieces."

He stormed out of the room, leaving us in an awkward silence as everyone glanced in our direction and then looked away, flashlights turning down to give me and Annie privacy.

I reached for her hand and tugged her against my body. "Hey, he's just angry. I know a lot about anger. It has a way of blinding you, consuming, let him feel it, he'll be fine tomorrow."

She let out a shudder and then an exhale. "Maybe I should go check on him."

"I'm sure one of the guys went after him." I was going to Hell for that. "Sit, relax... preferably on my lap."

I could almost feel her roll her eyes. "I think I'll just sit next to your... lap."

"Your loss."

"Or gain," she said softly. "It just depends on how you look at it."

She seemed distant.

And I only had Tank to blame.

Well, that and my shitty treatment of her for the past year.

I took a deep breath and leaned back just as the lights flickered back on, only to have Junior turn them down again and announce we were watching Elf.

What was it about the dark that made you less brave?

That suddenly stole your breath from your lungs?

Had you counting the beats of your heart as they picked up speed.

Measuring the inches between your fingertips and someone else's?

Nothing had changed, and yet everything had, as the necklace I wore nearly burned a hole through my chest.

A reminder of my past.

And the fact that I still could have a future where I wasn't so miserable, I destroyed everything in my path because I could, because I hurt.

I leaned back against the couch while Annie sat ramrod straight, watching the movie like she'd never seen it.

So instead of watching what I'd seen over and over for years.

I watched her.

Every expression.

Every small smile.

Every sharp intake of breath.

And what I saw was beautiful.

I hated myself more than I'd ever admit out loud in that moment.

She'd given her fucking pearls to a dirty grave, her pearls. Something that meant everything to her, which meant Claire had meant everything to her as well, but I'd missed it.

Fuck. I'd missed it all. And I had no idea how to even begin to fix it other than to show her rather than use the words she no longer trusted.

She laughed a truly happy laugh that slid over me and inside me and made me long for more.

I put a hand on her thigh and then slid it up past her hips to her shoulder as I leaned in and whispered, "You're really pretty."

She froze.

A trickle of unease went down my spine.

Slowly she turned, and with trembling lips, said, "I can't."

"Can't what?" I smirked.

"Play." She swallowed and looked down at her hands. "I can't play a game I don't know the rules to. So if you could just…" She licked her bee-stung lips. "Just watch the movie, and be my friend… I can—I can handle that, but anything else just feels like a game where I don't know the rules, one I'm bound to eventually lose. And Ash…" Her eyes were sad. "I don't have much left to lose."

My stomach sank. "But we're friends… right?"

She was quiet for a minute and then put her hand on mine and whispered, "Friends."

My hands shook to grip hers, to tug her against me and kiss her, to give her multiple gifts.

How ironic that the very thing I wanted to give her.

She didn't want.

It was too late, wasn't it?

I was too late.

Always too late.

Even with her heart.

CHAPTER
Twenty-Three

"Death is the golden key that opens the palace of eternity." —John Milton

Annie

For the rest of the movie, the air between us was charged… and so awkward I wanted to cry. Ash wasn't necessarily distant. He just seemed… sad.

So many times, I wanted to elbow him, force him to tease; even being mean would have been nice.

Instead, he was polite.

And I kind of hated it.

It wasn't like I wanted the asshole back. I just didn't know where we stood. And was the one who'd said friends, and I couldn't honestly live with myself if I just forgave everything so easily.

Sure, was I attracted to him?

The dirt would be attracted to him.

Was I half in love?

Yes.

Was it dangerous to my heart, soul, and sanity? Absolutely.

I had fled the country and freaking cut my hair because of that asshole, because of that *night*.

"Until the stars fall," his voice whispered in my head.

I wanted to scream as heat swept across my cheeks. Being drunk did nothing for his stamina. If anything— No, I couldn't go there, I couldn't even process it, because if I did, I'd start to relent, I'd get weak, and I had sworn to myself in Italy that I would never be a victim again, that I would fight for me.

So even though I wanted to give in so bad…

He needed to earn me.

To earn my trust.

"Hey," Serena interrupted my train of thoughts. "Want a ride back home?"

I stupidly looked around for Ash and realized he'd fallen asleep on the couch right next to me. My heart deflated a bit.

Ugh, I needed to get a handle on the whiplash of emotions I had concerning him.

"Yeah." I nodded and smiled. "That would be great, thanks."

Serena eyed me and then Ash, her eyes missing nothing as she licked her full lips; how purple lipstick looked sexy on her, I had no clue. Paired with her long platinum hair, tight jeans, and cropped white sweater, and I felt like I should be pushing a shopping cart through an alleyway. "Cool, let's go. Junior's driving."

Junior shot us both a wink then gave us his back as we all trailed behind him out of the theater room. Associates nodded in our direction as we passed; I would never get used to that.

Used to the way they bowed as if I was royalty too when I was the pauper who didn't even have her own bank account.

I straightened my shoulders.

Not for long.

Just graduate.

Stay safe.

My future was always hard to look forward to, especially now that I saw flickers of Ash in it.

Damn it.

It was starting to snow as we made our way outside past the expensive sports cars and toward Junior's new Uris Lamborghini SUV. Had someone told me a year ago that this would be my life getting in a car that cost more than two houses combined, I would have rolled my eyes and then burst into tears for giving myself hope even in my dreams.

Junior opened the back door; I scooted across the leather then did a double-take when Serena did the same thing.

"Um…" I tucked my hair behind my ears; some of it fell forward anyway. "Hi?"

"Hey." She clapped her hands. "All right Junior, chop, chop, places to go, people to ruin."

"Yeah, yeah." He chuckled, and the engine roared to life as he pulled around the circular driveway and out the gates. "I'll just be up here ignoring whatever the hell Serena thinks you guys need to talk about." His gorgeous jaw flexed as he smiled and then winked those nearly aqua eyes through the rearview mirror.

"I know." Serena sighed. "He's too pretty, right?"

"I'm all man," Junior grumbled.

"Yes, all man, congrats, you have a penis. Oh, also you have one job. Drive!"

"Driving." He held up one hand, keeping the other on the wheel.

Before I could take another breath, Serena whipped her head around and locked eyes with me; it was like a freaking tractor beam, her stare. "What did you do?"

"Wait, what?"

"To Ash." She crossed her arms. "He's acting human, he actually cracked multiple smiles today, and Junior swore it was either the second coming or he's the anti-Christ. So which is it?"

"Um… neither?" I bit my lower lip. "And what makes you think it was me?"

"The look," Junior interrupted. "He had the look."

"What's the look?" I made air quotes.

Serena mimicked me and leaned in. "It means he's seeing only one thing right now, and that one thing isn't pain, or anger, or destruction, it's…" She hesitated, only for Junior to answer.

"It's his queen."

My throat hurt, burned with the need to say something like *it's not me, I wish it was, but there's too much hurt, too much destruction, blood, carnage…* instead, I said nothing.

"Whatever it was," Junior said from the front seat, "thank you."

"N-no problem, I mean really it wasn't—"

Serena reached out and touched my arm. "It was. It is. He's… acting human."

I smiled sadly down at where her black fingernails touched my fair skin. So different, weren't we? And yet still so human, in need of one thing. Love. "His humanity was never the problem… it was his guilt."

The car turned down the long road leading to Chase's compound, and gravel crunched beneath the tires, the only sound breaking the silence that had fallen.

Lonely.

I was still lonely.

"Sometimes." I began talking again like she was my therapist, and Junior, our freaking driver. "It just takes pain, recognizing pain. Nothing more. Nothing less."

Junior brought the car to a stop and put it into park. "All right, princess, your castle awaits."

I smiled. "Thanks for the ride." I unbuckled my seatbelt and opened the car door, then felt a tug on my arm as Serena pulled me back against her in a gruff hug, rasping in my ear. "Thank you."

"He's my friend," I said, unable to move. I'd always loved Serena, but I'd been closer to Claire than Izzy. "I would do anything for him."

"And we would do anything for you," Junior spoke for her. "Remember that. Even though you aren't blood, you're family, so you may as well be. We protect our own… you don't have to be alone anymore, Annie. Now, your loneliness is a choice, all right?"

"And yet it doesn't always feel that way," I said sadly.

"Then don't fucking let it." Serena let me go and nearly shoved me out of the car. "And give him hell."

"Why do people keep saying that to me?" I wondered out loud.

Junior barked out a laugh. "Because he deserves it."

"Preach." Serena winked and then hopped out of the back and moved to the passenger side of the SUV. "We mean it… we've got you."

"I know you do," I said softly. "I just need time to believe it."

"That's fair, princess, that's fair." Junior saluted me, and then they were driving away.

Suddenly exhausted, I yawned and walked the short distance to the front door. It was open as usual before midnight, plus the place was completely surrounded by fencing, all thirty acres.

That and cameras and, according to Ash, guns.

Yay us.

At least we were safe.

I smiled at the thought.

Safe.

I'd never been so safe in my entire life—including when the bomb had been sent in the creepy stuffed horse.

As much as I wanted to just crash, I knew I needed a shower, so I took my time in stripping my clothes and going into the en suite bathroom.

Steam filled the room as I thought about the day.

About the weird convo with Serena and Junior that a year ago would have had me in tears of complete fear and confusion.

And now… now I felt strong.

Life was so strange, wasn't it?

I washed the day away, and shut off the shower, grabbed a towel, and dried off, wrapping the towel around my body as I went back into my room.

"You left," Ash said from behind me.

I jerked upright and banged my ankle against the bed stand, then stumbled backward toward the bed, finally sitting on it and crossing my legs like I planned on a graceful fall. "What are you doing?"

"Making sure you're okay." His massive body was leaning against the doorframe. I hated how he seemed to swallow it whole, with his dark jeans and tight shirt.

I equally hated how delicious his tattoos looked in the moonlight like he was some sort of punishing deity sent down to wreak havoc on us mere mortals.

His whiskey-colored hair seemed to come alive in the flicker of light still on in the bathroom and spilling into my bedroom.

I clutched my towel tighter. "Well, I'm safe, so you can just... go."

His eyes flickered with amusement. "But I just got here."

"Hah." I crossed and uncrossed my legs awkwardly. "At least let me put on some clothes then?"

"Negative." He shrugged. "I like you... a bit unsure. Plus, I can see almost completely up your right leg until it goes dark, and my memory is really fucking good."

I grabbed a pillow and chucked it at him.

He caught it with one hand and a laugh, then tossed it to the floor and continued walking toward me.

Self-preservation had me jolting from my bed because my heart was completely on board with dropping the towel and begging him to kiss me.

To say *my* name.

Not hers.

To know, without a shadow of a doubt, that he was kissing *me.*

Loving *me.*

Asking the stars to stay in the sky—for me when he'd only ever begged the sky to stay for Claire.

I sucked in my bottom lip and backed toward my bookcase,

naturally stumbling into it because my focus was completely on his predatory body and the way he seemed to almost dance through the night air.

Something crinkled beneath my foot.

Frowning, I looked down.

Oh no!

"Annie…" His voice was low. Deadly. "Are those my fruit snacks?"

My stomach dropped as his eyes locked on mine with an intensity that was so terrifying I nearly stopped breathing. "No. Nope. They're, mine, totally mine."

He bent down and grabbed one of the packages that had spilled from the bin in my bookcase. "Really? Because I write down the date of each box I purchase, and this matches what I wrote down in my dream journal that day."

"What?" My knees knocked together. "You write it down?"

"Did you miss the dream journal part?" He looked up with a grin on his face. "And I'm shitting you. I know they're mine because I've been missing almost an entire box for a week…"

"Maybe…" I shrugged. "I bought my own."

"You know you're the worst liar ever, right? Like if I asked you to tell me the sky was brown, I think you'd stutter halfway through and then look away and lamely try to change the subject."

"That's not true!" Asshole! "Plus, they're mine. Finders keepers."

"Ohhhh, is that how this game works?" He was right in front of me, all masculine perfection, flawless full pout, a strong jaw that I wanted to reach out and touch then slap because it was so perfect. "I find it, I keep it?"

"Yup." I lifted my chin.

His arms came around me in a flash, and then his forehead touched mine. "Found you. Keeping you."

My lower lip trembled. "That's a really manipulative way to try to get your fruit snacks back."

"Is it working?" He pulled me tenderly against his chest. "What if we trade?"

"I have nothing more to give."

"Ohhh…" His eyes searched mine. "I'm not so sure about that."

I tried to keep my towel tightly wound around me, but his eyes were hypnotic demons from hell that had me loosening my grip to the point that I had one hand holding it in front of me, pressed between our bodies, touching the necklace I gave him.

She would always be there.

And I was okay with that.

As long as I was there too.

"Ash," I warned.

"I was going to give you your present… do you still want it?"

"Is it a puppy?" I joked, trying to break the sexual tension between us. I needed to stay strong.

His eyebrows shot up. "I think a puppy would take too much of your attention away from me. I mean, you're already commandeering my fruit snacks; what if I got you a puppy and you started ignoring me or provoking me on purpose?"

I snorted out a laugh. "Admit it, you'd like it."

"I admit everything." His arms tightened around my body; I had to tilt my head up to see him. "I admit I'm an asshole, but I think you like me that way. I think me being polite scares the shit out of you."

"Because you aren't polite," I blurted. "You're mean."

"I know."

"And cruel." I just kept going. "You're the definition of a selfish asshole who thrives on others' pain."

"True and true," he admitted.

I sighed. "You're supposed to get mad."

"Why would I get mad at my own twisted truth? If you want to make me mad, just try to change me; that will make me mad. But you don't want the gentleman..." He pressed forward, his lips against my cheek as he whispered. "You want the sinner."

I closed my eyes as my knees weakened.

He gripped the towel in one hand, tugging it away from me.

My breaths came fast and shallow. "What are you doing?"

"Making you fall..." Just as he said it, the towel pooled at my feet, and then his hands were cupping my face. "Look at me."

I opened my eyes, terrified of what I'd see. "I'm looking."

"I'm not," he said simply. "And I won't look. I swear to you I won't look until you're ready because I know this is too soon. I know I sliced over and over again and never even attempted to stop the bleeding. I know that now... So I'm not going to look even though it's fucking killing me. I just want you to know that you're beautiful. That I care. That I won't stop caring even if you shove me away the way I did you." His thumbs moved against my jaw. "And Annie?"

I couldn't trust my voice. My tongue felt thick, my throat dry.

"You aren't alone." He shook his head. "Not anymore."

He released me and turned away like he was leaving.

"Wh-what about the fruit snacks?" I asked.

His dark chuckle said it all. "I'll get even... one day..."

"Ash!'

The door clicked shut behind him.

And I knew.

Sleep... would be completely futile, maybe for the rest of my life as I fell against my bed completely naked and wanting.

Him.

Always him.

Only him.

And as I looked out my window, I watched the stars.

And wished.

Begged.

Prayed.

That he'd be mine...

"Until the stars fall.." I whispered into the night.

CHAPTER
Twenty-Four

"Death is not the greatest loss in life. The greatest loss is what dies inside of us while we live." —Norman Cousins

Chase

January

"Things are better, then?" Phoenix asked just after New Year's.

I glanced out the window as the snow continued to pile itself around Chicago and shook my head. "They're hard to read."

Phoenix snorted out a laugh. "Welcome to your twenties."

"Were we ever that young?" I wondered out loud.

"No," Tex said from his spot in the corner half-assed watching Dante and Nixon playing chess. Andrei and Valerian were deep in a discussion about Russian politics, and Sergio was reading a medical text that would probably scare a sane human.

Dom was at the door watching, guarding as always.

And there I sat.

It was the first time since her death that I wished I would have trusted more, trusted my friends, my family, the bosses.

We'd been to hell and back, over and over again, and yet, this secret wasn't mine to keep, wasn't mine to tell. And yet I knew, in the way that Phoenix sometimes looked at me—he knew I wasn't the same.

Would never be the same after that day in the hospital, when the life left her eyes when she was lost to him.

My son.

My fucking son.

With his broken heart, spirit, soul.

I pounded the desk with my fist, gaining everyone's attention before I even realized what I was doing.

"Someone's panties in a twist?" Andrei grinned like he wanted to pick a fight.

But Nixon?

Nixon just shot me a cool stare that said. *"Stop hiding."*

"What would you do…" I stood and stared out the window. "If someone you loved asked you to sacrifice everything at the risk of your own happiness?"

"Er, asking for a friend?" Tex joked.

I heard a muffled "ouch," so clearly someone hit him.

"Seriously." I lowered my head. "How do you even begin to unravel that?"

Phoenix spoke first. "If they truly love you, they don't ask you to sacrifice what makes you… *you.*"

"Damn." Dante laughed. "Phoenix just rose from the ashes a poet. Okay, Lord Byron, while I agree, it just depends on circumstances."

"No." Nixon was next. "I disagree. You give everything up

for those you love at the risk of your own happiness; to do anything else isn't love."

I barked out a laugh. "Yeah, yeah, you won Trace, you're such a dick sometimes." He laughed with me. "You're lucky I love my wife."

"And you're lucky you do too. Otherwise, I'd kill you for loving mine," Nixon said so casually I had to flip him off.

I meant it.

My wife was… everything Trace wasn't.

She was perfect.

Mine.

But that didn't mean Trace wasn't still one of my dearest friends that I just so happened to kiss back in college.

Someone cleared his throat, and then Sergio spoke. "I would have done anything and everything for Andi—in the moment." He drew a deep breath and released it, then added, "But in that moment, would it have been fair in our relationship? There must always be a balance, Chase, especially in this lifestyle."

I nodded, crossed my arms.

Continued looking out at the snow.

"Brother," came Andrei's voice. "At the risk of getting the shit beat out of me… you can't measure love. It simply has no scale, so every situation is going to be different depending on the ask."

I hung my head. "And if… the ask was death? Then what?"

The room was silent.

The clock ticked in the distance.

I squeezed my eyes shut as I felt the room fill with tension, and then Phoenix's voice… "What did you do?"

My truth.

My life.
My son.
With a shaking voice, I whispered, "I killed her."

CHAPTER
Twenty-Five

"What we have done for ourselves alone dies with us. What we have done for others and the world remains and is immortal." —Albert Pike

Ash

One Week Later

"Wake up!" My dad's voice was tense, worried—afraid. I jerked awake and stared into his icy blue eyes. I saw nothing but terror there, nothing but uncertainty. "What's wrong?"

"Emergency meeting. Now."

"With who?"

He swallowed and looked away with shaking hands. "Everyone."

"All the bosses?" I didn't mean to question, but it was rare to have actual meetings. Dinners were one thing, but meetings? A commission?

"Yes." Dad tossed me a pair of jeans from the floor and said, "Get ready."

"For what?"

He stopped at the door and whispered, "War."

I immediately thought of Annie as I hurried to brush my teeth, then threw on a beanie, dressed in dark jeans and a gray T-shirt, and stumbled out of the guest house.

By the time I arrived at the kitchen, it wasn't just all the bosses who were present, but all the cousins—even the younger ones.

"What the hell is going on?" I asked in a cold voice. "Because right now, it looks like we're planning another fucking funeral." Where was Annie?

My stomach dropped.

My heart stopped beating.

Eyes furiously darting around the room until I saw her holding Kartini's hand.

Kartini?

I mean, she was young, only seventeen but, why Kartini?

And that was when I saw it.

The dust on some.

Dark smudges on others.

Blood on a few.

What the hell had happened to my family? And why was Kartini shaking?

"Someone. Talk. Now." I was losing control fast. Something snapped within me, imagining the smudges on Annie, the fear in her eyes.

Did Annie have blood on her?

What the hell would cause everyone to look this morose?

"Someone…" Tex shuddered and glanced at King, who

had smudges of burnt something across his face. His eyes were rimmed with red, his jaw locked like he was afraid if he opened it, he'd scream. "Someone sent one of those shitty white horse bombs to every single one of the cousins. Most of them knew what to do, but they were on timers, so they went off anyway... Had they not been warned because of the one at Ash's ..."

I clenched my fists. "So who do we go after? Who are we killing?"

I was ready.

Adrenaline surged through my body.

Nobody threatened what was mine.

Nobody.

"That's just it." Tex sighed and ran a shaky hand through his copper and brown hair. "We still have no intel; it's like they're off-grid."

Tank chose the worst timing ever as he let himself into the house, the door nearly coming off its hinges. "Is everyone okay?"

His eyes darted around the room, finally settling on Kartini as he seemed to sigh in relief.

I wanted to shout, *"with no thanks to you!"* But I kept silent.

I watched.

Waited.

"Yes," Dad finally said. "We're just trying to figure out what's the safest route..."

Tank immediately jumped into action. "I can get agents to surround your property; you know they want the bigger fish, the violent squirmy one." He pulled out his phone. "Just give me a minute."

"No." The voice was feminine. Familiar. Shocked, I watched as Annie made her way into our circle as if she'd been a part of this life for an eternity. "You can't involve them."

"Annie." Tank's face fell as his eyes softened toward her sealing his fate of getting punched in the face later. "This isn't the same."

"You don't know that." Her teeth chattered. "Just because you have protection doesn't mean you're protected. And if they're smart, they'll just wait until your guard's down… and you can't live your life that way—just waiting, for the other shoe to drop, just waiting for that next hit, the next shove, the next draw of blood." her voice caught on a sob.

I reached for her; thank God she let me pull her against me. Her body shook as she spoke. "You draw them out…"

She smelled like smoke.

My fingers dug into her hair.

Someone was dying that day.

"Them?" Phoenix said in obvious interest. "And who are they? Do you know?"

She squeezed her eyes shut, I tried to turn her toward me, but she jerked away and then looked up to my dad. "Do you know?"

He was silent, his eyes guilty as hell.

"Do you?" Her voice was softer now. "Do you? Does he?" She pointed to Phoenix, who sighed heavily. "You do, right? It's why you took me in?"

"Okay." I was losing my mind. "Can someone please tell me what the fuck is going on?"

"She was my target because of her adoptive dad." Tank pulled out a chair and sat like he held the weight of the world on his shoulders. "He was a De Lange recruit; they adopted the orphans and wanted to brainwash them, train them against the other families."

The very Family that we'd tried to flush out.

That wanted us dead more than anything just because they'd fucked up and been left with nothing.

My own dad, the executioner that went after their families all those years ago and cleansed the family lines only to grow a heart and let the kids live, make better choices, survive.

A mistake, people said.

Grace, he'd snapped back, a man broken and beaten, who still saw the value of human life despite the horror around him.

I'd heard the story a million times.

"You're De Lange?" I couldn't keep the hiss of pain out of my voice. Was history just repeating itself?

She lowered her head. "No. I'm—"

"She's Sinacore," Dad answered in a calm voice that had me ready to throw furniture. "Her father wanted to move up in the De Lange line... but they couldn't get pregnant, so..."

Andrei's eyes softened as much as they probably could as he took in the scene, she was related to him, and he never knew; she'd been threatened all this time, and he hadn't protected her.

I knew that guilt well.

So. Well.

A tear slid down Annie's cheek. "He whored out my mom to a Sinacore underboss... and she got pregnant. Only they fell in love, and my dad, he never forgave her for it and never forgave me for being born." She fell into gut-wrenching sobs. "H-he killed her the day the men came and stole me from my house, and she said, she said..." My arms went around her as I held her tight, refusing to let her go despite our curious audience. "She said the only Family I could trust were the Abandonatos."

Had the moon fallen from the sky?

The sun?

The stars?

In that moment, I couldn't have moved as my brain replayed every single shitty thing I'd done to her, said to her, been to her.

My throat all but closed up.

She'd seen me as a hero.

And I'd been nothing but the villain.

I'd reveled in it.

I'd punished her.

"How old were you?" I rasped.

"Nine," came her damning response. "He killed her, then killed himself, and Tank was undercover as a high school student next door. I didn't know it then, but I was adopted or taken because of my bloodline; nobody wanted a girl that old. I was so excited to leave my life behind, and then—"

"Hell," Tank finished. "Fucking. Hell." He stood to his feet then. "They tortured those kids, they wanted information, but they were so young." He slammed his fist onto the table. "The FBI did whatever they could to gain the protection those kids needed—your fucking protection."

"And you've known?" I asked. "This whole time? Fuck how old are you?"

Tank shook his head. "Found out before I came here… the FBI thinks the horses are a way at getting back at the FBI for attempting to gain protection for the De Lange orphans." He sighed. "And not as old as you think, regardless of what you think, I was a child prodigy when it came to math, was recruited sickeningly young by the government." He swallowed. "Our best guess is they want to get even."

"Shit," Nixon said from his seat. "So they want retaliation?"

"We think so, yes," Tank admitted sadly. "It's the only thing that makes sense. Several of the De Lange Family are still living and went underground after we busted Annie's family. Most of the kids that you know, that you're training, were adopted under those pretenses. That's why they'd die for you guys, they have nothing left, no protection, no family—and they're pissed, all they wanted was love, and all they got was used."

The door opened again as six of the De Lange recruits slowly walked in. Four guys, two girls.

The last remaining kids of the De Lange line, each of them had been training under us for the past year and a half—all of them made leaps and bounds as they swore their fealty to me—to the Family.

All while going to Eagle Elite and learning skills we'd need them to perfect later on in life. They lived under Phoenix's roof too, safer that way, but I'd only ever seen them as leeches.

Pawns.

My own foot soldiers.

And now?

Now I realized I'd never taken the time to ask their names, their ages, backgrounds because that had been Tank's job as trainer, his punishment.

But me? I was their leader.

Not my dad. Not the Capo.

Me.

I was who they looked to.

And I was the one they were looking to right now.

"We just heard." Dylan, I think his name was Dylan ran a hand through his shoulder length jet black hair. "Just tell us what we need to do."

I hesitated, my eyes darting to my father's and back.

It was a moment that usually the bosses would take—they'd plan, they'd tell us how to execute it, and we'd be fine.

But right now.

Right now, all of the bosses curiously stared at me, as if it was my turn to truly step up to the plate, to own my heritage of the Abandonato Family.

"Annie's right," I found myself saying. "By hunting, we leave ourselves exposed. Besides, we won't even know exactly who we're looking for."

"So?" Junior crossed his arms. "We just wait?"

I narrowed my eyes. "When were you going to have an engagement party?"

Junior swore. "That? That's what you focus on right now?"

I held out my hand. "Hear me out… rumors constantly circulate about how much of a douche you are."

"Oh good, I like this conversation. Please continue." Junior threw his hands in the air . Standing next to him, Dylan smirked.

"It's true, right?" I eyed the eighteen-year-old kid, who gave a reluctant nod. "I'm sure you were told we were spoiled rotten rich kids with silver spoons poking out of our asses. And while ridiculously exaggerated, if that's what they think, then let's give it to them, make them think we're lowering our guard." I had everyone's full attention now. "We throw a party downtown, make sure security is undercover, control the location, and we draw them out… just like Annie said. Besides, waiting for the monster under the bed is way more dangerous than reaching beneath and crushing his skull while he thinks you're sleeping."

"Creepy allegory," Junior muttered. Then he shrugged and

conceded, "But accurate."

"So?" I faced my dad. "You guys feel like handing over those credit cards now?"

"Oh." Dad grinned. "Annie's already got one."

"The hell!" I rolled my eyes. "You made me wait until last year!"

"She's a careful spender." He grinned.

Annie shifted in my arms; I could feel her nerves at being the center of attention— I should let her go, I should set her away from me; instead, I pulled her tighter.

Refused to stop touching her.

Because she was here.

Alive.

Breathing.

And I found that my heart needed a reminder of all of those things as my brain tried to plan a way to take down anything that threatened my blood—my soul.

I searched the bosses' faces, and then my cousins', each of them had their own reason for ending this—now.

"So?" I grinned at Junior. "You ready to play arrogant prick with too much money and a bimbo on your arm?"

"Hey!" Serena shot me a glare. "Let them think I'm stupid; it will give me time to shove my stiletto into their eye sockets and hear them scream."

"Graphic," Maksim muttered under his breath, while the rest of the cousins seemed to be uncertain.

"It's a good plan." I looked at my dad. "We'll pair off." I clung to Annie then. "Nobody's alone. Sergio can fit us all with earpieces, and if nothing insane happens then, we still get to party."

"No drinking," Dad pointed out.

"I would never drink and shoot." I gave him a grin.

Junior frowned. "But what about that time—"

"Not now," I snapped, earning a shit-eating grin from both Junior and Maksim while King shared a look with Valerian—one I knew all too well. He still struggled with the power difference between the two. King may be the future Capo, but for now, his brother was already a boss, in charge of countless families and a fortune, and I knew it weighed heavy on him, seeing it change Valerian in a way that made him age beyond his twenty-one years and nearly look identical to the other bosses.

It needed to end.

Whatever the hell this was.

"The moms won't like it," Nixon finally said as if peering into the room next door where they were with the younger kids. "But I agree with Ash—and Annie—draw them out, before they surprise us again."

Annie exhaled.

"Tomorrow night, The Regis, Scary Dad—"

He groaned.

"Think you can make it happen for your very favorite son?"

"Only son." The corners of his mouth tilted up into a smile. "And of course, what's the use of being a Senator if you can't abuse some power every once in a while."

Tex burst out laughing. "Good one."

"I was being serious," Dad grumbled.

"Every once and a while?" Nixon added. "That's like saying it was an accident when you shoved someone's feet into cement last week and dropped them into Lake Michigan…"

My dad just grinned. "He slipped."

"Scary bastard," Junior muttered under his breath, earning an equally terrifying wink from my dad.

Andrei spoke next. "I'll help make arrangements, and it goes without saying—dress the part, children."

"You're literally a year under forty," I pointed out.

He adjusted his tie. "And yet..." He eyed my outfit up and down.

"And yet, what?" I asked.

"Oh, that was it." Phoenix jumped in. "He was insulting your outfit without using words; we've been working on his bedside manner, lately."

"It shows." Tex did a slow clap.

"Parents," I grumbled. "Keep us updated, and until the party, everyone stays here, agreed?"

"Sure thing," Dad said smoothly. "Kartini can stay with Annie in her room, and we'll set..."

As his voice trailed off with all the arrangements, all I kept thinking was over my dead body.

She wasn't going to leave my side.

Even if it meant I was tying her up and throwing her over my shoulder, then hiding her in my closet.

I winced. Somehow I went from protective mode to serial killer, all within the span of a few seconds.

Welcome to the mafia.

I half expected for someone to yell out, *"And break!"* Like we were playing our annual football game against the dads, but instead, everyone slowly dispersed.

Annie moved to pull away from me.

"No." I held her firm.

She glanced up at me. "But, your dad said—"

"And I say no." I licked my lips and stared at her full mouth. "Don't make me repeat myself."

"You're such a damn bully." She squirmed beneath my

regard, trying to get out of my grasp.

My eyebrows shot up. "Did you just say damn?"

"Maybe." Her cheeks flushed. "Look, I need to go help Kartini get settled in; she's terrified right now."

"So am I." I lied. "Petrified of my own shadow, can't trust me not to shoot at anything that moves, and it's going to get dark later, which means I'm going to be even more scared, and I don't want to have to army crawl all the way back to the house and up the balcony stairs just to beg you to sleep with me and make the monsters go away."

Her eyes narrowed. "What's it like?"

"What's what like?"

"Being the monster you're actually afraid of?"

I tipped my head. "Touché."

Her smile was faint. "On that note…"

She tried getting away.

Again.

If I wasn't so arrogant, I might honestly feel offended that she struggled to get away from me every few minutes.

"Son." Dad walked over to us. "A minute?"

"Sure." His expression wasn't the least bit cheerful.

Great.

He turned his icy cold stare to Annie. Amazing how his face transformed into a smile. "Annie, why don't you go help Kartini get settled in? I'll send Ash after you later."

"Good, threaten her with my presence. That will make her want to stay." I sighed.

She pulled herself away from my body without a backward glance and made a beeline for Kartini, looping their arms together as they made their way down the hall.

"Sit." Dad pointed to one of the wooden chairs at the

kitchen table.

We were alone again, just me and him, and about a billion secrets that I'd probably never know holding a constant wave of tension between us.

"Whoever's after you—they know you're lethal…"

"A compliment? And here I thought you were about to give me another terrifying discussion on sex."

He winked. "Saving my next one for later."

I exaggerated a shudder. "Please don't."

His fingertips drummed against the table, he looked over his shoulder and then leaned forward onto his thighs, clasping his fingers together like he was about to tell me someone died. "We need Sergio to start a rumor… a rumor that will reach their ears, eyes, something that would make the enemy curious, something that would make you vulnerable."

A ripple of awareness washed over me, trickling down my spine. "Okay… where are you going with this?"

He bit down on his lower lip. "She trusts you to keep her safe."

"Who?"

"Don't play dumb; it's a shit look on you, son."

"Annie." I actually looked away, afraid if we locked gazes he'd see too much, the bitterness, the anger, the protectiveness, the fear, the need for more, and… the loneliness; it was all there on the surface every time someone said her name.

"You're going to need to revert to your asshole self."

"And so soon after pulling my head out of my ass. Lovely," I grumbled.

He sighed. "It will need to look real, like your spiraling, like you're using her—get a hotel room. Pretend to be drunk. Keep her safe, but appear aloof, everyone will tell you to sleep it off. You'll need to be cruel, Ash. You'll need to be—"

"Myself." My heart sank. "Let me just tell her so she knows, I can't and won't do that to her again, Dad—"

"If she knows, her responses won't be real. You have tonight… and then tomorrow…" As his voice trailed off, he sighed and met my gaze.

My chest felt so tight it was hard to breathe. "What you're saying… it makes sense, but I can't just—"

"What's going to keep her safe, Ash? What's going to keep your cousins safe? What's going to work better? You flirting with a pretty girl and being a gentleman, or stepping off the ledge and letting your guard down. I don't need you to kiss the girl—I need you to make her cry."

I clenched my fist, feeling all the blood drain from my hand as my jaw locked in place, teeth grinding, I finally answered. "I'll do it."

"She'll understand, son."

I snorted out a laugh. "Or she'll never forgive me because she'll never trust my word again."

My dad stared me down longer than what felt comfortable for any sane human, then said. "If she loves you. She'll understand. This is the job, Ash. It's what you do. It's what you're good at. She needs to get that, see that if she wants any part of this life—sacrifices must be made."

Well, if that wasn't a severe case of deja vu.

"That it?" I stood.

"Yeah, that's it…" He jerked his head toward the stairway. "Now go do what you've been dying to do since I started this painfully long conversation—grab Annie and spend some time with her. And Ash… make it count."

I forced the anger back down, just barely. "Yeah, I'll get

right on that."

I was maybe five steps away from him when I heard him say. "I'm proud of you, son."

"I hope you still say that after I break her heart."

"Her heart was never in question of getting broken."

I froze. "What?"

"Yours, however…"

I shook my head, refusing to look back. "You can't break what's barely been salvaged and broken, Dad."

"You're a fool if you think your heart was anything but whole, before Claire, during Claire, and after Claire. She never had the chance to break you—Annie does."

My heart pounded against my ribs. I didn't know what to say, so I said nothing and kept walking, and when I finally made it to Annie's room, I didn't have the energy to even try to digest whatever cryptic words my dad had said to me.

Instead, I just barked, "You." Like a complete caveman. I pointed at Annie and did this weird grunt that had Kartini looking at me like I was going insane, which honestly, I felt like I was at that point.

"I think he's trying to communicate," Kartini whispered. "Quick, if he starts beating his chest, look away, or he'll see it as a challenge to his dominance."

I flipped her off with both hands.

"Look at the male homo sapien as he uses his fingers to communicate what his words cannot… interesting, very interesting."

"I hope to God you fall in love with someone who can train you, I really do." I sighed. "Annie, let's go, you're my *let's not get killed buddy*."

Annie paled. "I'm not sure I like that title. Can we come

up with something happier?"

"Ah, ah, ah, ah, staying alive." Kartini did a little dance. "No?"

"No," we said in unison.

She crossed her arms in annoyance. "Fine, fine, I'll be okay all by myself, in this large room after getting nearly blown to bits by a stuffed animal, no big..."

"Don't worry, Tini, Tank will be back soon to babysit."

She lunged for me.

I jerked back against the door.

She was tiny.

But Sergio had taught her how to pack a punch.

Footsteps sounded down the hall, then stopped behind me. I glanced over my shoulder. "And God provides!"

"Huh?" Tank glared.

"You're the sacrificial sheep..." I grinned. "Oh, and she's singing Stayin Alive, so good luck with that."

I grabbed Annie by the hand before she could protest, and then I rubbed the middle of my chest with the other.

I had less than twenty-four hours to show her the real me, the one who was finally letting go—getting the closure I needed, the one who was still trying to give her a damn present she clearly didn't even want.

Twenty-four hours before the monster came back.

And I wondered if she'd ever forgive me for using her to draw out our enemies. I couldn't help but think about Claire.

About how I forced her hand.

And I didn't want to force Annie.

She was too—sweet. Too pure.

Claire had seen the necessity of the parts we played—but I knew she hated it.

Which meant it would destroy Annie to have to do the same.

Right?

Then again, last year she had offered herself up when I needed her, but that was just a ruse, right? To be useful? To make out?

I wiped my hand down my face.

"Slow down." Annie jogged after me.

"Sorry, just wanted to make it to the pool house before it rained."

She stumbled and looked up. "There's like one cloud."

"Well, you never know." I gave her one last tug, and then we were at my door, going into the house, and I was shutting it behind us, pressing her up against it.

I looked into her big blue eyes and said my truth then.

Said what I should have said months ago.

I cupped her face, my forehead touching hers as my thumbs flicked her bottom lip. "I need you."

Her little gasp was all the invitation I needed as I pressed my body against hers, and then my mouth, sliding my tongue past any protest she may have had.

And taking.

Stealing.

Keeping.

"Mine," I whispered. "Mine."

I pushed my hands under shirt and then very slowly ran my fingertips down her sides, breasts, nipples. My tongue lined the outside of her ear, and I held her close and murmured, "I'll stop when you can't take it anymore, and then… you get your present."

"This isn't it?"

A dark chuckle was the only answer I offered.

"You don't have to, you know…" she whispered. "You don't owe me anything—"

I pinched her nipple, and she threaded her finger into my hair then tugged.

"You still don't get it. I want you. I *need* you." I studied her eyes, looking for… I didn't know what. Because I was terrified she would tell me no.

She searched my gaze; it was like she was raking through the mess that was my soul like she would know all my secrets.

I didn't care.

"Then take me," she murmured.

She didn't have to say it twice.

CHAPTER
Twenty-Six

"No one gets out of here alive." —Jim Morrison

Annie

H e was claiming me.
　　Kissing me.
Hands in my hair, mouth sliding against mine, his lips massaging gently, beckoning me to open.

And I hated it.

I hated all of it.

Because he was being gentle on purpose—as if that was what I wanted.

I hated myself now too, because I should be jumping for joy, but instead, I wanted to slap him across the face and ask him to treat me like—like he had.

As if I was Claire's ghost.

Oh, God.

Sick to my stomach, I pulled back. "Ash…"

His eyes flickered to my swollen mouth and then back up again, and something shifted.

"You don't want this." He stumbled back.

"I want this. I just don't want it *like* this," I said stupidly.

His grin was almost cruel again like I'd offended him, which I probably had. "Then how do you want it, perfect little princess? It's cute that you think this is really up to you, that you get a say."

I glared. "Amazing, is this your first time getting turned down?"

"Is this your first time getting turned on?" he countered.

"You're an asshole!"

"And you're a fucking liar!"

My hand went flying. He caught it midair and flipped me around, pinning my chest against the wall, his body pressing me there, his breath hot on my neck. "If I remember correctly." He had both hands prisoner above my head, while his other hand cupped my ass and squeezed.

I let out a little gasp, my body bucking against him.

"Sensitive." His chuckle was dark perfection.

My body shuddered.

"Run," he whispered in my ear before tugging it with his teeth. A sharp pain sliced through my skin as his nose trailed down my neck. "Run, but remember… finders keepers."

"Ash—"

"Annie."

"I don't think—"

"Ten, nine, eight—"

"Crap! Ash, let me explain. I just meant that—"

"Seven." He gripped my ass again and then pulled away,

leaving me still straining back toward him. "Six."

Slowly I turned.

His gaze raged.

His posture was rigid.

His jaw clenched.

This was Ash.

This was *my* Ash.

This was what I needed.

What he craved.

"Five." His eyes flashed.

And I ran.

I missed the doorknob about seventeen times, and then I was running as thunder sounded overhead. Rain started to pour from the one dark cloud? Really?

I nearly slipped as I sprinted around the pool.

Four.

Three.

Two.

I knew he was coming.

Could feel him at my back.

Was too afraid to look over my shoulder.

And then I was tackled into the soft grass near the hammock.

"Down we go…" He didn't give me any time to process what he was doing as he slid my dress up past my hips then hooked my legs around his neck.

Anyone could see us.

Anyone!

His smile was possessed as a rough hand slid up my thigh, jerking my legs apart harder, exposing me to him before deft fingers ripped my underwear.

Rain poured.

His chest heaved as water dripped from his jaw down onto my body.

I lifted my chin in defiance.

And then he lowered his head in reverence.

Followed by worship.

His tongue was hot against my skin, almost too hot as he spread me wide.

And partook.

My body shook as memories of that night flooded my vision like the very raindrops cascading down both of our bodies, cleansing us from the inside out.

Maybe the rain was washing away my one unholy act of taking what wasn't mine to take, for giving a gift that wasn't mine to give.

I had sinned.

My loneliness was my punishment.

And his tongue was my jailer.

He gripped my ass so hard with his fingertips I cried out. He answered with a growl against my sensitive skin. He flicked his tongue over me, and then he fucked me with that tongue.

It was primitive.

Angry.

It was all Ash.

In every way that mattered.

There was nothing beautiful about this moment—and everything brutal and exposed.

He pulled back just enough to lock eyes with me as he continued his assault, setting my nerves on fire. His eyes heated as I let out a moan, needing more, needing so very much more. His hands firm, he held me captive as the rain drenched us both, and his mouth locked onto me.

His beautiful mouth punished.

And I reacted to each tug of his lips, each suck, each swirl of his tongue, over and over again; he took me to the stars only to stop just as I was falling back again.

"Ash." My body wept along with the weather. "Please!"

"You don't get to tell me." He pulled away, mouth wet, eyes crazed. "You don't get a say in how you want me or how you get me."

"You're so arrogant!"

"Yes," he snapped. "I'll take you hard. I'll take you gentle. But I'll decide how you need it, how you want it, and when…" A hand pinched my ass while another slid up and roughly cupped my breasts, massaging them as he lowered his head again. "I decide how I worship you."

I cried out as he slid his hand from my ass to between my legs, massaging with his palm. "Right there."

He pulled back and winked.

"You, you jack—"

He dipped his head.

He used his tongue like a weapon.

His hands like an instrument.

And when I came apart all over his face, his fingers, his tongue, he lifted his head toward the sky as if he wanted the universe to see evidence of what he'd done, as if he'd just made a sacrifice, there on the dirty ground with my legs wrapped around him.

A throat cleared. "I hate to break up whatever weird pagan ritual you guys got going on out here, but… DoorDash is literally pulling up right now." I about died when I looked over at Maksim, who had a hand covering his eyes, and King, who was staring down at his phone with a smirk across his face.

I fell back against the grass and sighed as Ash slowly lowered my legs and, in a move I didn't see coming, crawled up my body and shielded me from not only the rain but their stares.

From the poor delivery guy.

From everything.

Then again.

That was Ash.

Protector.

Monster.

Bully.

Mine.

CHAPTER
Twenty-Seven

"I'm not afraid to die, I just don't want to be here when it happens."—Woody Allen

Ash

Hours after tasting her—and I couldn't even eat dinner—because nothing would feel as good pressed against my tongue, occupying my mouth.

Had I lost my fucking mind there for a minute?

Yes.

Had I felt slightly guilty at the fear in her eyes?

Maybe.

But I knew her.

I knew Annie.

I was trying to ease her into it, trying to seduce her the way she deserved, with pretty kisses from a gentleman, not cruel bites from a villain.

And yet, that was what her body craved.

What I wanted.

There would be time for gentle.

One day I'd take hours.

But today was not that day.

And there was something so fucking familiar about the way her moans reached my ears, how her thighs clenched around my face like I'd visited her temple many times before.

What the hell?

I was still stumped.

Horny as hell.

And trying to fit the pieces together.

"Until the stars fall." I shook the phrase from my head.

Claire had said that, no, wait… she always said until the sky falls.

I froze.

Had I been that drunk?

"So." Maksim plopped down on the couch next to me. After dinner, we'd all gone to the theater room to Netflix.

I wanted to chill.

But Annie had been avoiding me since our foray into public fornication. Not that I blamed her.

The poor DoorDash driver asked if we needed an ambulance, only to have Maksim say. "Do they treat blue balls now?"

"So." I crossed my arms.

"That trick." He sniffed and looked away, then back at me. "You know where you had like one hand here." The fucker touched me on the chest. "And then the other… you know…" He nodded. "Lower—"

"Touch my dick, and I'm cutting yours off."

"Bro! At least be comfortable enough in your sexuality to

know that if I wanted dick, I'd tell you."

"That oddly doesn't make me feel better, Maks."

He snorted out a laugh. "Bet you're not feeling better at all. How are the balls? Sad? Tight? Blue?"

"Did you have a reason for being here?"

"So that move—"

"Yeah, I'm going to have to stop you right there. And you want to know why?"

He frowned. "Because it's a trade secret? Trademark move?"

"No." My jaw clenched. "Because I refuse to teach you something or even discuss something that you may or may not attempt on my fucking *sister*!"

He visibly paled and held up his hands in surrender. "It's not like that."

Izzy chose that moment to walk by and go. "Oh, it's exactly like that."

"She's lying!" he roared. "We haven't even—"

"Kill him, Ash." She batted her eyelashes. "Do it for your fave sis."

I reached for him.

He stumbled back and shot her a glare. "Grow a heart, Jezebel!"

"Grow a bigger penis, small fry!"

Junior grabbed Maksim by the collar and shoved him in the opposite direction. "I swear the hormones just make it harder to deal with them."

Izzy opened her mouth to most likely yell, but Serena clapped a hand over it and whispered. "Just walk away, yes in that direction, oh look, wine!"

"Shit, they're worse than you guys used to be," I grumbled. "And that's saying something, and who the hell asks for oral sex tips when screwing my sister?"

Junior barked out a laugh. "It's not like they're together anymore."

"Thus the animosity." I shook my head. "He's just pissed I made Dad cut down the tree by her window."

Junior held out his fist. "I approve of this cock block."

I hit his fist with mine. "Thank you, I do try."

He glanced over his shoulder and leaned in. "So a little bird—"

"Cut the shit, we both know King's the bird who told Valerian who probably told you…"

As if hearing his name Valerian sped over to us, sat down, and leaned in. "You went down on her in the rain?"

Junior smirked. "Nice."

"No, not nice! She could have caught a cold… holy shit, just tell me to stop talking. Am I turning into an old man now? Is that what being boss has done to me?" Valerian grumbled.

"Saw a gray hair, didn't wanna freak you out." Junior shrugged.

"Son of a bitch." He shot to his feet and stomped out of the room, most likely in search of a mirror where he'd find out he had nothing but perfect hair, then come back and try to pick a fight with Junior, which, let's be honest, ever since he'd become a boss could be a tough fight for Junior to win.

Not that I'd ever tell Junior that.

"He's gonna punch you when he comes back." I leaned back into the leather couch and put my hands behind my head.

Junior grinned. "I sure hope so; we don't want the Petrov boss getting soft." He was quiet a minute and then, "So you and Annie…"

"Saw that coming…"

"Yeah, well…" His eyes searched mine. "Can I ask a question and not get punched in the dick for it?"

I shifted uncomfortably. "Depends on the question."

"Are you just… oh shit, I'm gonna get hit, I just know it—but are you fucking with her?"

"The hell?" I shoved his chest. "No!"

He exhaled. "Good, because I heard it was you behind all those horrible tweets, not that I blame you for wanting whatever retribution or revenge you could get. I just wanted to make sure that you weren't being a sadistic asshole."

My stomach churned. "You're right, I was responsible for the tweets, but—"

A gasp sounded behind me.

Junior's eyes widened. "Annie…"

"Fuck." I jumped to my feet only to have her slam her hands against me, sending me sailing backward.

"YOU!" she yelled. She never yelled. Her face was red, tears were already streaming down her cheeks. She was never supposed to know. "You did that? To me?"

"Yes," I said quietly. "But you don't understand—"

"Fuck you!" Serena moved to stand behind Annie. "How could you be such a prick!"

Junior slowly moved away from me.

And when I looked up, it was to see my entire family backing Annie.

Not me.

"I had my reasons," I finally said.

"Nothing," Annie yelled. "And I do mean NOTHING excuses that level of bullying. God, I can't believe we just—" She covered her mouth with her hand and choked out a sob. "You've been lying this whole time, haven't you? Playing me? Playing my emotions. I trusted, I thought, after that... after..." She stumbled forward.

I caught her before she collapsed against the floor.

Everything that could go wrong went wrong.

The night before I needed her to hate me.

Well, at least my dad got that part right.

She would go into the next evening wanting me dead.

I just hoped this conversation wasn't a bad omen.

I picked her up in my arms, ignoring the protests from everyone around me. As much as I wanted to take her back to the pool house, I knew that my chance was gone.

Tonight I could have been the nice guy and still failed at that given the chance.

And now I was the monster again.

The monster she needed me to be tomorrow.

Maybe that was my curse.

My cross to bear.

That in life, I'd never be the hero.

Always the villain, no matter what choice I made or who I tried to protect—hell, the one time I'd tried to protect someone, to truly take care of them—she'd been killed.

I carried her to her room.

Blanketed in darkness.

Counting my sins.

And when her eyes flickered open, I sat her on her bed and looked away; I couldn't stomach looking at her in the eyes, seeing the betrayal there, as if I'd singlehandedly plotted her downfall up until this point.

"Go," she whispered, her voice hoarse, cracking at the end like she was just barely holding it in. "I quit."

"Don't." I reached for her hand then stopped halfway

across the duvet. My hands felt frozen, paralyzed, in need of hers, in want of her warmth, and all I had was the cool touch of the bed. "Don't quit."

"As you know, my dad was a bad man. He murdered my mom, took his own life, and basically gave me away. And then I got taken in," she said so wistfully I wanted to hug her. "I thought maybe things were taking a turn for the better, I mean getting fostered out? Adopted even at my age? Miracle." She let out a long sigh. "She told me about the great Abandonato Family, about how they protect their own, how even in the midst of darkness, your dad, the great Chase Abandonato, did the right thing—he set the broken free. And I knew, I just knew if I saw your family, touched someone, said something, that my dreams would come true. The ones my mom placed there. Not dreams of being rich or famous, no, I just wanted, I just wanted to feel safe." Her voice quivered. "It's amazing how far you're willing to crawl through the mud just to hear that word, feel that protection…" Her voice cracked again. "And then I met you, and you were this larger than life… thing. Strong. Intense. Beautiful. Mean."

"Annie."

"No, let me finish." She moved on the bed, by my calculations, probably away from me. Away from my warmth. My protection. My arms. "I saw you, really saw you. And I knew that no matter what, you'd protect, you'd kill for blood, so even when you were mean, even when you made me cry when all I wanted was to be loved. I told myself it was okay because I was safe."

I hated myself.

I hated everything about me in that moment.

The man I was.

The man I'd become.

All for what?

"But now…" She let out a shaky breath. "Now I know… I'll never be safe, protected, always alone, and that's okay because it's worse when you hope. Worse when I see you every day and imagine a world where I have someone fighting with me, side by side, someone who, regardless of how violent— would protect me like my mom said. Maybe that's the danger with your stupid white horses… men come riding in on them pretending to be your savior, and it's too late… too late to realize that they were the villain the entire time."

My body seized, afraid to breathe. "I was angry."

"I know."

"I wanted to hurt you."

"I know."

"That's not me, not anymore."

"People don't change overnight, Ash. That's still you—just muted by whatever you think we have."

"Annie." Panic edged its way into my voice. "Don't do this."

"I can forgive a lot of things, Ash. Betrayal is one thing… but you went a step further, didn't you? You stole my hope."

I squeezed my eyes shut. "Annie Sinacore—sent to me. To us."

"Annie Sinacore," she repeated. "Deceased. Tired. Done."

I stood then slowly turned to face her, letting my rage show on my face. "I blamed you. I hated you. And managed to love you at the same time. Two warring emotions in my soul. Two hearts. Guilt and shame. Right and wrong. So even if you quit me, I'm not quitting you. Maybe you've lost your hope, but that doesn't mean I've lost mine. I will fight for you,

Annie Sinacore. I will win you. This villain. This monster. This destructive King."

"We'll see." Her whisper was cunning, angry.

"Yes," I vowed. "We will." I walked over to the door and flicked off the lights. "Sleep well tonight, because tomorrow we war."

"What the hell do you think I've been doing, Ash Abandonato? Sitting out of the fight? Open your eyes—we've been in a war since the day I moved here, since the day I —"

She didn't finish.

Thunder roared overhead.

Rain poured.

And a memory surfaced.

Of Annie yelling at me by the pool.

Of hot lips.

Cold nights.

"Say goodbye, Ash, you have to say it." She clung to my skin, *smelling like sunshine. "You must!"*

"I can't!"

"You must!"

I thrust into her and screamed her name. "Claire, Claire, Claire."

With every thrust, her body relaxed into me, clung to me like a second skin.

And with one final moment of clarity. "Until the stars fall."

"Until the stars fall," I found myself saying under my breath.

Not to Claire.

But to Annie.

My Annie.

CHAPTER
Twenty-Eight

"Death is the graduation of the soul." — Sylvia Browne

Chase

"*A*re we going to talk about it?" Phoenix pulled out a chair next to me as I sipped my whiskey—neat.

"Nope." I took another sip. "Talking just makes it true, and you already have your answers, don't you?"

A pregnant pause lingered between us. "You should have given him a choice, Chase."

"I did. I gave him a choice every time he chose to believe the lies. Every time he drank the fake truth like a medicine when it was a fucking poison. As a father, you can't shove your kids in the right direction; you can only be there to help them decide what path to take."

Phoenix dropped the black folder onto the kitchen table. "If tomorrow goes south—"

"If it goes poorly, we have precautions in place. I've made sure of it."

"Made sure of it how?"

My chest ached where my heart should be. "I made sure that this time—his choice was black and white. I made sure of it because my son deserves it—and with that, we'll draw them out. Believe me."

"I'm afraid to." Phoenix grabbed the bottle of whiskey in front of me and poured himself a glass. "I'm afraid politics have corrupted your mind."

"Nah, just my soul, my mind's extremely safe," I joked.

He tipped the drink back. "You don't mean to start a war, but you could, couldn't you?"

Guilt pounded into me. "Quite easily."

"Peace is dangerous."

"More so than war." I sighed. "And all my cards are finally on the table. Let everyone know the truth of my sins—of his. Let them know how far we'll go to protect our own. And in the end, anyone who's stupid enough, greedy enough, to want our kids—will burn in hell."

He clinked his glass against mine. "It's a gamble."

"I never gamble, Phoenix. I merely win."

"Cocky bastard."

I lifted my glass. "I'll drink to that."

CHAPTER
Twenty-Nine

"Death is certain. Life is uncertain."—English Proverb

Annie

I spent most of the next day wondering if I should go smack Ash in the face or beg him to do it again.

My emotions warred with each other, and I felt weird asking Izzy or Serena for any sort of advice—we were all so different; the only one I was maybe a little bit like was Violet, but since Valerian was a boss, they were staying at their own compound with a bunch of super scary looking Russians.

Which left me...

Kartini.

The girl who snuck her vape pen past her dad and was right now taking a few drags before stripping completely naked and putting on her dress for the party.

I glanced away. "Is that a tattoo?"

"Which one?" She asked in what seemed like a bored voice.

What had happened to her?

I mean no judgment, but before I left for Italy, she was dancing on her dad's shoes and looking up at him with stars in her eyes. She was the gorgeous teen who had the world and every guy her age hanging on her every word.

And now?

Now she had streaks of blue in her hair.

Tattoo's on her fingers.

And she was getting high under the watchful eye of all the bosses who were already stressed out enough as it was. Nothing made sense, and again, no judgment, *you do you* and all that, but still.

It seemed so out of character.

And her parents adored her.

Indulged her.

Maybe that was the problem?

"Hellooooo." Kartini popped up in my line of vision with an amused expression, her pupils large. "You sure you're not the one high right now?"

I gave my head a shake. "Sorry, just thinking about tonight."

She crossed her little arms and snorted. "Why? You think you're going to get lucky?"

"No!" I all but yelled and then. "I mean, why would I think that?"

"Oh, I don't know, maybe because of a certain cousin of mine..." She twirled her hair and then pulled a tight white body con dress over her little body. "...ate more Annie than pizza last night if you get my drift." She winked.

"Huh?" I played dumb. "I don't know what you're talking about."

She cackled out a laugh then threw a brush at my face. I ducked just in time while she wagged her finger back and forth, her nails long, pointed, black. "Nope, you can't pull that shit with me. Hell, it would have been better if anyone else would have seen you guys, any of the girls would have had that entire scene on lockdown, but King and Maksim?" She examined her nails. "You may as well have had two pre-teen girls spying on who held hands with who during skate night."

"Skate night?" I frowned.

She snapped her fingers. "Keep up. It happened. I'm sure it was magical, and as much as Ash's tongue anywhere near my person makes me want to barf until I die—I can at least admit that he's hot—but pretty much all Abandonatos are." She put her hands on her hips as if to say, exhibit A. "So," she began as she plopped down on the bed. "Is that what you're wearing after one of the most notorious bad boys to ever walk the streets of Eagle Elite University had his head between your thighs less than twenty-four hours ago?"

I opened my mouth, then shut it. "It's cute." I self-consciously tugged at the simple black turtleneck sweater dress. It was form-fitting, and it was frigid outside, so I figured it worked, plus I looked good in black... Or so I thought until Kartini made a face that pretty much made me feel like a nun—and not a hot sexually repressed one, but one who thumped people over the head with Bibles and lost her virginity at the ripe old age of fifty after one wild night at the local biker bar.

"Whoa." Kartini laughed. "That a fantasy of yours or what?"

"I said that out loud?"

"Sadly, yes." She wrinkled her nose. "My ears might never recover. I think my ovaries are sad now. Is that what it means when your stomach hurts really low, and you taste metal in your mouth?"

"What? No!" I rolled my eyes. "Never mind. Yes, this is what I was planning on wearing." I was tempted to do a little twirl but restrained myself at her horrified look.

"No." She shook her head, stood, slowly walked around me. "No." And then. "SERENA!"

"Shhhh!" I clapped a hand over her mouth, just as Serena magically appeared at the door with Izzy.

Both of them stared.

Longer than I would have liked.

Kartini pointed. "Can she wear that after last night?"

"No," they said in unison, then both started talking at once.

"I mean, it's Ash; you can't just wear a turtleneck after Ash!" Serena proclaimed.

"It's like wrapping yourself in a really sad, sad blanket with no hopes of ever being naked again. Don't get me wrong, you're hot, but I digress—it's Ash." Izzy nodded.

"Ash." Kartini shrugged. "I rest my case."

I ground my teeth and counted to three. "Fine, it's Ash, whatever that means." They gasped.

"That's why he likes her." Serena beamed. "All right, strip out of that nice sweater dress my grandma got me for Christmas when I was in the sixth grade, and I'll be back with something that will make Ash want to set anyone on fire who looks at you, breathes within ten feet of you, basically any male or female that has eyes."

"It's really all I ask." Kartini yawned.

I didn't know how it happened.

One minute I was clothed.

The next, I was naked, and three sets of hands were tugging at my hair, my clothes, extremely tall pumps with red bottoms were slid onto my feet, and then I was getting shoved out the door.

I never got a chance to see what I looked like.

All I felt was heavier makeup than usual.

Tall like a baby giraffe when all I wanted was to look like a gazelle.

And I could barely breathe.

They'd somehow shoved my size eight short little body into a short white cocktail dress that had literally no back and a plunging neckline down the front that required copious amounts of double-sided tape and showed a serious amount of side boob.

A gold necklace dangled between said boobs.

And a tan faux fur jacket was dangled on my shoulders.

"It's time!" Serena grinned once I was shuffled into the kitchen, and we somehow went from Fashion Barbie playtime to Military Barbie boot camp as each of the girls hiked up their skirts and started packing in multiple utility knives, small guns, needles—I didn't even ask because I was too busy gaping.

Serena kicked up her leg across Junior's lap as he hiked something smoothly up her thigh and then strapped another gun between her thighs.

"Thanks baby." Serena air kissed him.

"I live to serve." He grinned but didn't even look up from loading his gun. King and Maksim were in the corner, basically doing the same. Kartini and Izzy finished in record time while Serena yawned and then stretched her arms over her head, gaining Junior's full attention. "Ready for our engagement party?"

His eyes zeroed in on her mouth. "Ready to get naked later?"

"Always."

"Can't un-hear this..." Maksim said from the corner.

Izzy glared. "I'll be happy to take care of that problem for you."

"What?" He frowned. "What problem?"

"Your ears." She made a slicing motion. "I'm positive I can make a clean cut on both sides of your ginormous head—amazing, you'd think your brain would be bigger."

He flipped her off. "Tell me again, what's bigger, Izzy?"

"OKAY!" Junior jumped to his feet. "Ash is already outside waiting. Word of warning, he's pissed; nobody knows why he's pissed." Almost all eyes turned to me, great. "But he is, and we need him focused, so try not to turn into his target practice on the way to the hotel. Everyone but Annie, hop into the Rover, and Annie, I mean it, he's in the zone, don't take it personally."

My chest tightened a bit. "That's okay. I think I'm used to his legendary mood swings by now."

"You're sure?" Junior's eyes flickered with something that almost looked like sadness, gutting me a bit, telling me everything I needed to know about my car ride.

Why did I even get ready?

Why was I even trying?

It would always be like this.

This push and pull.

This need for me to go to him when he always told me to run.

Stupid.

I was seriously so stupid.

I needed to move.

It was the only option.

Any one of the bosses would take me in—I'd be safe anywhere, right?

Maybe I was jumping to conclusions, though? I wondered as I made my way outside to his waiting Tesla.

Maybe I was the exception? Not the rule? Hah, said every girl out there when they think they can change the hot guy who has no morals.

My heels clicked against the concrete as I walked toward him. Ash looked like something out of a magazine. Tall, dark, handsome—lethal. How many weapons did he have under that perfectly tailored black suit?

He wasn't wearing a tie, which meant his chest tattoos were on full view as I took careful steps toward him. The last thing I needed to do was trip in my heels and skin both knees.

His aviators hid his eyes from me.

And I hated that I'd turned into the exact girl that needed to see the guy check her out—see his eyes dilate with pleasure.

I gripped the faux snakeskin clutch in my right hand and forced a smile. "Ready?"

The only movement he made was the slight tick in his jaw; his hands were still shoved in his pockets, his body relaxed and yet tense. "Who dressed you?"

"Wow." I gritted my teeth. "You look nice too, thanks. Oh, what was that? You'll get the door for me?"

He still didn't move.

After multiple curses under his breath that had me blushing in embarrassment, he pushed away from the car and jerked open the door in one fluid movement. "Get in."

A year ago, I think I would have started to cry all over again, or at least felt the burn behind my eyes.

But tonight?

I was pissed.

Because I could see where he'd taken me against the grass, where he'd chased me, just like I could envision the pool where we nearly had sex but never finished. Or his bedroom. His bathroom.

I could count on both hands the amounts of times he'd given me this exact expression, only to act on it then blame me afterward as if I was some succubus out to lure him into my web of sex and pain.

The engine didn't roar to life when he got in. He simply pulled out of his driveway and never once looked in my direction or tried to make small talk or even say, *"Hey, last night was weird, am I right?"*

Instead, he drove.

I sat, painfully aware of my own breathing and of the tight dress.

I should have worn the stupid sweater dress.

Then again, how dare he make me feel like a whore! It was for him! Only ever for him, and he couldn't even smile?

The drive downtown was short, maybe sixteen minutes, and with each passing second, I got more and more angry to the point that all I could focus on was strangling him or just knocking that perfect smile off his face and stepping on his sunglasses, kicking off my heels and running in the opposite direction.

Ash pulled the car aggressively into the Regis while I pulled out my phone and sent off a text that may as well be a breakup.

Then again, like everyone said.

All I'd had was his face between my thighs.

His heart?

He'd buried that a long time ago, in a grave next to the church he built for the only girl to ever hold it.

And it was time.

That I finally let him go, just like I had her.

> Me: Can you arrange for me to live somewhere else?
>
> Chase: ...Are you sure that's what you want?

"Annie!" Ash snapped his fingers. "We gotta go, stop snapchatting for like two seconds, all right? There's photographers, and I have an image to uphold."

I reared back like I was staring at a monster.

And without thinking twice, deleted the NO.

And as I slowly got out of the car looked down and typed YES.

CHAPTER
Thirty

"Sometimes when we think God has written The End,
what he really means is The Beginning." —Wes Michels

Ash

My focus was complete shit.

I'd nearly blacked out when she walked toward me in that dress. I'd never been so damn thankful for sunglasses to steel my expression. Her hips, breasts, and even more so, the brave face she wore reminded me that she was trying to be strong in a world that preyed on the weak. She was beautiful. Brave. Stunning. And she hated me.

"Remember," Dad had reminded me again that morning. "Your cruelty has to sell this, Ash. It has to be believable. Every reaction she has, every moment anyone's watching the hurt in her eyes, the chaos in yours, they'll see weakness, they'll approach her—you, either or. You protect your cousins at all cost, and in this little sting, you take the fall. You wanted to be their King—now prove you can rule."

"I won't let you down, sir." I held my head high all day. This was my chance to prove to the bosses I could take down our enemies without bloodshed, using my cousins as bait—I'd earn my reputation as ruthless—and I'd outsmart even the most genius enemy.

I'd almost been cocky about it.

Until I saw the dress.

Until I saw the hurt in her eyes.

Until I noticed the way she tried to tug her dress down like it was indecent—which it was, but only because I was so distracted.

I almost missed the hotel valet completely, then really did snap when I saw Annie texting.

Was it Tank?

Had he seen her yet?

Fuck!

I hadn't meant to be short with her, I just—I felt like I'd been on the edge of this cliff, waiting to fall for her waiting for some sort of heavenly permission to feel again, and now something snapped in me.

It felt right.

And yet, the timing was all wrong when it shouldn't have been.

Had I earned her trust—really earned it, she'd know this was a ruse, that there was more, so much more than the surface, than the parts we played.

But she'd been in Italy.

And I'd been a giant dick ninety-nine percent of the time drowning so heavily in my own pain that I never got a chance to tell her.

This was the job.

My job.

I wasn't just the assassin; I was the arrogant son of a bitch son to Chase Abandonato; I had the world at my fingertips—and expected my subjects to bow.

Because the only thing worse than showing weakness.

Is showing strength.

It makes your enemies that much more angry and willing to take you down at any cost—even if it meant their own lives.

I tossed my key to the valet and then pulled a crisp hundred dollar bill out of my pocket and shoved it into his hand. Then I patted him on the cheek. "There's more where that came from."

As promised, the press was waiting outside the main doors to the lobby. I wrapped an arm around a tense Annie and grinned at them. "Just can't stay away from me, can you?" I kissed the top of Annie's head. "Guess our secrets out then, huh sweetheart?"

Her stunned expression was priceless. Had I not been sick to my stomach over the way I was treating her, I might laugh.

I waved my hand away. "Sorry guys, private party tonight, no press."

"Ash!" A woman yelled my name. "Who's the girl? Is it too soon after your girlfriend's death? It's only been over a year!"

Annie tensed, then clung to me like I was her human shield.

"Too soon?" I snorted. "It's never too soon to fuck." I squeezed Annie tight and kissed her neck. Her shocked expression was absolute kryptonite for the cameras as they fired off and started lobbing more questions at us than I could answer.

I slid my hand down to her ass only to have her elbow me in the gut. I laughed and gave her a stern look, then continued walking her into the private restaurant we'd blocked off for the night.

Champagne was flowing.

Quite literally coming from a champagne tower down the middle. A giant black and white cake sat over next to the bar where associates and our "friends" walked around and toasted to the mafia queen.

Serena had a black crown on.

It fit her well.

And how Junior was able to be wearing all black while carrying around a red scepter that doubled as a blade was beyond me.

The theme was gothic chic.

And they worked the crowd like they've always done at Eagle Elite.

Make them want.

Make them crave.

Make them bow.

Mere mortals didn't hold a candle to our influence, money, power, and just being in that room meant you had a chance.

Small.

But it was there.

You were rubbing shoulders with us.

The excitement in the room was like a drug as the music picked up in the background, Kaleo, Way Down We Go pumped through the system.

I took a glass of champagne and downed it, remembering my dad's two drink rule. The rest of the night, I'd have tonic and lime and appear to be drunk.

There was a bottle of gin back there that was just sparkling water.

Lucky me… because with the way Annie looked, I could really use a drink.

Izzy waved her over, gave her a wink, and I felt her pull away from me.

"Not a chance," I hissed. "Or have you forgotten?" I snickered in her ear. "I licked you—you're mine."

"You asshole!" Annie jerked away from me, tears filled her eyes, and then they narrowed in on me, really saw me.

I met her stare with one of my own.

People were watching me.

They always did.

Even if this was about Junior and Serena's engagement—I was the assassin, I was the one they wanted; arrogant, weak.

So I grabbed another glass of champagne and downed it while holding Annie captive, her large blue eyes calculating in a way I'd never seen before.

She was either going to knee me in the junk or knee me in the junk.

So I taunted her more.

Because I was sick.

Because sometimes I craved her tears the way I craved her touch.

Tears meant she was still fighting.

They meant she still cared.

They meant I was something.

And I realized in that moment.

Claire had never cried over me.

Not fucking once.

She'd gotten angry.

But she'd always gone along with everything I did.

And if she was upset, she'd suggest another option.

She didn't fight me.

She didn't fight for me.

She didn't fight for us.

Fuck.

"Ash…" Annie moved to cup my face. I purposely jerked away and dropped the glass to the floor.

Annie jumped back.

I slumped forward like I was already drunk and whispered gruffly, taking her face between my thumb and forefinger. "Dance with me."

"There's no way you're drunk," she hissed.

"How would you know? You've made it your job to ignore me all day, right? I make you com—"

She shoved at my chest then cupped a hand over my mouth; I bit each fingertip, God she tasted good.

I was drunk for sure.

On her.

I leaned into her even more, my body practically wrapping itself around hers. "What if I've been drinking since I drank you? What if I was pissed that your taste left my lips? Jealous of yours?"

Her cheeks burned red.

"I fucking love your taste, Annie. Tell you what. Let's do a little test; you only eat and drink what I fucking tell you—and then, I feast." I let go of her chin. "On you. It can be a… guessing game?"

Annie looked from left to right. "What are you doing?"

"You." I shrugged. "If you don't run away, then again, I did like watching you try last night…"

"Start counting, and I swear on all that's holy—"

"One." I winked. "Two." I jerked her against my chest and then pulled her roughly toward the dance floor, moving my body against hers, flipping her back, so her ass was pressed against every hard inch of me.

She let out a gasp.

I felt that gasp in my fingertips as they held firm beneath her breasts, keeping her steady, and I felt it in my soul as the rush of air left her mouth.

We were gaining more and more attention.

Good.

I flipped her around, dipped her, and then slid my hand up her thigh until I gripped bare ass cheek. I kept my face impassive, but I was dying inside. "No underwear?"

"I forgot?"

"Sure, you did." I chuckled against her neck, then pulled her to her feet and twirled her again. "Just like I forgot mine."

Her eyes narrowed. "Huh?"

"Too many clothes between us." I gripped her body tight against mine as we moved in sync. "Always too many." At her light sigh of exasperation, I looked over her head and saw several faces that were familiar and two that were not.

Security?

We hadn't hired outside security.

Annie shoved hard at my chest when I wasn't paying attention; her clutch went flying across the dance floor. Her phone tumbled out.

I reached down to grab the phone before someone stepped on it while she grabbed her purse.

And I saw a text from my dad.

Chase: I can move you into Phoenix's house

tonight. Is that good for you?

"Fuck. No." I typed back before I could think otherwise, and then I completely broke character or maybe just lost my mind as I reached for Annie and tossed her over my shoulder, phone still in hand.

We moved through a crowd of people.

I was losing my shit.

She couldn't go.

She couldn't.

Music flooded the bathroom hall as I kicked the door open. "OUT!"

The few men that were in there washing their hands ran.

I set her down and very slowly turned the lock in place on the door. "Explain this."

I waved the phone between us.

"Give that back." She glared.

"No," I barked. "Not until you tell me why!"

"You don't deserve to know!" she screamed. "You're a horrible human being who plays with people's emotions, their hearts, you get them to trust you, to love you, and then you just, you just—" Her chest heaved.

And I completely fucking lost it.

I charged, picking her up over my shoulder again and slamming our bodies against the brick wall next to the sinks. Her legs wrapped around me to hold on.

"How?"

"How what?" A tear slid down her cheek.

"How did I get a perfect creature like you—to possibly love me?"

She shook her head and then turned it to the side so I couldn't see her eyes, pissing me the hell off, and just when

I didn't think she was going to answer, she spoke in a clear, soft voice. "Lonely recognizes lonely, sad recognizes sad, desolate recognizes desolate... Lost." Her eyes met mine then. "Recognizes lost."

My mouth collided with hers in an angry force of teeth and pain as I stole kiss after kiss from her.

From this perfect girl.

With hair she probably cut just to piss me off.

With a body she hid from others because of the pain only I knew too well.

Her bruises had been on the outside, from the monster who had adopted her.

My bruises were on the inside, from the monster who commanded me—demanded blood—needed the war.

After all, a King isn't at peace unless he's fighting for it.

And I'd been fighting ever since Claire died.

And now?

Now I was tasting it.

Touching it.

My hands gripped her ass; I was so hard I couldn't think straight, didn't want to think, didn't want to plan, beyond this—beyond us.

"I had you once," I said against her mouth. "And I left you."

"Ash." Her lips parted as I kissed a trail down her neck, between the valley of her breasts. "You're still..." I sucked one of her hard nipples through the material of her dress, wetting it with my tongue, flicking it, then sucking again.

"I'm still what?" I chuckled darkly.

"Literally the devil."

I pulled back and slowly pressed her harder against the

wall, gripped her chin with my hand, eyes locked. I nuzzled her neck and whispered. "Care to sin?"

When she gasped, I invaded again, my tongue fucking her mouth the way I wanted her body.

Who the hell was I kidding?

I wanted everything.

And I was going to fucking take it.

She was mine even before I wanted it before she knew it.

Always.

"Mine," I growled like a monster, then rested her body against my pinned knee as I shimmied her tight dress past her hips.

She moved against my leg.

"Take it," I encouraged. "You're only making it easier for me to take you."

With a whimper, she fell forward, her forehead resting against my shoulder as she panted with need.

"Unbuckle my pants," I ordered.

Her blue eyes locked on mine in a challenge, a standoff that would decide everything between us.

And then she reached down and jerked open my belt, painfully, purposefully, hitting every hard inch of me as she roughly tugged it open, followed by the button of my trousers.

Without looking away, she gripped me.

It took every ounce of strength not to whimper, collapse against her, to beg for more of what I'd been needing.

Her.

We made zero sense.

I'd thought.

And now I realized.

We were the only thing that did make sense in this cruel world.

Fallen King and his Orphan Queen.

As she roughly pumped me, I leaned forward, biting down on her shoulder—my teeth would leave marks, the way her touch would imprint on my soul.

"Hard. Fast. Painful." I barely got the words out. "This isn't making love, Annie. This is a claiming."

Her eyes fell to my mouth as she whispered. "Then what are you waiting for… claim me."

I shoved her hand out of the way, pressed her up the wall, and then impaled her on me, sliding all the way down, until I was home.

In heaven.

Her heat was slick, ready for me, clenching me like she was afraid I was going to pull out and away.

Maybe because so many other times I had.

But now?

Now I was taking.

I moved her up, down, then reached up with my right hand and shoved it into her hair, messing it up, tugging it, refusing to let her be tame anymore— not even letting her hair even be tame as I held on and forced her to ride me.

"Ash, I'm already." Her eyes were wild, unfocused.

A bead of sweat ran down my temple. "Good."

"I need more." She begged so prettily, so perfectly, how could I not lift her onto the counter and pray it was clean as my hips bucked against her.

"So much." She panted. "It's so much."

"It's us." I barely got the two words out as I tried to hold myself at bay, tried to make sure she got where she needed to go, but it was too much.

Because it was us.

It was explosive.

It was all sorts of pain.

And pleasure.

And beautiful violence that we both needed.

I tugged her hair again. As she arched back, memories assaulted me of when her head hit the mirror last time we were like this.

I would kill to stay inside her forever.

I spread her thighs wide, gripped her, felt her body sucking me in, holding me hostage as she let out a scream.

My. Name.

Passion, heat, untold secrets, and lies—truths shattered between us as I followed her release.

Both of us panting, I cupped her face gently with my hands, ready to confess.

To reveal it all.

When I heard the slight tick of the lock on the door turning.

Her eyes met mine, wide with fear.

I pressed a finger to my mouth and pulled out of her, then shoved her behind me into one of the stalls, quickly pulling up my pants, flattening them, and grabbing my gun, hiding it in my jacket as I pretended to throw water on my face.

I gripped the countertop then as water dripped off my chin, noticing the reflection in the mirror.

I didn't recognize him.

But he looked... rough.

A balding head with greasy skin, a black suit that clearly

wasn't made for him, and from what I could see, a really shitty Glock that he had hidden inside of his jacket like he was going to shoot me executioner style.

"The door was locked." He pointed behind him.

"Yeah, I was jacking off." I shrugged. "Sorry, not sorry."

He frowned and started to look behind me.

A gasp sounded.

Annie?

He moved.

But so did I.

I flew into action, grabbing him by the throat and slamming him against the bathroom countertop, and then against the mirror as glass went flying.

His gun went off.

With a grunt, I broke it free from his grip and it scattered across the floor.

Blood poured from his head wound as he smiled at me like he had the upper hand. "You will lose, Abandonato."

"You the dipshit sending horses?" He frowned as I stood to my full height. "Oh, sorry, you're probably a bit slow. Um, not drunk, still a jackass, working on it, maybe I'll get therapy, who knows… oh and in case you're still confused." I smacked him on the cheek. "We all have a part to play, which I'm sure you're associates are experiencing in three, two, one—"

The bathroom door burst open.

"Heard gunshots." Valerian had his gun trained on us along with Junior, Tank, and Serena.

"Kill me." The man shrugged. "I don't care. I won't talk."

"That's okay," Tank sneered from his position. "The FBI already moved in ten minutes ago… we have three of your men ready to give us everything as long as they don't get life."

His face paled. "They wouldn't dare."

"They already did." Tank put his gun away and pulled out his badge. "You're officially under arrest for—"

"D-dad." Annie's voice sounded on a gasp as she moved out of the stall and stumbled to my side.

His face darkened with hatred. "You? You're still alive after I sold you to those De Lange men?" He let out a laugh. "Ah, of course you are; you always were such a resilient bitch. What? Did you whore yourself out like your mother did to one of ohhhh—" He eyed Ash. "I see... sex for protection, clever, clever—"

"I love him," she said in a low voice. "And you died, I saw the reports, you killed Mom then killed yourself before I went into the system before those men came to the house!"

"The system and those hired men should have taken care of my problem—you." He sneered. "A Sinacore under my roof!" He spat, "MINE! You were too dangerous to keep the older you got."

Annie lifted her chin.

She didn't cry.

She just stared at him.

At this man that forced her mother to go to another man to have a baby.

I imagined her pain.

I wanted to end him.

I searched the floor for the gun, and that was when I noticed she was holding it as if she wasn't afraid, as if she'd held one before.

Of course.

Italy.

"Tank." She said his name, making me want to roar with

anger. "Please leave."

"Aw shit, Annie—"

"I'm in this now, right?" she asked in a shaky voice.

"Blood in," I said gently. "No out."

She lifted the gun. "You murdered my mom!"

He held up his hands. "You don't have the guts, you're spineless, gentle, just like her, wouldn't even hurt a—"

Two shots fired.

Directly.

Into.

His.

Dick.

She didn't miss.

He howled with pain, collapsing to the floor, blood went everywhere, and then with shaking hands, she dropped the gun and lifted her chin. "Death would be too kind."

He screamed her name as I reached for her hand and nodded to Junior. "Clean this up, will you?"

He cracked his knuckles. "With fucking pleasure."

"Think of it as an early wedding present." I patted him on the shoulder.

"I knew we were best friends for a reason." He grinned, shutting the bathroom door behind him.

I didn't give Annie time to think.

To panic.

I just grabbed her by the hand and walked us through the lobby nodding to the associates I knew would clean up and listen to every word from Junior.

And when we got to the elevator.

I looked back.

Tank stared at us.

He sighed, and then he called into his lapel. "All clear."

"Thank you," I mouthed as the doors closed.

He nodded his head, and then he was back in FBI mode.

"I can't believe I just did that." Tremors rocked Annie from head to foot.

"I can. I knew you had some rage inside you." I pulled her into my arms. "Now, let's go wash it all off."

"The blood?"

"No." I kissed the top of her head. "The rage."

CHAPTER
Thirty-One

"Unable for the loved to die, for love is immortality."—
Emily Dickinson

Annie

I still felt him between my legs.

Tasted his lips.

And then I saw it.

Him.

The dad I was born with.

The one that basically trafficked me into another Family
like an item sent to the Goodwill… or the trash.

I collapsed against Ash.

With a curse, he lifted me into his arms.

We made it to the penthouse suite, or I assumed so since
it said PH, and as we walked down the hall, several associates
were stationed at each exit like Ash had been planning this all
along.

"I may be the devil," he muttered. "But that doesn't mean I didn't want to give you heaven after your descent into hell."

I frowned as he tossed his card to a cousin standing by our door. "Hey Dom, can you let us in and then just guard..."

Dom grinned. "That why you gave us all earplugs?"

"It's because I care," Ash teased.

"Asshole," Dom groaned. "You know we're not allowed to silence anything that happens in that room, but..." He smiled at me. "...I swear we'll conveniently forget anything ever happened."

"Excellent." Ash moved into the suite, the door clicked behind us.

The room was ginormous.

With a panoramic view of the city and Lake Michigan.

"You like it?" Ash whispered, setting me on my feet.

I nodded. "Did they have this available last minute or—"

Ash scoffed. "I'm not an amateur; I booked this yesterday." My eyebrows shot up. "And paid off the rich dude who was supposed to stay overnight."

A bucket of champagne was waiting next to two flutes on the main living room table.

It made a popping sound when he opened it.

"We can talk about my job—what I do for the Family other than kill, or we can wash off the night, order room service, and put on something that makes girls feel better... Hallmark? That Netflix princess one?"

My jaw dropped as I stared at him. "You weren't drunk. You were... pretending..." Heat swamped my face. "In the bathroom were you pretending too—"

"Wow, my dick thanks you for the compliment, but you can't pretend something that big, hard..." he winked. "Pulsating."

I groaned.

"What? Too far?"

"You always go too far," I pointed out.

"I thought that was part of my charm?"

I shrugged, lifting a hand to tuck my hair only to realize it was trembling. Ash was at my side in an instant. Taking my hand, pressing it against his cheek. "It's over."

"He sold me."

"He'll burn in Hell," Ash said softly. "Devil." He patted his chest proudly. "I know things."

I laughed and then rested my cheek over his heart, absorbed its steady beat. "So, you really are the protector of the family, drawing everyone out with your asshole ways."

"Of course, you'd figured it out." He rested his chin on my head. "Most people just think I'm mean, family included"

"You are mean," I pointed out. "But it's a necessary cruelty."

"Mmm..." His arms held me tight. Protecting me. Holding me close. "Annie?"

"Yeah?"

"Since your dad's the asshole who threw you away—does that really mean I get to keep you?"

I froze, a smile forming on my face as I pulled back and looked up into his eyes and whispered, "I'd start counting—you have to catch me first."

"Ten." His eyes flashed. "Nine."

I had no idea where I was running.

Only that no matter what direction I went in.

It would end up in his arms.

Always.

The gleam in his eyes was my undoing.

"Catch me," I taunted.

And then I ran.

I ran down the hall took, a left, and ended up in a gorgeous bathroom.

Trapped.

It was modern.

A huge tub was in front of me.

Normally I'd give in.

Tell him he won.

Instead, I decided to crawl in and hide.

I leaned my head back, my legs slightly spread since I couldn't straighten them.

"Hmmmmm…" Ash's deep voice sent chills down my spine. "Where could my little Annie have gone?"

I bit down on my bottom lip to keep the joy inside—which was nearly impossible.

Because Ash.

My Ash.

My tormentor.

Mine.

Was chasing me.

His gorgeous head of whiskey-colored hair fell over his forehead as he leaned over the tub and then lowered himself in, over my body. Wordlessly, he nudged my head aside as he started filling the tub with cold water, then hot.

I waited, teeth chattering as water swirled around us, as the warmth of his body kept me secure, safe.

And when it turned hot, when he turned those icy blue eyes back on me, he pressed a kiss to my forehead and then lowered my hair back into the tub.

"You were baptized in fire… in rejection. In horror." He lifted my head, heavy with water, cradling my neck as he whispered. "And now, bathed, baptized—pure."

I reached for him.

He grabbed my body, our mouths slammed together as water sloshed around the bath.

I moved onto him, straddling his body as we tried to tug our wet clothes away. They were suddenly offensive, separating us.

He gritted his teeth as he kicked his wet pants down.

The sound of the tub filling was like a white noise of passion as I lifted my dress over my head and tossed it to the wet white marble ground.

Our clothes joined.

And then so did we.

In that tub.

Mouths fused.

Bodies flushed.

Hot.

One.

"Finders…" He thrust into me. "Keepers."

"Good." I forgot my own name, only able to say his, over and over again. "I'm yours."

He flipped us around, so I was pressed back against the tub wall, and then he surged like the water, filling me deep, pinning me, his eyes fierce, his muscles taut.

In that moment, he wasn't cruel Ash.

Assassin.

Mean.

He was a god.

King.

Mine.

CHAPTER
Thirty-Two

"Mostly it is loss which teaches us the worth of things."
—Arthur Schopenhauer

Ash

It didn't seem real. Having Annie actually in my arms—no arguing.

Quiet.

The light of the moon filtering past the thick black hotel curtains as I pulled her into my arms and then the sheets over both of us. I couldn't stop staring at her, at how peaceful she looked.

Earlier tonight, she'd looked ready to raise hell with barely a scrap of gorgeous white dress wrapped around her body like a snack.

Now? Now she was naked against me, her skin pink from the bath, her lips swollen from the kisses.

I ran my hands through her short dark hair. "Be honest, you cut your hair because you wanted to kill my soul, right?"

She stilled, then looked up at me, her eyes flickering. "You hate it."

I sighed and kissed her head. As far as she'd come with her confidence, I needed to remember that she still needed the words, the actions, needed me to tell her how beautiful she was. How mine she was. I was owned. As cliche as it sounded, she was what I needed without even knowing, so I gave her the gentled words as I pulled her against me. "I love everything about you; I just feel like this was a giant fuck you, Ash..."

Her laugh had me smiling as she leaned up and flicked my chest, her blue eyes sparkling. "It was."

I gripped her fingers and kissed each one. "Then again, it backfired when I didn't recognize you. Shit, I'm an idiot." I fell back against the bed as she splayed halfway across me.

Her fingertips spread across my chest. "Say it again."

I reached for her hand. "Hell no, my ego's extremely fragile post-sex."

She jerked her fingers away and punched me in the chest; I caught her hand and kissed her fingertips again, then grabbed the remote. "So, what will your poison be?"

"Anything torturous... you deserve it after putting me through that tonight. The way I see it, I should have full control of the remote."

"And yet..." I pulled it back. "Who's holding it?"

She batted her eyelashes at me. "Who's holding you?"

"Damn it." I sighed. "So what will it be?"

Her smile was conniving; my dick and I liked it because her eyes were hooded, her breaths came in short pants, and we remembered what that felt like, and I wanted her again.

"Something that makes you want to jump out that window like It's a Small World at Disneyland..."

"And I'm the devil," I grumbled as she brought me back from my wicked fantasies. I wouldn't trade it though. I loved it. Loved that we were talking, loved that I was holding her, that she knew me, saw me, not as the cruel playboy assassin, but just me. "So?"

"Die Hard?" she offered.

"Very funny."

"No look." She pointed at the TV. "It's on, and I love Bruce Willis."

"Are you trying to get laid again?" I pulled her until she was flush against me. "Because it's working... honestly though, that may have been the hottest thing I've ever seen."

She frowned up at me, her face makeup-free, clean, beautiful. "Die Hard?"

I rolled my eyes. "Not Bruce, you holding a gun, and I still get rock hard imagining you dressed up as a librarian."

"I never dressed up as a librarian." Her pretty eyes narrowed into a confused frown that had me wanting to reach up and kiss her.

I grinned mischievously. "We sure about that? Because my vision's extremely clear," I groaned. "I fucking loved it, daydreamed about pulling your hair about a million times."

She gave me a shove. "Wow, imagine had I just grabbed my favorite ruler out of my bag and smacked you with it then bit into an apple..."

"Fuck." I flipped her onto her back, collapsed my body weight against her. "Only as long as you tell me to try to be quiet while I sink into you behind a stack of dusty books."

She burst out laughing. Free. She was free. "Let me guess

you're going to shove them all off the desk."

"There really isn't any other move for that situation, Annie." I gave a serious nod. "And I am a fucking professional."

Her eyes heated. "Die Hard in the background... You... in my mouth."

I completely froze, afraid I'd ruin the moment by being an ass again, and then I blurted, "Are you sure? It's been a long night and—"

I allowed her to shove me to the side of the bed, and then she was ducking under the covers as I tried to mutter out. "I'm an idiot, just kidding, carry on, shit—"

"Finders Keepers." Her lips moved against my cock.

"Yes," was all I could squeeze out. "Hell... yes."

I dug my fingers into her short hair.

And I vowed to keep her forever.

CHAPTER
Thirty-Three

"Do you wish to be remembered? Leave a lot of debts."
—Elbert Hubbard

Ash

We spent all night talking.

And then not talking at all.

And then sleeping, only to wake up again and kiss.

"So you thought your dad died?" I whispered between kisses.

"Mmm…" She kissed me back and then shrugged. "He killed my mom then himself; apparently, he just killed her and had it all set up, I can't believe he'd do that, but his hatred for her was deep. She ruined his plans. She was supposed to go to Luis Sinacore, get pregnant with a son, and come back to him. Instead, she got pregnant with me, fell in love, then had such a horrible labor, according to my dad—I ruined her. Broke her."

"Not true," I whispered. "He may have thought you broke

her, but you put me back together again."

She cupped my face. "It's impossible, you know."

"Fixing me?"

"Being drawn to you." Annie sniffled. "Even when you're a complete ass who deserves to get strangled to death."

"Harsh." I put a hand across my chest; she gripped it and held it tight.

"I mean it." Her eyes were clear, focused solely on me. "I wasn't terrified when I first met you, I told myself it was terror, but it was something else it was…" She chewed her lower lip, sucking it in and out, then finally a bright smile. "It was you. Maybe there's no way to explain Ash Abandonato, except he's dark when he needs to be, light when it's asked of him—hero and villain. I can't imagine you any other way."

I kissed her swollen mouth. "I hate that I wasted time, that you were gone, that I sent you away." I frowned then. "Why did you leave?"

It was the first time I saw uncertainty in her eyes. "Not tonight… later… I'll tell you later."

"Promise?"

"Always." She kissed me.

And I spent the rest of the morning smiling like a fool, then the rest of the afternoon ready to consume her again only to get blindsided by every single cousin with a party at my pool house.

Apparently, we were trending on Twitter for a while, me and Annie, and her horrified expression in that gorgeous dress as I kept her close.

Booze was set up around my kitchen, pizza, pasta—basically anything and everything Maksim could order in with his DoorDash app.

And everyone was there.

My friends.

My family.

We split up the party—the bosses were all with my dad in the house playing ping pong, which still weirded the shit out of all of us because what the hell happened to poker? I mean, mafia? Really?

They even had a fucking chalkboard with their tournaments.

Weird. So weird.

I grabbed a whiskey and coke and sat on my couch while Annie and Serena laughed in the corner.

She belonged.

Here.

With me.

Anywhere else just seemed, such a waste, of a good person, of her. And I needed her goodness, her ability to challenge me even when she was scared. I needed someone who knew themselves, knew themselves well.

"So funny story..." King plopped down next to me, wearing a black beanie and a shirt that said. Fight me. "Junior here saw a ghost last night."

"Shut the hell up," Junior groaned and downed the rest of whatever he was drinking; he grabbed the remote and changed the channel to some weird reality show shit that had the girls animated instantly. "Hate that guy."

"Whyyyyyy?" Maksim groaned. "Why are we watching The Bachelor?"

"Oh, I don't know." Izzy appeared behind us. "Are you jealous, Maks? Because he has balls, and you have... whatever you have down there... dangling between your sad, pathetic legs?"

She blew him a kiss.

I whistled. "Bro, not that I want you having sex with my sister, but what the hell did you say to her to get her so hostile."

"I have this answer." Tank strolled in with a beer and groaned. "He called her a what was it? Dirty whore. Yup, I think I got it right."

I glared at Maksim. "Are you fucking kidding me?"

"TWO SIDES, MAN!" Maksim yelled. "To every story! And we're getting sidetracked; Junior saw a ghost!"

All the guys quieted while Valerian burst into laughter. "Yeah, a ghost, okay... and after Christmas, how rare..."

Junior shuddered like he was scared shitless. Junior of all people. He was never scared. Scary, yes, scared, no.

"Are we sure?" Valerian grinned. "That it wasn't Maksim dressed in cosplay again."

"That was once!" Maksim yelled.

"And fucking hilarious," King added. "Your outfit was see-through."

"Jingle Balls, Jingle Balls," I sang, earning a pillow in my direction with a yell that Christmas was over.

"Adrenaline." Junior nodded. "It had to have been adrenaline because it really did scare the shit out of me. I didn't sleep all night, but I think, and not to bring up past shit, but I think it just had to do with us bringing part of our enemies down last night. So much was tied in with Claire." He shot me a sad look. "She died because we were targets, and I think my subconscious was just... sad all over again, for you, us, her."

Misery washed over me, and then Annie waved at me from her spot in the kitchen.

Fresh start.

We could have this fresh start.

It could be different.

Maybe it wouldn't be the same, but did that make it any less beautiful? No. Not with Annie. With her, it would still be... glorious. Like a sunrise.

I caught her eye, and with a laugh, she strolled over and wrapped her arms around my neck from behind.

I tilted back and lifted my chin, meeting her halfway with a kiss that had everyone groaning around us.

I couldn't stop smiling.

And I hated how long it took me to get to this place, with myself, with her.

My emotions were overwhelming as I held her close, and I knew nothing. Nothing in the world would change this.

Ever.

CHAPTER
Thirty-Four

"Sometimes you will never know the value of a moment until it becomes a memory."—Dr. Seuss

Chase

The Past: The Day of The Accident

"Tank," I barked into the phone. "I'm busy; what is it?"

He was quiet. Was he crying? Not breathing?

"Tank," I ground out.

"She's... she's okay."

"Who?" I roared. Imagining my daughters, my wife, anyone I loved getting hurt had me crushing the phone until I was sure it would crumble into tiny pieces of dust.

"Claire." He sighed. "I mean, she looks rough, but she's okay... at least I think she is, the doctors aren't... they aren't fully sure yet because there could be some internal damage."

"Fuck!" I roared. "What the hell happened?"

"Cut brakes, meant for Ash, you need to get down here, Nikolai's already seen her, but she's asking for you."

Those words.

Those damning words.

"Okay." I hung up.

I slid my phone into my pocket.

I stared out the kitchen window.

The same one I watched my son play outside with his siblings, the same one I saw him walk through with Claire on his arm, declaring her his.

The same window.

The same fucking window I saw so many things through.

And yet, they were never clear, were they?

Altered, yes they were altered by the angle of the sun, the moon, the thickness of the glass; I only saw what I wanted.

I only saw what I needed to see.

So did Ash.

And Claire?

She only saw Ash.

Until she didn't.

Until. She. Didn't.

Did she ever even realize it?

Memories assaulted me then of a moment so long ago when I'm sure Luca or Frank, the original bosses, stared out a different window and watched me walk in, with Trace on my arm, after Nixon's so-called death.

I claimed her as mine.

I wanted her.

I wanted her too much.

And then I realized it wasn't my path.

Nixon had known, though, and he'd been willing, he'd

been what I couldn't be, and I hadn't even realized it until that moment.

I'm sure they watched like I did then.

I'm sure they were silent like I so often was.

Letting all of us figure out the pain on our own, knowing we would suffer, knowing there would be tears, blood, pain.

But knowing, in the end, it would be worth it.

"God." I clutched the kitchen sink and lowered my head. "Forgive me… Forgive me…"

"Everything okay?" Luc came up behind me, sliding her arms around my middle, holding me tight, resting her head against my back.

All roads had led to her.

The excruciating pain had been worth it.

The moments of darkness.

When I thought I knew what was best for me, for family, for everyone around me.

But the universe knew.

Hell, maybe God took pity.

But they led me to her.

"Something's happened," I whispered, my voice shook. Because my son.

My son would suffer.

And I couldn't see past his pain—to hers.

"Claire's been in an accident."

Luc gasped then hugged me tighter. "What hospital? We need to go. Now!"

"Yeah." I lowered my head, in prayer, in reverence, in forgiveness. "One more minute, Luc. Give me one more minute to be the father I need to be, for the son I never deserved."

"Chase, what—"

"The sun..." I held her tight. "It's beautiful today... like a new beginning."

"A new beginning," she agreed. "Are you sure you're okay?"

No. "I have you. How could I not be?" I turned and crushed her against me. "Our son needs us now. I need you."

She looked up at me with wonder in her eyes and said, "Where else would I be? Than by your side?"

She confirmed it.

My wife.

Her words.

Her confidence.

A half-hour later, I walked into that room, and I sat while machines hummed and beeped all around us.

I reached for her hand, and I squeezed.

She squeezed back.

The door closed as Nikolai cleared his throat. "I'm ready."

I sighed.

But she squeezed.

So I nodded my head.

I left that room.

Ten minutes later, Nikolai was back out, and my son was running down the halls, tears streaming down his face.

And all I could think was.

What in God's name.

Had. I. Done.

CHAPTER
Thirty-Five

"That it will never come again is what makes life so sweet." —Emily Dickinson

Annie

I t felt right.

Being with them.

In that room.

Drinking, celebrating, letting my guard down. About a dozen times, Ash glanced over, his eyes full of heat.

He was wearing a tight black T-shirt and skinny jeans, barefoot with his tats showing and his hair all mussed—and he'd never looked so wrecked and sexy.

I'd had my hands on that body.

My fingers combing through that unruly hair.

Mean? Yeah, but he was *my* mean.

He crooked his finger.

I rolled my eyes even as my feet took me over to him as I

wrapped my arms around his neck from behind. He lifted his chin for a kiss, and I gave, fully, willingly, because he was mine.

Because finally, we were moving on. Both of us, together.

With the memory of her, a dangling necklace of hope between our bodies.

One that told us both that we could grieve.

Love.

Move on.

And still, have a part of her.

His lips moved against mine; he tasted like whiskey and coke and all things Ash. How did a person have a taste? He somehow did, like bad decisions you'll never regret even if you end up in prison.

Damn Abandonatos.

I swear they were an addiction in and of themselves.

"Pool," he whispered against my neck. "Five minutes?"

My breath hitched. "But everyone's here…"

"Like that stopped me the first time." He nipped my neck. "Run."

With a giddy laugh, I took off toward the door earning groans and cursing from everyone as if they knew exactly what sort of game we were playing.

"Hey, Serena," I heard Junior call. "Run!"

"Hey, Junior," she called back. "Run, Bitch."

I heard scrambling.

Something like a knife clattering against the floor.

Laughter.

And a body getting tackled against the stairway.

Ash was mine, but maybe they were mine too.

I smiled, jogged back to the house, opened the sliding glass door, and paused as all the bosses were playing ping pong.

Like they literally had three tables set up.

Sweat was pouring like wine.

The wives were in a corner playing cards.

Everyone looked up.

I bit down on my lower lip. "Scary mafia, party of one."

Chase pointed his paddle at me. "Tell no one."

I held up my hands. "Yeah, your secret's safe with me."

He nodded and then turned to his opponent, Dante, the Alfero boss. "You let me beat you, and I'll give you the new Lambo."

"Nope, old man." He winked. "I'm young and impressionable."

"You're in your thirties!"

"Careful, don't wanna break a hip," he teased.

Chase yelled.

Tex yelled on Chase's behalf, and I laughed as I ran up the stairs really quick to grab a swimsuit and some sweats—even though I wouldn't need them—to cover my body, after all, it was January and freezing.

I pulled my hair into a short ponytail and vowed to let my hair grow out, for him and me, because I'd loved my hair.

My cheeks were red, my lips nearly bruised from all the kissing, and I wore it with pride.

The mark of Ash.

The one I'd always wanted.

He'd seen me.

Treated me with respect when it counted.

Killed, actually killed my adoptive dad when he saw the bruises.

And he kept Claire's promise.

He watched over me, even while it hurt.

As he bled all over the floor, he still watched over me.

As he tried to get his revenge, he still hugged me.

"You're not his anymore," I whispered into the universe. "Maybe you never were... maybe, Claire." I sniffed. "Maybe you were just the path that led to him, to my forever."

I swiped the tears on my cheeks and turned off the lights since I'd be spending the night with Ash. I ran down the stairs and laughed as Chase yelled at Dante for cheating, and the wives all started pouring wine.

Luc winked in my direction.

How had I gotten so lucky?

I went from lonely—to ginormous, insane, Italian family.

I was still smiling when I left the warmth of the house for the frigid chill outdoors.

I was about to call out Ash's name since he was just standing there when I heard him say.

"Claire."

I almost corrected him... maybe he was having a moment of—

"Hi Annie," the voice said.

I turned.

And there her ghost stood.

I stumbled backward onto the cement, scraping my hands in an effort to catch myself.

And yet Ash just stood there like a statue.

"I, um..." Claire had lighter hair; she looked thinner, but otherwise, the same gorgeous friend.

My only friend.

"I, um, have a lot to say, but..." Her eyes went to Ash.

His jaw was clenched.

As were his fists.

"Claire?" Tears streamed down my face.

And then, selfishly, it hit me.

I let myself hope.

I let myself love him.

I let myself fall.

And the love of his life was standing right in front of him, as if resurrected, looking gorgeous, healthy.

Whole.

Her smile was sad but bright, beautiful, and I'd never felt more like an interloper, an impostor in my life.

"Ash?" I asked, maybe pleaded. I just needed him to tell me it was okay, that I just needed to calm down, to breathe, that this was all just a horrible mistake, that he knew she'd been alive and still fell for me, still loved me.

But he said nothing.

Too stunned?

Too happy?

I scrambled to my feet. "Ash?"

Slowly, he shook his head.

I reached for him and then stopped myself as my heart sank to my stomach, then down to my feet only to crash against the concrete.

He'd built her a chapel.

I'd left her my pearls.

I started walking backward until my tears made it impossible to move without swiping them away, then running.

I gripped the sliding glass door, stumbled inside, unable to breathe and unable to focus as I collapsed onto the ground.

Luc was there in seconds.

Then Chase.

I clawed at the kitchen floor, and then I screamed. Was

that scream mine? Was this person me? Sobbing so hard she couldn't breathe.

"Hey, hey." Sergio slapped me lightly on the face. "Take deep breaths, calm…"

Tex and Phoenix shared a look, then Andrei was moving toward the door cursing up a storm.

But my focus went to Chase.

His eyes fell to mine.

In apology.

In knowledge.

So I closed mine.

So he couldn't see my pain.

Or notice how the last remnants of my heart that were truly Ash's just collapsed within themselves, leaving me nothing but darkness and despair.

Alone.

My fault.

My mom said to trust the Abandonatos.

And I gave them everything.

And now.

I had nothing.

Nothing but a heartbeat inside a shell of a body.

And still, Ash wasn't here.

And why would he be?

I swayed to my feet, shoving past everyone as I numbly walked up the stairs and into my room—possibly the last night I'd be there.

I went to the bathroom and turned on the faucets—both of them.

Then the shower.

And once the sound of water falling was almost too

much—I screamed.

Until I wanted to die.

And in the furthest recess of my mind, I heard a voice whisper—you just did.

"Is this yours?" Chase held up a pregnancy test. "I wanted to ask before I went to my daughter's..."

I burst into tears. "I can't, Chase. I can't. I tried. I wanted to help. I love him. I'm so sorry."

He pulled me into his arms.

The missing piece of the puzzle.

"Sadly, so ironic, isn't it?" Chase said mysteriously. "This is Ash's?"

I couldn't trust myself to speak, but I could nod. "I was trying... he thought I was... someone else."

Chase's jaw flexed. "Fucking ruined him."

Ruined me, I wanted to say. Instead, I said in a small voice, "Please, please just... send me away."

"You're under our protection... but okay."

I still remembered that night, six weeks later, when I sent Chase the text that was still so painful that I wanted to die again.

It was the first time I contemplated it as I typed.

"Miscarriage."

He'd made sure I had family around me.

I had the best doctors.

He called every day.

But all I kept thinking was this happened because my mom, the only person I trusted in my life, said to go to the Abandonatos.

And all Ash had ever done was hurt and live up to his name, Abandon.

CHAPTER
Thirty-Six

"Sometimes the heart sees what is invisible to the eye."
—H. Jackson Brown Jr.

Ash

"What. The. Hell." Junior roared from behind me, and within minutes all the bosses were filing out of the house, surrounding us.

And there she fucking stood.

My angel.

My demon.

My dream.

My nightmare.

It was impossible to hear anything past the roar of my own pain and anger as Claire stared me down like she fucking belonged in my yard after all the carnage she'd left in her wake.

"Why?" It was all I could say.

Her eyes darted around to the audience we now had.

She lowered her head. "I saw the news, the tweets, about you and Annie." Her smile was sad. "Not really what I had in mind when I said protect her."

I heard myself growl like an out of body experience.

She held up her hands. "I wasn't supposed to come back, not like this, never like this, but then I, just, I realized that maybe." Tears filled her eyes. "Maybe I was too scared. Wrong." Her eyes fell to someone behind me. A hand touched my shoulder.

I imagined my dad.

Junior.

Maybe even Valerian.

But it was Tank.

Tank of all people that looked ready to rage a war on one small female. He gripped my shoulder and stood there.

And then, Junior followed.

Maksim.

Serena.

Valerian.

Until all of my cousins stood by my side, adding their strength.

Claire let out a shudder. "I thought so. But it was worth it. Because I realized..." Tears spilled over her cheeks. "That you were always worth it, and I didn't deserve you, I didn't understand. I let myself... create this perfect life in my head, and then it didn't happen, and I resented you—all of you, so I went to your dad." She hiccupped out another sob, covering her mouth. "I messed up so bad that I couldn't come out of it."

"What?" My voice was hoarse. "Did you do?"

Her eyes were clear as she whispered. "I lied about being pregnant, I thought it would force your hand, get us out, make things normal, and then I realized my mistake, but it was too late. I was too late."

My entire body went rigid and then deflated like she'd just stabbed me in the heart a million times over. "You lied about our baby?"

"Yes."

"I PROPOSED!" I roared, slamming my hand against my chest as Tank held me back. "I FUCKING LOVED YOU!"

She burst into heavy sobs. "I loved you too… but not, not enough to give up actual life away from this, not enough…" She sobbed. "Not enough."

"I'm sorry then." I found my voice. "I'm sorry I proposed with a two million dollar ring. I'm sorry I built you a fucking chapel to get married in. I'm sorry I did everything, everything in order to be enough for you. I'm sorry you had to fake a baby." My voice cracked. "My baby!" I lunged again. Tank held me firm, Junior gripped my other arm. "My money. My house. My love." I shook my head as a tear spilled onto my cheek. "I'm sorry I mourned someone who thought nothing of walking away. I'm sorry. Not you. You're weak. Not sorry."

She fell to the ground. "I snuck in on Nikolai's plane, I just…" She cried. "I wanted to see you, and then you were so happy."

Tank growled. "Because that's what people fucking do when they're family, Claire! They weep, mourn, fight, hate, move on, and love, only to repeat it! How fucking dare you do that to my family! To my friend!"

Stunned, I looked over at him, his chest was heaving, his eyes full of tears. "How dare you!" He repeated.

And then it was me holding him back.

Tank.

Our FBI agent.

Adopted brother.

Friend.

He defended me.

Like he'd done Annie.

I almost laughed like an insane person because what the ever-loving hell was I even doing?

Mourning someone who never really existed in the first place? Who lied? Who chose herself and her vision of her future over me?

"It's okay." I patted Tank on the back and then turned to my dad. "You knew?"

"Me." He nodded. "Nikolai. Her request. As you know, per our rules. If you want out. You have to die. The accident was real, her injuries… were not."

"And Annie?" I roared. "What about her?"

"Innocent." She gulped. "I just… She was abused, I wanted to help her, and I knew that since I had to die—you would."

"I did." I nodded. "I am."

"I know." Her lower lip trembled. "I'm not sorry for loving you."

I almost sneered, *"you should be."*

But I wasn't that man anymore.

Because of Annie, I was different.

So I gave her a sad smile and said. "I'm not sorry either—because your selfish love—brought me her."

Claire sucked in a sob, her eyes filling with tears. "I know that now."

"Junior," I barked. "Take her to the airstrip." I pointed at my dad. "And you. You fix what needs to be fixed." My eyes searched for Phoenix. "Make sure her identity is intact." I

snapped my fingers. "Sergio, I need all cameras blocked from
the airstrip to our house; if she needs a new identity, do that
too. Keep her safe." I looked back. "To hurt her would hurt
Annie."

"Right away... boss." Junior smiled.

And the old bosses, the ones I had no business even talking
to, let alone ordering around, moved.

They moved into action.

And as I rushed toward the house.

Toward her.

I heard Phoenix and Nixon both mutter. "King. The true
Abandonato heir."

"Mine," Dad said with love, authority, affection.

"Yours," I whispered, hoping Annie, in all her confusion
and anger, somehow heard me. Felt me.

Knew me.

My soul.

My heart.

It was hers now.

Hers.

CHAPTER
Thirty-Seven

"They did not leave your life, I moved them." —God

Annie

Rain suddenly started to pour outside.

Reminding me that maybe it was a bad omen.

Loving him, in her place, in mine.

Selfishly wanting him but needing him to stop drinking his life away or taking pills.

She'd done that.

So I hated her in that moment.

I hated that he'd love her.

He'd marry her in that perfect chapel with the fireflies and my mom's pearls; she'd get everything for hurting him.

For breaking Ash—she'd earn him.

And I couldn't love that.

Or be okay with it.

But what could I do?

She was the love of his life, and I was the orphan girl who literally didn't stop wanting him, needing him, pushing him, caring for him.

I was basically the nurse until she was all better and decided to come back and actually own up to her horrible mistakes.

How the hell was she even alive?

Thunder roared.

Rain fell.

Just like my tears.

Just like that first night, I tried to take her place—not for me, for him.

A door opened, and then Ash's voice sounded. "Are you trying to flood the house now, or is this another weird fetish?"

I looked up, vision blurry. "W-what are you doing here?"

Slowly, Ash went to the shower, turned it off, peeled his drenched shirt over his head, and tossed it to the floor in a loud *thunk*. He went to the sinks next, his eyes never leaving mine, and then he knelt next to me and smiled. "Kind of live here."

"What?" What was happening? Where was Claire? Why was he here? In my room?

"In this house," he corrected. "Not this room, keep up." He reached for my chin and tilted it up toward him. "They should be gone by now."

"What? Huh? What are you—" I fought against him, but he held me tight.

And just like the rain, I fell.

Every last tear just released from my body as I banged him with my fists, wishing he would love me more, knowing he couldn't.

"I hate you!" I yelled. "I hate you!"

"I know." He gripped me tighter against him. "I know."

"Leave then!" I shoved against his chest, but he refused to move. "Just leave! Go with her! Be happy!"

"But I'm not!" He set me on my feet. "Not without you. I go nowhere without you. Don't you see? This is how it's meant to be. You and me. I didn't see it before. I refused to. I ignored the signs, the fights, everything, because how could someone, how? Just how?" He sighed, lowering his head until it touched mine. "She lied about the baby."

I gasped and immediately touched my own stomach. "Wh-what?"

"She lied." He kissed my head. "It was her twisted way of thinking I'd change my mind about my job—the one you saw and experienced the other night."

"But why?" I couldn't fathom it. "Why?"

He kissed my head again. "Exactly why I love you."

"No!" I shook my head. "I can't do it, Ash, I can't do some goodbye screw before you leave me, I can't, I can't! Please just go!"

He started carrying me down the stairs despite my fighting him and then stopped at the bottom. "Where the hell would I go?"

"With Claire!" I screamed in defeat. "Why are you still here?" So she lied, that didn't mean he didn't love her!

"Oh Annie, I thought I told you before... when that bomb was in my room, when you were there with your light, your goodness." He tilted my chin up toward him and whispered. "Because here is where you are."

His mouth covered mine.

I gasped; his tongue was invasive, his body hot.

The cool night air hit me as he carried me outside. "I thought I said pool in five minutes—"

"But Ash."

"We can talk later," he whispered. "Until the stars fall."

I froze beneath his kiss. "Ummm."

"You." He kissed me again and then, "It was you wasn't it? That night? Not Claire?"

Tears fell again. "Yes, and I'm so sorry. I got pregnant, and I didn't tell you, and I told your dad, and then I lost him—"

Ash went completely still next to me. "Wh-what?"

I'd never heard him stutter before or miss a beat.

Rain poured down around us as I yelled. "I'm sorry."

"For getting... what?"

I pulled away. "Pregnant. Obviously, it wasn't planned, and you were so mean to me, so hurt..." I hugged myself or attempted to, but he just refused, pulling me into his lap and kissing every inch of my face. "It's okay—I lost the baby, in Italy."

"No! No!" he roared, hands shaking, body pale as his swollen lips descended. "Never. It will never be okay. What the hell? You did that alone? Without me? And I was... I was..." He stumbled a bit.

I clung to him as he lowered us fully clothed into the warm pool, near the shallow end where our chaos started over a year ago. "Ash, really."

"Annie... really," he deadpanned. His expression softened. "You lost a baby—our baby—without me by your side. That's unforgivable. I really am the devil."

"Ash." I sighed. "Really, you're here now... right?"

"I'm not leaving your side." He vowed as his voice cracked. "And as of right now, you're not leaving mine."

"But—"

"Mine." He captured my mouth. "Forever."

I pulled back with a sad smile. "And Claire?"

"On a flight out tomorrow," he said without remorse. "I'm not saying that we don't have a lot of shit to go over, but I do know one thing." He kissed me roughly again. "It's you. And if she in all her mistakes brought me you? I can't be mad. I can't."

I laughed, and then a tear escaped. "That was very romantic for such an asshole."

His smile was sad. "I try." He spun me against the shallow end stairs. "Now, let me show you how much I love you."

"Drown me in it, Ash, drown me." I whimpered as he pulled me into the deep end and started to kiss.

Clothes came off in slow motion.

And then it was just us.

Finally joined.

Him pressing me up against the wall, my hair a tangled mess as he tugged and pulled. My lips parted as his tongue met mine.

And as the rain poured.

As he thrust into me.

I welcomed him home.

To our home.

"I missed you when you were gone..." he confessed. "I missed you every day."

"I missed you too," I cried out when he kissed down my neck, his fingers finding my core. "So much."

Baptized.

Reborn.

Or maybe just... living.

He was mine.

I was his.

Regardless of the past.

This.

This destructive chaos was our future.

*H*ours later, I was sprawled out across him. "You awake?"

"Yeah." His voice was hoarse. "You?"

"Obviously." I laughed.

"Asking me to leave this life... my family," he started. "It's like taking a knife to my heart. It's in my blood. My veins. My bones."

"I would never ask you to," I said simply. "First off, the world's a safer place with your rage firmly in it—and second he asks, well second, how could anyone be upset over how you protect your blood? Your family? It's heroic."

"I kill people." He groaned.

I smiled against him. "When you put it that way..."

"Does your dad know she showed up?"

"Oh, he heard us yelling at each other at about the same time Phoenix, Tank, and every other boss came running out half-drunk and confused and by then Junior and Serena had run out of the house, and well let's just say Claire had a lot of sorries to say—she owes you one too. But not now."

"I don't. I can't." Panic rose in my chest. "I don't know if I can see her."

"Your choice." I kissed her on the nose. "According to a very apologetic and sad text from Scary Dad, her flight back to New York leaves in the morning."

I tried to keep it in but couldn't. I just couldn't. "How could she?" And then. "I gave her my pearls, I gave—"

"About that." Ash made a face in the dark. A guilty face. A rare face. "I kind of couldn't stand to see you lay the only thing your mom had given you down into the dirt, so I replaced them with a fake set and had yours cleaned. They're in the right drawer of my nightstand."

"What? You did that?"

Ash ignored my question with one of his own. "One more thing." He kissed my lips softly. "Did I hurt you... that night?"

"You freed me," I found myself saying.

"Until the stars fall," he whispered.

I froze. "You mean the sky?"

"No." He shook his head. "I like this version better—our version. Until the stars fall."

"Until the stars fall," I whispered against his skin.

EPILOGUE

"Life is not a problem but a reality to be experienced."—
Soren Kierkegaard

Tank

I rode with Annie to the airport.

I saw her confront Claire.

There were tears.

Yelling.

Hugging.

And then... this huge part of Ash's life, of Annie's, just flew off.

It was better that way.

For everyone. For the healing that needed to take place, though, I knew, it had wrecked a lot of us, made our trust just a bit frayed.

Especially when it came to me still being in the FBI, playing both sides as much as I could.

Which left me here, at the Capo's compound celebrating Spring Break and drinking wine, just waiting for the other shoe to drop.

"Listen up!" Serena pulled out a whistle and blew it while everyone was groaning from hangovers for the last night. "We're going on a trip!"

"My mouth literally tastes like sand and not the nice kind full of colors but the rotten kind and shit, whoever that is, stop mouth breathing!" Maksim groaned.

"It's the cat."

"We don't have a cat." Ash fell back against Annie like he needed about a million more years of sleep after all their noise last night in the bathroom during movie night. It's like they never slept.

Only. Sex.

As if on cue, something randomly meowed. The hell?

"Who the fuck stole a cat last night?" Valerian roared.

Maksim looked down at the scratches on his chest. "I admit nothing until my lawyer is present."

"He just wanted some pussy," King piped up and then burst out laughing, earning groans from everyone around them.

I was still seeing double thanks to no sleep after trailing behind Kartini, who did nothing but taunt me at every single opportunity. When she wasn't wearing low cut outfits, she was talking about another tattoo or piercing, and when she wasn't drinking, she was vaping, and when she wasn't doing any of those things, she was dancing or binge-watching.

She was the epitome of a sleep study for the FBI—survive her, and congrats, you can do your job without going insane.

So a vacation?

Sounded incredible.

Thank God I wouldn't have to go.

"So we decided to elope." Serena grinned. Was she seriously still talking? "And all of you are going to be there, and we do mean all of you." I literally hid behind a bottle of booze only to earn a glare from Serena that said she could clearly see what I was trying to do.

"Looks like we're gonna be spending a lot more time together then, huh, Tank?" Kartini squeezed my thigh.

My body shook. Yup, I was definitely going to puke.

"I uh, have a thing." I lied out my ass.

"Change it." Serena glared, clearly eavesdropping. "Or I'll march my ass right up to headquarters holding my hot pink gun and—"

"Fine..." I groaned.

"Your gun is pink?" Annie asked.

Serena just shrugged. "Feminism?"

"No, that's not really how that works..." Violet and Annie shared a grin before Serena had everyone's attention again.

"Come on, it will be fun!" She shrugged. "Plus, some of the bad guys are gone; Ash isn't acting like he's possessed anymore because he's actually eating normal food and getting regular sex from someone who loves him and isn't a soul-sucking virus—" She took a deep breath. "—Sorry not over it."

"Meh." Kartini and Izzy both waved her off.

The guys grunted in unison.

Because in the grand scheme of things? Real, fucking, shitty thing to do to someone you claim to love.

"Sooooo?" Serena clasped her hands together. "Come on, assholes, just say yes."

"Yes." Everyone said with the excitement of no sleep and

too much alcohol, and I could have sworn before I closed my eyes and drifted off to sleep again, Kartini grinned over at me and said...

"Welcome to hell big guy, welcome to hell."

WANT MORE
RVE?

Did you enjoy Destructive King?
Then check out these other Mafia Romances!

The Eagle Elite World encompasses three separate series that can each be read on its own: Eagle Elite (Italian Mafia), Elite Bratva Brotherhood (Russian Mafia), and Mafia Royals (the next generation). Pick a couple you want to know more about and enjoy!

Eagle Elite
Elite (Nixon & Trace's story)
Elect (Nixon & Trace's story)
Entice (Chase & Mil's story)
Elicit (Tex & Mo's story)
Bang Bang (Axel & Amy's story)
Enforce (Elite + from the boys POV)
Ember (Phoenix & Bee's story)
Elude (Sergio & Andi's story)

Empire (Sergio & Val's story)
Enrage (Dante & El's story)
Eulogy (Chase & Luciana's story)
Exposed (Dom & Tanit's story)
Envy (Vic & Renee's story)

Elite Bratva Brotherhood
RIP (Nikolai & Maya's story)
Debase (Andrei & Alice's story)
Dissolution (TBA)

Mafia Royals Romances
Royal Bully (Asher & Claire's story)
Ruthless Princess (Serena & Junior's story
Scandalous Prince (Breaker & Violet's story)
Destructive King (Asher & Annie's story)
Mafia King (Tank & Kartini's story)
Fallen Royal (Maksim's story)
Broken Crown (King's story)

Rachel Van Dyken & M. Robinson
Mafia Casanova (Romeo Sinacore's story)
Falling for the Villain (Juliet Sinacore's story)

ACKNOWLEDGMENTS

This is the part that's so freaking hard for me to do.

Because it takes a village.

It does.

It takes so many people to help get a book out there.

And then there's the husband, two kiddos (YAY, we added a newborn to the mix—NO STRESS, lol).

And even then, as I'm sitting here typing this, I'm like, how did this book even get finished? After writing until 5 am, having poor Jill going, heyyyyyyy this is great, but maybe don't fall asleep while your hands are still on the laptop next time, m'kay?

This book was destructive.

To my sanity.

To my time.

To everything.

Because it needed to be felt, and sometimes we aren't in

the best headspace (looking at you 2020) to experience those things. So to anyone reading this right now, just know, I feel you, I see you (you aren't invisible). Yes, it sucked, but yes we can power through anything just like Ash did—just like you will.

Wow, I think I just got confused between an acknowledgment and church, but here's the thing. You're gonna be okay, and sometimes we just need someone to tell us that.

The end.

Jill, you were so patient. Thank you for being such an ear for this story and not judging me when I literally needed about a billion voice texts with you to even flush out how we were gonna do this and how it was gonna go down. I kept your notes when you said THIS, EPIC, YES, they won't even know what's coming because it encouraged me so much as I wrote.

To my husband, Nate, and my sons, you are my everything. Thank you for your constant encouragement and patience. Nate, thanks for always being like it's cool, go ahead and DoorDash! Again.

For the millionth time this month.

I always thank God because without him, man, I would be so lost (yet again looking at 2020). I'm so thankful for my faith and for what it's brought me in such tumultuous times.

Thank you to my beta readers, Tracey, Yana, Jill, Kristin, Krista, Stephanie, Georgia, Candace—you guys make my job so much easier with your amazing feedback!

To the Rockin' Readers, man, you guys are like family; you KNOW you are. I'm so thankful for our safe space and basically the best group on Facebook, so many strong women and men in that group. I am nothing without you guys!

To the rest of my admins, my team Angie, Heather, Dannae, Becca, new Heather P, lol.

To my ARC team and my bloggers, I so appreciate you taking time out of your busy schedules to even read my books. I'm so thankful.

If you wanna follow my shenanigans, I'm horrible at Tik Tok, but on Insta @RachVD and on Facebook/Twitter. YOU ROCK! Blood in, no out.

ABOUT THE
Author

Rachel Van Dyken is the #1 New York Times, Wall Street Journal, and USA Today bestselling author of over 90 books ranging from contemporary romance to paranormal. With over four million copies sold, she's been featured in Forbes, US Weekly, and USA Today. Her books have been translated in more than 15 countries. She was one of the first romance authors to have a Kindle in Motion book through Amazon publishing and continues to strive to be on the cutting edge of the reader experience. She keeps her home in the Pacific Northwest with her husband, adorable sons, naked cat, and two dogs. For more information about her books and upcoming events, visit www.RachelVanDykenauthor.com.

ALSO BY
Rachel Van Dyken

Elite Bratva Brotherhood
RIP (Nikolai & Maya's story)
Debase (Andrei & Alice's story)
Dissolution (TBA)

Mafia Royals Romances
Royal Bully (Asher & Claire's story)
Ruthless Princess (Serena & Junior's story
Scandalous Prince (Breaker & Violet)
Destructive King (Asher & Annie)
Mafia King (Tank & Kartini)
Fallen Royal (Maksim's story)
Broken Crown (King's story)

Rachel Van Dyken & M. Robinson
Mafia Casanova (Romeo Sinacore's story)
Falling for the Villain (Juliet Sinacore's story)

Kathy Ireland & Rachel Van Dyken
Fashion Jungle

Wingmen Inc.
The Matchmaker's Playbook (Ian & Blake's story)
The Matchmaker's Replacement (Lex & Gabi's story)

Bro Code
Co-Ed (Knox & Shawn's story)
Seducing Mrs. Robinson (Leo & Kora's story)
Avoiding Temptation (Slater & Tatum's story)
The Setup (Finn & Jillian's story)

Cruel Summer Trilogy
Summer Heat (Marlon & Ray's story)
Summer Seduction (Marlon & Ray's story)
Summer Nights (Marlon & Ray's story)

Players Game
Fraternize (Miller, Grant and Emerson's story)
Infraction (Miller & Kinsey's story)
M.V.P. (Jax & Harley's story)

The Dark Ones Series
The Dark Ones (Ethan & Genesis's story)
Untouchable Darkness (Cassius & Stephanie's story)
Dark Surrender (Alex & Hope's story)
Darkest Temptation (Mason & Serenity's story)
Darkest Sinner (Timber & Kyra's story)

Ruin Series
Ruin (Wes Michels & Kiersten's story)
Toxic (Gabe Hyde & Saylor's story)
Fearless (Wes Michels & Kiersten's story)
Shame (Tristan & Lisa's story)

Seaside Series
Tear (Alec, Demetri & Natalee's story)
Pull (Demetri & Alyssa's story)
Shatter (Alec & Natalee's story)
Forever (Alec & Natalee's story)
Fall (Jamie Jaymeson & Pricilla's story)
Strung (Tear + from the boys POV)
Eternal (Demetri & Alyssa's story)

Seaside Pictures
Capture (Lincoln & Dani's story)
Keep (Zane & Fallon's story)
Steal (Will & Angelica's story)
All Stars Fall (Trevor & Penelope's story)
Abandon (Ty & Abigail's story)
Provoke (Braden & Piper's story)
Surrender (Andrew & Bronte's story)

Curious Liaisons
Cheater (Lucas & Avery's story)
Cheater's Regret (Thatch & Austin's story)

Covet
Stealing Her (Bridge & Isobel's story)
Finding Him (Julian & Keaton's story)

The Consequence Series
The Consequence of Loving Colton (Colton & Milo's story)
The Consequence of Revenge (Max & Becca's story)
The Consequence of Seduction (Reid & Jordan's story)
The Consequence of Rejection (Jason & Maddy's story)

The Bet Series
The Bet (Travis & Kacey's story)
The Wager (Jake & Char Lynn's story)
The Dare (Jace & Beth Lynn's story)

The Bachelors of Arizona
The Bachelor Auction (Brock & Jane's story)
The Playboy Bachelor (Bentley & Margot's story)
The Bachelor Contract (Brant & Nikki's story)

Red Card
Risky Play (Slade & Mackenzie's story)
Kickin' It (Matt & Parker's story)

Liars, Inc
Dirty Exes (Colin, Jessie & Blaire's story)
Dangerous Exes (Jessie & Isla's story)

Waltzing With The Wallflower — written with Leah Sanders
Waltzing with the Wallflower (Ambrose & Cordelia)
Beguiling Bridget (Anthony & Bridget's story)
Taming Wilde (Colin & Gemma's story)

London Fairy Tales
Upon a Midnight Dream (Stefan & Rosalind's story)
Whispered Music (Dominique & Isabelle's story)
The Wolf's Pursuit (Hunter & Gwendolyn's story)
When Ash Falls (Ashton & Sofia's story)

Renwick House
The Ugly Duckling Debutante (Nicholas & Sara's story)
The Seduction of Sebastian St. James (Sebastian & Emma's story)
The Redemption of Lord Rawlings (Phillip & Abigail's story)
An Unlikely Alliance (Royce & Evelyn's story)
The Devil Duke Takes a Bride (Benedict & Katherine's story)

Other Titles
A Crown for Christmas (Fitz & Phillipa's story)
Every Girl Does It (Preston & Amanda's story)
Compromising Kessen (Christian & Kessen's story)
Divine Uprising (Athena & Adonis's story)
The Parting Gift — written with Leah Sanders (Blaine and Mara's story)

RACHEL VAN DYKEN
www.rachelvandykenauthor.com